# THE GOLDEN SPUR

*Also by Dawn Powell, available from Vintage Books*

THE WICKED PAVILION

ANGELS ON TOAST

# DAWN POWELL

# The Golden Spur

WITH AN INTRODUCTION BY

Gore Vidal

VINTAGE BOOKS

A Division of Random House, Inc.
New York

FIRST VINTAGE BOOKS EDITION, FEBRUARY 1990

Introduction Copyright (c) 1989 by Gore Vidal
Copyright © 1962 by Dawn Powell

Library of Congress Cataloging-in-Publication Data
Powell, Dawn.
The golden spur / Dawn Powell.—1st Vintage Books ed.
p.   cm.
ISBN 0-679-72687-X
I. Title.
PS3531.0936G65   1990
813'.52—dc20                           89-40283
CIP

Manufactured in the United States of America
10   9   8   7   6   5   4   3   2   1

*For Margaret De Silver*

# DAWN POWELL, THE AMERICAN WRITER

## Gore Vidal

Once upon a time, New York City was as delightful a place to live as to visit. There were many amenities, as they say in brochures. One was something called Broadway, where dozens of plays opened each season and thousands of people came to see them in an area which today resembles downtown Calcutta without, alas, that subcontinental city's deltine charm and intellectual rigor.

One evening back there in once upon a time (February 7, 1957, to be exact), my first play opened at the Booth Theatre. Traditionally, the playwright was invisible to the audience. One hid out in a nearby bar, listening to the sweet nasalities of Pat Boone's rendering of "Love Letters in the Sand" from a glowing jukebox. But when the curtain fell on this particular night, I went into the crowded lobby to collect someone. Overcoat collar high about my face, I moved invisibly through the crowd, or so I thought. Suddenly a voice boomed...tolled across the lobby. *"Gore!"* I stopped; everyone stopped. From the cloakroom a small, round figure, rather like a Civil War cannonball, hurtled toward me and collided. As I looked down into that familiar round face with its snub nose and shining bloodshot eyes I heard—the entire crowded lobby heard: *"How could you do this? How* could you *sell out* like this? To *Broadway!* To *commercialism!* How could you give up *The Novel?* Give up the *security?* The security of knowing that every two years there will be—like clockwork—that *five-hundred-dollar advance!*" Thirty years later, the voice still echoes in my mind, and I think fondly of its owner, our best comic novelist. "The field," I can hear Dawn Powell snarl, "is not exactly overcrowded."

On the night that *Visit to a Small Planet* opened, Dawn Powell was fifty-nine years old. She had published fourteen novels, evenly divided between accounts of her native Midwest (and how the hell to get out of there and make it to New York) and the highly comic New York novels, centered on Greenwich Village, where she lived most of her adult life. Some twenty-three years earlier the Theater Guild had produced Powell's comedy *Jig Saw* (one of *her* many unsuccessful attempts to sell out to commercialism), but there was third-act trouble, and despite Spring Byington and Ernest Truex, the play closed after forty-nine performances.

For decades Dawn Powell was always just on the verge of ceasing to be a cult and becoming a major religion. But despite the work of such dedicated cultists as Edmund Wilson and Matthew Josephson, John Dos Passos and Ernest Hemingway, Dawn Powell never became the popular writer that she ought to have been. In those days, with a bit of luck, a good writer eventually attracted voluntary readers and became popular. Today, of course, "popular" means bad writing that is widely read while good writing is that which is taught to involuntary readers. Powell failed on both counts. She needs no interpretation, and in her lifetime she should have been as widely read as, say, Hemingway or the early

Fitzgerald or the mid O'Hara or even the late, far too late, Katherine Anne Porter. But Powell was that unthinkable monster, a witty woman who felt no obligation to make a single, much less a final, down payment on Love or the Family; she saw life with a bright Petronian neutrality, and every host at life's feast was a potential Trimalchio to be sent up.

In the few interviews that Powell gave she often mentioned as her favorite novel—surprisingly for an American, much less a woman of her time and place—the *Satyricon*. This sort of thing was not acceptable then any more than it is now. Descriptions of warm, mature, heterosexual love were —and are—woman's writerly task, and the truly serious writers really, heartbreakingly, flunk the course while the pop ones pass with bright honors.

Although Powell received very little serious critical attention (to the extent that there has ever been much in our heavily moralizing culture), when she did get reviewed by a really serious person like Diana Trilling (*The Nation*, May 29, 1948), *la* Trilling warns us that the book at hand is no good because of "the discrepancy between the power of mind revealed on virtually every page of her novel [*The Locusts Have No King*] and the insignificance of the human beings upon which she directs her excellent intelligence." Trilling does acknowledge the formidable intelligence, but because Powell does not deal with morally complex people (full professors at Columbia in midjourney?), "the novel as a whole...fails to sustain the excitement promised by its best moments."

Apparently to be serious a novel must be about very serious—even solemn—people rendered in a very solemn—even serious—manner. Wit? What is that? But then we all know that power of mind and intelligence count for as little in the

American novel as they do in American life. Fortunately neither appears with sufficient regularity to distress our solemn middle-class middlebrows as they trudge ever onward to some Scarsdale of the mind, where the red light blinks and blinks at pier's end and the fields of the republic rush forward ever faster like a rug rolling up.

Powell herself occasionally betrays bewilderment at the misreading of her work. "There is so great a premium on dullness," she wrote sadly (Robert Van Gelder, *Writers and Writing*, Scribner's, 1946), "that it seems stupid to pass it up." She also remarks that it

> is considered jolly and good-humored to point out the oddities of the poor or of the rich. The frailties of millionaires or garbage collectors... Their ways of speech, their personal habits, the peculiarities of their thinking are considered fair game. I go outside the rules with my stuff because I can't help believing that the middle class is funny, too.

Finally, as the shadows lengthened across the greensward, Edmund Wilson got around to his old friend in *The New Yorker* (November 17, 1962). One reason, he tells us, that Powell has so little appeal to those Americans who read novels is that "she does nothing to stimulate feminine daydreams [sexist times!]. The woman reader can find no comfort in identifying herself with Miss Powell's heroines. The women who appear in her stories are likely to be as sordid and absurd as the men." This sexual parity was unusual. But now, closer to century's end than 1962, Powell's "sordid, absurd ladies" seem more like the comic Carol Burnett than the dread Alexis of *Dynasty* fame.

Wilson also noted Powell's originality: "Love is not Miss Powell's theme. Her real theme is the provincial in New York who has come on from the Middle West and acclimatized himself (or herself) to the city and made himself a permanent place there, without ever, however, losing his fascinated sense of an alien and anarchic society." This is very much to the (very badly written) point. Wilson finds her novels "among the most amusing being written, and in this respect quite on a level with those of Anthony Powell, Evelyn Waugh, and Muriel Spark." Wilson's review was of her last book, *The Golden Spur*; three years later she was dead of breast cancer. "Thanks a lot, Bunny," one can hear her mutter as this belated floral wreath came flying through her transom.

Summer. Sunday afternoon. Circa 1950. Dawn Powell's duplex living room at 35 East Ninth Street. The hostess presides over an elliptical aquarium filled with gin, a popular drink of the period known as the martini. In attendance Coby—just Coby to me for years, her eternal escort; he is neatly turned out in a blue blazer, rosy-faced, sleek silver hair combed straight back. Coby can talk with charm on any subject. The fact that he might be Dawn's lover has never crossed my mind. They are so old. A handsome young poet lies on the floor, literally at the feet of E.E. Cummings and his wife, Marion, who ignore him. Dawn casts an occasional maternal eye in the boy's direction, but the eye is more that of the mother of a cat or a dog apt to make a nuisance. Conversation flows. Gin flows. Marion Cummings is beautiful;

so indeed is her husband, his eyes a faded denim blue. Coby is in great form. Though often his own subject, he records not boring triumphs but improbable disasters. He is always broke, and a once distinguished wardrobe is now in the hands of those gay deceivers, his landladies. On this afternoon, at home, Dawn is demure, thoughtful. "Why," she suddenly asks, eyes on the long body beside the coffee table, "do they never have floors of their own to sleep on?"

Cummings explains that since the poet lives in Philadelphia he is too far from his own floor to sleep on it. Not long after, the young poet and I paid a call on the Cummingses. We were greeted at the door by an edgy Marion. "I'm afraid you can't come in." Behind her an unearthly high scream sounded. "Dylan Thomas just died," she explained. "Is that Mr. Cummings screaming?" asked the poet politely as the keening began on an even higher note. "No," said Marion. "That is not Mr. Cummings. That is Mrs. Thomas."

But for the moment, in my memory, the poet is forever asleep on the floor while on a balcony high up in the second story of Dawn's living room a gray, blurred figure appears and stares down at us. "Who," I ask, "is that?"

Dawn gently, lovingly, stirs the martinis, squints her eyes, says, "My husband, I think. It *is* Joe, isn't it, Coby?" She turns to Coby, who beams and waves at the gray man, who withdraws. "Of course it is," says Coby. "Looking very fit." I realize, at last, that this is a *ménage à trois* in Greenwich Village. My martini runs over.

To date the only study of Dawn Powell is a doctoral dissertation by one Judith Faye Pett (University of Iowa, 1981). Ms. Pett has gathered together a great deal of biographical material, for which one is grateful. I am happy to know, at last, that the amiable Coby's proper name was Coburn Gilman, and I am sad to learn that he survived Dawn by only two years. The husband on the balcony was Joseph Gousha, or Goushé, whom she married on November 20, 1920. He was musical; she literary, with a talent for the theater. A son was born retarded. Over the years a fortune was spent on schools and nurses. To earn the fortune, Powell did every sort of writing, from interviews in the press to stories for ladies magazines to plays that tended not to be produced to a cycle of novels about the Midwest, followed by a cycle of New York novels, where she came into her own, dragging our drab literature screaming behind her. As doyenne of the Village, she held court in the grill of the Lafayette Hotel — for elegiasts, the Lafayette was off Washington Square at University Place and Ninth Street.

Powell also runs like a thread of purest brass through Edmund Wilson's *The Thirties*: "It was closing time in the Lafayette Grill, and Coby Gilman was being swept out from under the table. Niles Spencer had been stuttering for five minutes, and Dawn Powell gave him a crack on the jaw and said, '*Nuts* is the word you're groping for.'" Also, "[Peggy Bacon] told me about Joe Gousha's attacking her one night at a party and trying to tear her clothes off.... I suggested that Joe had perhaps simply thought that this was the thing to do in Dawn's set. She said, 'Yes: He thought it was a social obligation.'" Powell also said that "Dotsy's husband was very much excited because the Prince of Wales was wearing a zipper fly, a big thing in the advertising business." A footnote to this text says that Dawn Powell and Wilson carried on a correspondence in which she was Mrs. Humphrey

Ward and he "a seedy literary man named Wigmore." Later, there is a very muddled passage in which, for reasons not quite clear, James Thurber tells Dawn Powell that she does not *deserve* to be in the men's room. That may well be what it was all about.

Like most writers, Powell wrote of what she knew. Therefore, certain themes recur, while the geography does not vary from that of her actual life. As a child, she and two sisters were shunted about from one midwestern farm or small town to another by a father who was a salesman on the road (her mother died when she was six). The maternal grandmother made a great impression on her and predisposed her toward boardinghouse life (as a subject, not a residence). Indomitable old women, full of rage and good jokes, occur in both novel cycles. Powell's father remarried when she was twelve, and Dawn and her sisters went to live on the stepmother's farm. "My stepmother, one day, burned up all the stories I was writing, a form of discipline I could not endure. With thirty cents earned by picking berries I ran away, ending up in the home of a kindly aunt in Shelby, Ohio." After graduation from the local high school, she worked her way through Lake Erie College for Women in Painesville, Ohio. I once gave a commencement address there and was struck by how red-brick New England Victorian the buildings were. I also found out all that I could about their famous alumna. I collected some good stories to tell her. But by the time I got back to New York she was dead.

Powell set out to be a playwright. One play ended up as a movie while another, *Big Night*, was done by the Group Theater in 1933. But it was World War I, not the theater, that got Powell out of Ohio and to New York in 1918, as a member of the naval reserve. The war ended before her uniform arrived. Powell wrote publicity. Married. Wrote advertising copy (at the time, Goushé or Gousha was an account executive with an advertising agency). Failure in the theater and need for money at home led her to novel writing and the total security of that five-hundred-dollar advance each of us relied on for so many years.

*Angels on Toast* was the first of Powell's novels to become, if not world famous, *the* book for those who wanted to inhabit the higher, wittier realms of Manhattan where Truman Capote was, later and less wittily, to camp out. It is 1940. War had begun to darken the skyline. But the city's magic is undiminished for the provincial Ebie, a commercial artist whose mother is in the great line of Powell eccentrics. Ebie lives with another working woman, Honey, who "was a virgin (at least you couldn't prove she wasn't), and was as proud as punch of it. You would have thought it was something that had been in the family for generations." But Ebie and Honey need each other to talk at, and in a tavern

> where O. Henry used to go...they'd sit in the dark smoked-wood booth drinking old-fashioneds and telling each other things they certainly wished later they had never told and bragging about their families, sometimes making them hot-stuff socially back home, the next time making them romantically on the wrong side of the tracks. The family must have been on wheels back in the Middle West, whizzing back and forth across tracks at a mere word from the New York daughters.

Brooding over the novel is the downtown Hotel Ellery, where for seventeen dollars a week Ebie's mother, Mrs. Vane, lives in contented squalor.

> BAR and GRILL. It was the tavern entrance to a somewhat mediaeval looking hotel, whose time-and-soot-blackened façade was frittered with fire-escapes,... its dark oak wainscoting rising high to meet grimy black walls, its ship-windows covered with heavy pumpkin-colored chintz.... Once in you were in for no mere moment.

In its remoteness, this world before television could just as easily be that of Walter Scott.

It is also satisfying that in these New York novels the city that was plays so pervasive a role. This sort of hotel, meticulously described, evokes lost time in a way that the novel's bumptious twentieth-century contemporary, early talking-movies don't.

> Another curious thing about these small, venerable, respectable hotels—there seemed no appeal here to the average customer. BAR and GRILL, for instance, appealed to seemingly genteel widows and spinsters of small incomes.... Then there were those tired flashes in the pan, the one-shot celebrities, and on the other hand there was a gayer younger group whose loyalty to the BAR and GRILL was based on the cheapness of its martinis. Over their simple dollar lunches (four martinis and a sandwich) this livelier set snickered at the older residents.

Ebie wants to take her mother away from all this so that they can live together in Connecticut. Mrs. Vane would rather die. She prefers to lecture the bar on poetry. There is also a plot: two men in business, with wives. One has an affair with Ebie. By now, Powell has mastered her own method. Essay beginnings to chapters work smartly:

> In the dead of night wives talked to their husbands, in the dark they talked and talked while the clock on the bureau ticked sleep away, and the last street cars clanged off on distant streets to remoter suburbs, where in new houses bursting with mortgages and the latest conveniences wives talked in the dark, and talked and talked.

The prose is now less easygoing than it was in the early novels, and there is a conscious tightening of the language although, to the end, Powell thought one thing was different *than* another while always proving not her mettle but *metal*. *Angels on Toast* ends with a cheerfulness worthy of Shakespeare in his *Midsummer Night's Dream* mood: everyone where he or she should be. I can think of no one else who has got so well the essence of that first war-year before we all went away to the best years of no one's life.

*The Wicked Pavilion* (1954) is the Café Julien is the Lafayette Hotel of real life. The title is from *The Creevey Papers* and refers to the Prince Regent's Brighton Pavilion, where the glamorous and *louche* wait upon a mad royal. From Powell's earlier books, the writer Dennis Orphen opens and closes the story in his mysterious way. He takes no real part in the plot. He is simply there, watching the not-so-magic wheel turn as the happy island grows sad. For him, as for Powell, the café is central to his life. Here he writes, sees friends, observes the vanity fair. Powell has now become masterful in her setting of scenes. The essays—preludes, overtures—are both witty and sadly wise. She also got the number to Eisenhower's America as she brings together in this penultimate rout all sorts of figures from earlier novels, now grown old: Okie is still a knowing man-about-town and author of the definitive works on the painter Marius, Andy Callingham is still a world-famous novelist (based on Ernest Hemingway), serene in his uncontagious self-love, and the recurrent Peggy Guggenheim figure is back again as Cynthia, an art gallery dealer. One plot is young love: Rick and Ellenora who met at the Café Julien in wartime and never got enough of it or of each other or of "the happy island," Powell's unironic phrase for the Manhattan that she first knew.

A new variation on the Powell young woman is Jerry, clean-cut, straightforward, and on the make. But her peculiar wholesomeness does not inspire men to give her presents; yet "the simple truth was that with her increasingly expensive tastes she really could not afford to work.... As for settling for the safety of marriage, that seemed the final defeat, synonymous in Jerry's mind with asking for the last rites." An aristocratic lady, Elsie, tries unsuccessfully to launch her. Elsie's brother, Wharton, and sister-in-law, Nita, are fine comic emblems of respectable marriage. In fact, Wharton is one of Powell's truly great and original monsters:

Wharton had such a terrific reputation for efficiency that many friends swore that the reason his nose changed colors before your very eyes was because of an elaborate Rimbaud color code, indicating varied reactions to his surroundings.... Ah, what a stroke of genius it had been for him to have found Nita! How happy he had been on his honeymoon and for years afterward basking in the safety of Nita's childish innocence where his intellectual shortcomings, sexual coldness and caprices—indeed his basic ignorance—would not be discovered.... He was well aware that many men of his quixotic moods preferred young boys, but he dreaded to expose his inexperience to one of his own sex, and after certain cautious experiments realized that his anemic lusts were canceled by his overpowering fear of gossip.... Against the flattering background of Nita's delectable purity he blossomed forth as the all-round-He-man, the Husband who knows everything.... He soon taught her that snuggling, hand-holding and similar affectionate demonstrations were kittenish and vulgar. He had read somewhere, however, that breathing into a woman's ear or scratching her at the nape of her neck drove her into complete ecstasy.... In due course Nita bore him four daughters, a sort of door prize for each time he attended.

The party is given by Cynthia now, and it rather resembles Proust's last roundup: "There are people here who have been dead twenty years," someone observes, including "the bore that walks like a man." There is a sense of closing time; people settle for what they can get. "We get sick of clinging vines, he thought, but the day comes when we suspect that the vines are all that hold our rotting branches together."

In 1962 Powell published her last and perhaps most appealing novel, *The Golden Spur*. As so often was the case with Powell, the protagonist is male. In this case a young man from Silver City, Ohio, called Jonathan Jaimison. He has come to the city to find his father. Apparently twenty-six years earlier his mother, Connie, had had a brief fling with a famous man in the Village; pregnant, she came home and married a Mr. Jaimison. The book opens with a vigorous description of Wanamaker's department store being torn down. Powell is now rather exuberant about the physical destruction of her city (she wrote this last book in her mid-sixties, when time was doing the same to her). But there are still a few watering holes from the twenties, and one of them is The Golden Spur, where Connie mingled with the bohemians.

Jonathan stays at the Hotel De Long, which sounds like the Vanderbilt, a star of many of Powell's narratives. Jonathan, armed with Connie's cryptic diary, has a number of names that might be helpful. One is that of Claire Van Orphen, a moderately successful writer for whom Connie did some typing. Claire gives Jonathan possible leads; meanwhile, his presence has rejuvenated her. Her career is revived with the help of a professionally failed writer who studies all of Claire's ladies' magazine short stories of yesteryear; he then reverses the moral angle:

> "In the old days the career girl who supported the family was the heroine, and the idle wife was the baddie," Claire said gleefully. "And now it's the

other way around. In the soap operas, the career girl is the baddie, the wife is the goodie because she's better for *business*. . . . Well, you were right. CBS has bought the two [stories] you fixed, and Hollywood is interested."

Powell herself was writing television plays in the age of Eisenhower and no doubt had made this astonishing discovery on her own.

Finally Cassie, Peggy Guggenheim yet again, makes her appearance, and the famous Dawn Powell party assembles for the last time. There are nice period touches. Girls from Bennington are everywhere, while Cassie herself "was forty-three—well, all right, forty-eight, if you're going to count every lost week end." She takes a fancy to Jonathan and hires him to work at her gallery. By the end of the novel, Jonathan figures out not only his paternity but his maternity and, best of all, himself.

The quest is over. Identity fixed. The party over, Jonathan heads downtown, "perhaps to 'the Spur,' where they could begin all over." On that blithe note Powell's life and lifework end, and the magic of that period is gone—except for the novels of Dawn Powell.

Grateful acknowledgment is made to the following people, who helped in the preparation of this volume: Howard Frisch, Al Silverman, Jacqueline Rice, Gore Vidal, and the staff at the Elmer Holmes Bobst Library at New York University.

# THE GOLDEN SPUR

# 1

THE HOTEL STATIONERY was Wedgwood blue like the wall-
paper, delicately embossed with a gold crest and a motto,
*In virtu vinci,* a nice thought, whatever it meant, for a
hotel. Nice paper, too. Paper like that could make a writer
of you, if anything could.

He took the whole pack from the desk and inserted it
among his other papers in the briefcase with his pajamas,
shirt, the monogrammed Hotel De Long ashtray, hand
towels, and dainty lavender soap. Too bad there were only
two hotel postcards left. Anyone seeing that view of the
De Long lobby, magnified beyond recognition, jeweled
with tropic blossoms, oriental rugs, divans, and liveried
pages would assume that seductive sirens and fabulous ad-
venturers lurked behind the potted palms. Actually, Jonathan had observed only a few old crones and decrepit gentlemen hobbling or wheeling through the modest halls
last evening. He chose, however, to believe the postcards.
That was the city as he had pictured it, and he wished he
had a stock of them to keep sending out as camouflage for
the cheaper quarters he had to find.

He addressed one card to Miss Tessie Birch, R.F.D.,
Silver City, Ohio.

"Dear Aunt Tessie. No time for good-by. Will write
when I get more leads. J."

His window was on a court within hand-shaking distance of other windows, but a wedge of the street below was visible and there rose the contented purr of the city, a blend of bells, whirring motors, whistles, buildings rising, and buildings falling. The stage was set, the orchestra tuning up, and in a moment he would be on, Jonathan thought. Curious he felt no panic, as if his years of waiting in the wings had prepared him to take over the star role. But it was more as if he were released from a long exile in an alien land to come into his own at last. In a window across the court he could glimpse a fair young man seated at a desk, idly smoothing his hair and smiling as if at some happy secret. The figure moved, and it dawned on Jonathan that the window was a mirror, the young man with the secret was himself.

He looked around to see if there was more magic to be discovered in the room. He'd certainly gotten his seven dollars' worth. Last night he had sat up till three, marveling at the new life so suddenly opened to him, trying to organize the plan he had outlined before leaving Silver City. Again he flipped through the fat little red notebook, on the flyleaf of which was written: CONSTANCE BIRCH, NEW YORK CITY, 1927. Beneath his mother's name was written: PROPERTY OF JONATHAN JAIMISON, NEW YORK CITY, 1956. The old names his mother had listed and those he had added from the references in her letters Jonathan had already checked in this year's telephone directory with little success. Beside each name he had jotted the connection with his mother and the last known address. Two names offered possibilities. The first was:

"Claire Van Orphen, author. Typed mss. Last Xmas card 1933. Care Pen and Brush Club."

The Pen and Brush Club, he had found, was right in

the vicinity, and a note might bring results. Second to Miss Van Orphen as a source was another but more famous writer, Alvine Harshawe, whose early work his mother had been privileged to type. She had continued to collect his press notices for years after she had returned to Ohio and married Jaimison, Senior.

"Copied Alvine's last act today and he was so pleased he took me to celebrate at The Golden Spur," she had written in her diary, which Jonathan knew almost by heart.

The Golden Spur still existed, he'd found, and Jonathan planned to ask there for Harshawe.

He knew the "Hazel" mentioned frequently in the diary had shared rooms on Horatio Street with his mother, and "George" had been her fiancé, a rich young lawyer. George's opinions on literature were faithfully quoted. He seemed to awe Jonathan's mother, but then she was awed by everybody she had ever encountered in New York, just as she found all places incredibly charming, such as the Horatio Street rooming house, the Hotel Brevoort (where George and Hazel took her to Sunday breakfast and where the public stenographer graciously gave her some work), the Black Knight, Chumley's (where all the great writers and artists congregated in better style than at The Golden Spur), the Washington Square Bookstore ("Alvine's friend Lois works there"), Romany Marie's, the Café Royale, and other romantic names that Jonathan could not find in the directory.

Tucking the priceless little notebook in his inside coat pocket, Jonathan considered the wisdom of trying to find Miss Van Orphen this very day. The wall clock registered eleven-forty. A printed notice advised that guests would be charged for another day after one o'clock. Better wait until he was settled in permanent quarters, he decided. No use fooling himself that the mystery of these many years could be unraveled in a day. Let's get on with it, then, he told himself, and picked up his briefcase.

The corridor appeared deserted, and he seized the chance to nip in an open door where he could see a stack of postcards on the desk. He had barely time to slip them in his pocket when an ancient hump-backed porter materialized in the doorway. His withered old neck stretched out of the De Long uniform like a turtle's, and the watery eyes under wrinkled lizard lids blinked suspiciously at Jonathan, the old nose sniffing stolen postcards, towels, ashtrays, and precious soap.

"I must have missed him," Jonathan said nervously.

"He checked out an hour ago," said the porter, suspicions allayed. "Maybe you could catch him at the funeral parlor."

"That's so," said Jonathan.

"Or maybe his home," offered the porter. "He was just staying here to fix up the Major's affairs, all that legal stuff. Did you come for the funeral?"

"Yes," said Jonathan. "I—I got the word in Ohio."

"The Major would have appreciated your coming all that way just to bury him," said the porter. "He was a great one for appreciating little favors like that. They don't come any finer than the Major is what we say here."

"That's what I always said," Jonathan agreed, edging out the door past the porter. Lucky to touch hunchbacks, he remembered. "I hope I'm not late for the funeral."

"You'll make it," said his friend with a dry cackle. "The Major wouldn't let anybody hustle him. Things have got to be done just right, you know how he was."

"That's so," said Jonathan and returned the smart salute,

grateful to the dead Major for his unexpected protection. He had one friend in New York, it seemed, even if the bond was a peculiar one. He was still glowing when he came out on the street. It was a wonderful July day created especially to surprise and delight the timid visitor. The street of old brick houses with their fanlights over white doorways, trellised balconies of greenery, magnolia trees, vined walls, cats sunning themselves in windows, was not so different from the residential streets in hundreds of home towns far away. Even little saplings on the sidewalk sprouted leaves, and pigeons strutted along the gutter until routed by a street sprinkler bearing a sign: KEEP NEW YORK CLEAN. A dirty but friendly baptism, Jonathan thought, brushing the mud from his trousers.

"Is this the way to Aunt Nellie's Carolina Tea Room?' a lady in a hatful of violets called out to him, leaning out of a taxicab door.

Jonathan was flattered to be taken for a seasoned New Yorker, and he pointed impulsively to a restaurant sign down the street. The lady beamed gratitude and with a flower-hatted companion clambered out of the cab, backsides first. The sign turned out to advertise MAC'S BAR AND GRILL, Jonathan saw on closer inspection, but maybe the ladies wouldn't know the difference.

Along the way doormen, decked out in more braid than banana generals, were being propelled by clusters of peanut-sized Poms and chows on mighty leashes, braking to allow each hydrant and every passing pooch to be checked. A dog was a necessity in this city, Jonathan deduced, and promised himself that one of these days he would have one, a Great Dane, say, something to give his doorman a real workout, a big-shot dog to show the world. He'd never had a dog, but now he would have everything the old Jonathan had never dared to want, for this was his city, and his mother's secret was the key to its treasure.

"I'm not a Jaimison," he murmured to himself over and over, and his stride grew longer, his head higher. "I could be anybody—*anybody!*"

Before him lay Washington Square.

Only eighteen hours in New York, and he loved everything, every inch of it. Ah, the square! He crossed Waverly and stood at the corner by the playground. He beamed at the ferociously determined child aiming a scooter straight at him, and jumped out of the way of a chain of girl rollerskaters advancing rhythmically toward him. An enormous-busted, green-sweatered girl with a wild bush of hair, black skin-tight pants outlining thick thighs and mighty buttocks, came whooping along, clutching the legs of a screaming bearded young man she bore on her shoulders.

"Let me down, now! Now you let me down!" he yelled, waving his arms. A short muscular girl with ape face and crew-cut, in stained corduroy shorts and red knee socks, ran behind, shouting with laughter.

"Didn't I tell you that Shirley is the strongest dyke in Greenwich Village?"

The big gorilla girl stopped abruptly, letting the young man fall headlong over her shoulders and sprawl crabwise over the green.

"Don't you dare call me a dyke!" she shouted, shaking the smaller girl by the shoulders.

The lad snatched the moment to pick himself up, with a sheepish grin at Jonathan, and tore down the street, combing his long, sleek locks as he ran.

"Go ahead, Shirley, pick up this one, go ahead!" the small girl yelled, pointing at Jonathan while she wriggled neatly out of her attacker's hands. Too startled to move for a few seconds, Jonathan saw the big girl's eye fall on him with a speculative smile. He clutched his briefcase and ran, the girls howling behind him. He made for the fenced-in space where the smallest kiddies, drunk with popsicles, were wobbling on teeter-totters or reeling behind their buggies. He knocked one of these live dolls over and quickly snatched it up in his arms as Big Shirley came toward him.

"Look out, he's going to throw the kid at you, Shirley!" the short girl yelled warning. "Come on, let's go."

They loped away, stopping for the younger ape to leap expertly onto Shirley's back. With a sigh of relief, Jonathan set down the howling child carefully.

"Thank you very much, sir," he said to the child, picking up the raspberry Good Humor his savior had dropped and restoring it to the open red mouth. He remembered that he hadn't had anything to eat since last night's hamburger in the station and he was ravenous. A benign white-haired old gentleman, wide-brimmed black hat on lap, black ribbons fluttering from his spectacles, sat on a bench reading a paperback copy of *The Dance of Life*. Reassured by the title, Jonathan coughed to get his attention.

"Could you tell me where I can get a cup of coffee here?" he asked.

Without looking up from his reading, the gentleman reached in his pocket and handed out a quarter before turning a page. Jonathan stared at the coin in his palm.

"Thank you, sir," he said. "Thank you very much."

How strange New Yorkers were, he marveled, but he would get used to their ways. He crossed the park and wandered up a side street. Golden letters on a window, where a menu was pasted, announced that this was Aunt Nellie's Carolina Tea Room. His two old ladies were several blocks off course, he thought, unless Mac of the Bar and Grill had set them right. Perhaps they were inside right now, jubilantly wolfing the farm-style apple-peanut surprise, home-boiled country eggs, barn-fresh milk, cottage-made cocoa, garden-good lettuce sandwiches. Rejecting these gourmet temptations, Jonathan turned in the other direction.

Lunch hour had filled the streets, and Jonathan studied the people, fearing they were frowning at his best gray tropical tweed because it was last year's style. His confidence melted even more—as his confidence always had a way of doing—after a couple addressed him in Spanish, and a girl asked him directions in Swedish. On second thoughts, he might be too dressed-up to pass as a native New Yorker. The standard costume seemed to be loose sport shirts and slacks, or even shorts proudly exhibiting knobby shins, hairy calves, and gnarled knees. Certainly these people were nothing like those natty cosmopolitans pictured in *Esquire* and the movies. As for the girls, he tried not to notice them. After his encounter in the park he figured that they must be a stronger breed than those back home.

Ah, New York! A flying pebble nicked him in the eye, and as he was blindly trying to shake it out he found he was caught up in a crowd around a demolition operation that took up the whole block. Evidently something dramatic was about to happen, for all eyes stared skyward intently. Maybe the Mayor himself was about to appear on the roofless tower and beg for their ears. Jonathan nudged his way to the front and stared upward too.

A giant crane was the star performer, lifting its neck heavenward, then dropping a great iron ball gently down to a doomed monster clock in the front wall of the structure, tapping it tenderly, like a diagnostician looking for the sore spot. Does it hurt here? here? or here? Wherever it hurts must be target for the wham, and wham comes next, with the rubble hurtling down into the arena with a roar. A pause, and then the eager watchers followed the long neck's purposeful rise again, the rhythmical lowering of the magic ball, the blind grope for the clock face, and then the avalanche once more. The cloud of dust cleared, and a cry went up to see the clock still there, the balcony behind it falling. "They can't get the clock," someone exulted. "Not today! Hooray for the clock!" The spectators smiled and nodded to one another. Good show. Well done, team!

Jonathan returned the congratulatory smile of the fat little man on his right bearing a bag of laundry on his back, and composed a graver expression for the scowling neighbor on his other side. This was a ruddy-faced, agate-eyed man, bare-headed, with gray-streaked pompadour and mustache, carrying an attaché case and a rumpled blue raincoat over his arm.

"Do you realize the bastard who runs that blasted contraption gets sixty dollars an hour?" he asked Jonathan. "Sixty dollars an hour—twenty, thirty times what a college professor makes. And time and a half for overtime. Figure it out for yourself. Seven, eight hundred dollars a day just for sitting on his can in that little box and pressing buttons."

"Is that a fact?" Jonathan asked, feeling richer at the mention of such large sums. He moved closer with the vague hope that money was contagious.

"Destruction is what pays today," said his neighbor, twisting his mustache savagely. "Wreckers, bomb-builders, poison-makers. Who buys creative brains today?"

"Nobody," Jonathan said, glad to know some answers.

"Name me one constructive, intellectual activity that pays a living," pursued the quizmaster.

"You got me," Jonathan said.

He accepted a bent cigarette from the pack offered by the man, who was now brooding silently.

"Can you tell me if there's something special about this particular wrecking to bring out such a crowd?" Jonathan asked.

The gentleman snorted.

"Of course I can tell you. In the first place this was a splendid old landmark and people like to see the old order blown up. Then there is the glorious dirt and uproar which are the vitamins of New York, and of course the secret hope that the street will cave in and swallow us all up."

Jonathan looked down uneasily at the boards underfoot.

"Dear old Wanamaker's." His companion sighed. "If I had paid their nasty little bill, perhaps they would never have come to this. Well, mustn't get sentimental."

Another avalanche of rubble roared into the pit.

"Eight hundred dollars a day is a lot of money for pushing buttons," Jonathan thought aloud.

"Entertainers must be paid," the other man said and walked away.

What a brilliant fellow! Jonathan thought, looking after him regretfully. He remembered that he was hungry and started looking for a lunchroom, rejecting one because it looked too expensive, others because they looked too cheap, too crowded, or too empty. After wandering up and down, he stood still finally in front of an auction gallery he had passed three times, pretending to admire a gold sedan chair. On the other side of the street was a great glass and chromium supermarket advertising its opening with valuable favors to be given away to every customer. He might buy a bun, he thought, thus entitling him to the valuable favor, and come back and eat it in the sedan chair. Or— Then a sign swinging out over a dark doorway next to the auction window caught his eye.

THE GOLDEN SPUR, he read mechanically and stared at the red and gold swinging horseshoe.

*The Golden Spur!* His mother's Golden Spur, the place she used to go to meet the Man, the place she went with her famous friends, but above all, the place where the great romance had started, the place, indeed, where Jonathan came in.

So the place did exist—not the grand Piranesi palace he had vaguely imagined, with marble stairs leading forever upward to love and fame, but a dingy little dark hole he must have passed before without noticing. He lit a cigarette with trembling fingers. If The Golden Spur was real, then all of it was real. His mother had stood on this very spot, and suddenly her image leaped up, not the pale face on the pillow he remembered from long ago, but the stranger, Connie Birch, the girl who had written the letters, the girl who met her lover in The Golden Spur. He saw her as she looked in the old snapshots, the thin, chiseled face with shining, appealing eyes (*Oh, do like me, do try to like me, please*), the coronet of thick fair braids, the parted lips half-smiling, the eager when-where-who expectant aura that must have attracted its own happy answers. This was the girl whose trail he must find, the girl who had written her sister (he had that letter with him too):

"Oh Tessie, please don't expect me to marry John Jaimison when I come home to visit because I don't care how he hounds me, my life is here. I've told you how lovely all the marvelous people I meet at Miss Van Orphen's are to me when I go there to type her stories. Hazel, the girl I live with, prefers a wild time at cabarets but I'd much rather listen to the important people at Miss Van Orphen's. Then there is the restaurant where the writers and artists go, The Golden Spur, and I've met the most exciting man there and Tessie, he's going to be famous and how could I ever go back to John after being in love with a really great man?"

Jonathan took a step toward the magic door and then stood still, desperately trying to steel himself for the part he had chosen to play and that had seemed so simple, so right, when Aunt Tessie had told him the truth in Silver City just forty-eight hours before.

"Once you get on the track, things will come to you like in a dream," Aunt Tessie had said. "Keep thinking of all those stories your mother used to tell you every night, stories about people and places she knew in New York, like that Golden Spur where she met all those famous ones. Think of the ones she used to find mentioned in the magazines, always cutting out their pictures and all that."

"I remember," Jonathan had said.

"I never got it straight in my own mind," Aunt Tessie had confessed. "Used to go in one ear and out the other like all those stories girls tell about their good times away from home, all those beaux, all fine men, all better than the hometown boys. 'After my time in New York,' your poor mother used to complain to me, 'how can you expect me to marry John Jaimison?' 'You were glad enough to get engaged to him before you went away,' I told her, 'and he did wait for you.' 'But Tessie, you just don't understand,

I see everything different now,' she kept at me, crying her eyes out. 'I'm used to geniuses, men with great minds, now, and John Jaimison doesn't think about anything but selling Silver City flour products. All he reads is sales letters, all he writes is orders. All he does is brag about the Jaimison family, and how they're the biggest old family in middle Ohio and how proud I'll be to be allowed at their family reunions. Oh, Tessie,' your mother says to me, 'you can't see me marrying John Jaimison and going to those awful reunions!' "

"Of course not!" Jonathan had answered Aunt Tessie "Why did you let it happen?"

"I said to her, 'Connie,' I said, 'what you say is true and I do understand how New York City changed your ideas about men, but honey,' I said, 'the point is he's still willing to marry you and in your condition you'd better snap him up, the sooner the quicker!' So!"

"Maybe he did suspect," Jonathan had said. "Maybe that was why he dumped Mother and me on you just three years after they married."

"John Jaimison turned her in just the way he turned in his car when it went bad," Aunt Tessie said. "He didn't suspect, he was just naturally a Jaimison, a small-minded man. He beefed about her turning tubercular on him as if he'd been sold a pig in a poke, and what a tussle it was getting money out of him for the doctors and you! Hard enough to catch him, and when I did he'd complain, 'You can't get blood out of a turnip, Tessie Birch,' and I'd say, 'Out of a Jaimison turnip you can't even get turnip juice.' But there, I never meant to tell you the truth about yourself!"

"I only wish you'd told me years ago," said Jonathan. "I needn't have gone to all those Jaimison reunions, with the old man bawling me out for not getting ahead, telling everybody that the Jaimison genius had skipped a generation. I only wish you could tell me who my true father was."

"I never thought it mattered, Jonny-boy," Aunt Tessie had said. "Connie told so many stories about New York. Don't you remember?"

"The bedtime stories she told got mixed up in my mind," he said. "The Golden Spur people weren't any more real than the King of the Golden River.'

"It'll all fit together," Aunt Tessie consoled him. "You'll find your answer."

"I'll find the answer," Jonathan repeated aloud, as if Aunt Tessie were right there before The Golden Spur urging him on.

Through a gap in the plum velvet café curtains he could see the bar and was heartened to recognize his friend from the excavation standing inside. He breathed deep of the heady New York air, that delirious narcotic of ancient sewer dust, gasoline fumes, roasting coffee beans, and the harsh smell of sea that intoxicates inland nostrils.

Then he pushed open the door.


A long bar stretched before him back to dark stalls with dim stable lanterns perched on their newel posts. Framed photographs of the great horses of old covered the wainscoted walls, horseshoes and golden spurs hung above the bar itself, and photographed clippings of old racing forms. Jonathan examined these souvenirs, noting that all that was left of the sporting past were the bowling alley ads posted on the bulletin board. These were overshadowed by notices of summer art shows, off-Broadway entertainments, jazz concerts, night courses in Method Acting, sketching, folk-singing hootenannies, poetry readings, ballet and language groups. Penciled scraps of paper were Scotch-taped to the wall, advertising cars, scooters, beach shacks, lofts, or furniture for trade or sale. Homesick Californian with driver's license asked for free trip back to North Beach. A new espresso café on Bleecker Street wanted a man to get up a mimeographed Village news sheet in return for "nominal" pay and free cakes and coffee. A Sunday painter offered free dental service in exchange for model. An unemployed illustrator would teach the Chachacha or even the Charleston for her dinners.

"Brother, she's hungry!" Jonathan heard a feminine voice say over his shoulder and turned to see a big girl with shrimp-pink hair laughing at his absorption. He drew away, embarrassed at being caught in tourist innocence.

The girl got her cigarettes from the cigarette machine and sauntered back to the dining booths, throwing him a friendly, mocking smile. He took a stool at the bar and saw, farther down, his neighbor from the excavation applying himself to a highball with deep satisfaction. Near him a man with a skimpy gray goatee, in a plaid shirt and scalp-tight beret, was reading a copy of *Encounter* with a beer in hand. He had a mountain of pennies stacked in front of him, and now he raised his glass for a refill. The bartender silently counted off fifteen coppers. Conscious of Jonathan's interest in this little game, the man looked up from his magazine and stared at Jonathan, frowning.

"Excuse me," he said. "You remind me of somebody."

"I do?" Jonathan asked, well pleased to look like somebody.

The man studied him, frowning, then shook his head.

"I can't place it," he said.

"My name's Jaimison," Jonathan offered.

"Don't know any Jaimison," said the man.

He looked like a real Villager, Jonathan thought in deep admiration, ageless, jaunty, wearing his faded bohemian uniform with the calm assurance of the true belonger. (I must scrap this tourist outfit of mine and get one like his, Jonathan thought.) He was somewhere between thirty and sixty; the bags under the eyes and deep furrows between the tangled brows might testify to dissipation instead of years, for the sharp-cut sardonic face was otherwise unlined, the figure trim.

"Two double Bloody Marys on the rocks, Dan," a female voice pleaded from the dark recesses of the dining booths.

"So Lize is back in the Village," said the Villager.

"They always come back," said the bartender. "Will somebody tell me why?"

As no one answered, Jonathan seized the opportunity.

"Alvine Harshawe, for instance," he said boldly. "Has he come back?"

The bartender selected a tomato-juice can from under the counter thoughtfully.

"I'll have one of those too," added Jonathan. "Bloody Mary."

"Harshawe, Harshawe," mused the bartender. "Must be a night customer. Harshawe, eh? Maybe he comes in here and I just don't know him by name. Lots of good customers, my best friends, I don't know the names."

"Dan never heard of Alvine Harshawe!" The shrimp-haired girl was back again, standing by the goateed man, watching her drinks being made. "Don't you love Dan for that, Earl? Imagine not hearing of Alvine Harshawe."

The girl picked up the two drinks the bartender pushed toward her.

"Writers don't come in this bar," she said to Jonathan. "Try the White Horse."

"Just a minute, Lize," said the goateed man reproachfully.

"I forgot about Earl here," the girl amended. "I mean the hardcover big shots—like Harshawe."

She retreated to the dark dining section again with her two gory potions, and Jonathan took the third.

"A writer's got to go where columnists can see him," the goateed Villager stated. "Alvine Harshawe could be dying of thirst in the middle of the Sahara. Suddenly there's an oasis, a regular Howard Johnson job, with fifty-nine flavors bubbling up in all directions. Terrific. But if Lenny Lyons isn't at it, I won't go, Alvine says."

"So he dries up, who cares?" said the bartender.

"Don't be silly, Lyons would be there all right," said the fellow named Earl. "You don't catch Alvine taking a chance on no publicity."

"Outside of this guy Harshawe being a big shot, what else have you got against him, Earl?" inquired the bartender, polishing the rimless spectacles that made him look like a respectable white-collar worker.

"What have I got against him?" mused Earl. "Why, he's my oldest friend, that's all."

"Now we're getting somewhere," said the bartender approvingly.

Jonathan, ears alerted, moved closer.

"Then he did use to come here?" he asked.

"Everybody used to come to the Spur," the man said carelessly, "until they could afford not to."

"Supposing we don't get these writers like Lize says," argued the bartender. "Who needs writers when we're already stinking with painters?"

"Painters have got to drink, especially these days," Earl observed. "A painter can't turn out the stuff they have to do now without being loaded."

The bartender subtracted a fresh supply of pennies from the board and pushed another beer across the counter.

"That's where you're wrong, Earl," he said. "I know more about artists than you do. After all, I'm the bartender here. The way I size it up is that they got to paint sober, then they're so disgusted with what they done they got to get stoned."

"And wreck the joint," said Earl. "Look at the crack in that table where Hugow and Lew Schaffer bashed it."

Jonathan looked admiringly at the damaged table indicated.

"The place sure seems quiet with Hugow out of town." The bartender sighed. "Ah, what the hell, painting's no kind of work for those guys. They got to let off steam, beat up their girl, kick in a door. It's only human nature as I see it."

"Sure," said Jonathan. "Human nature, that's all."

"Artists get away with more human nature than anybody else," Earl muttered morosely to Jonathan.

"Hugow sure gets away with murder," the bartender agreed. "Dames? They're all over him. What's he got?"

"Same thing he always had," Earl said. "Only it works better now that his stuff sells big, now that he's the champ."

"Hugow's a great guy. Why shouldn't he be making up for all his bad times?" The bartender turned to Jonathan for agreement. "Can you blame him? You know Hugow."

"No, I'm afraid I don't know any artists," Jonathan

said, flattered at the assumption. "Is he a great painter?"

The question seemed to require thought.

"He gets away with it," finally said the bartender. "I guess that's great enough."

The gentleman who had spoken to Jonathan at the excavation had kept to himself at the end of the bar but was listening.

"Art is all you hear in this bar nowadays," he explained to Jonathan. "We used to have brains. Real conversation."

"Speakeasy days," said Earl. "Brains, bathtub booze, and blind staggers. We had our champs then, too."

Jonathan longed to have the discussion continue, but Earl had scooped the last few pennies into his pocket and vanished before Jonathan could summon up the courage to ask about the champs of those other days, for one of them must have been his true father. His head throbbed with vague anticipation. He felt as if he had just pushed the magic button that was to open up the gates to his mother's past and his own future.

What and who was waiting to guide him? he wondered. He knew he would follow without any questions, no matter where he was led. His guides were closer than he knew.

# 2

Lize Britten and Darcy Trent having lunch at the Spur, stuck with each other at last, meant that the season was over, the summer drought was on. It meant that all the men—or the men Darcy and Lize shared—had taken to the hills, gone off on their Guggenheims, off to Rome or Mexico or Greece, off to Yaddo, MacDowell, Huntington Hartford, back to their wives or mothers for a free vacation.

There was nobody left in town except the outsiders, the summer faculties and students of the university, the deserted husbands, the tourists, and the creeps. From Hudson Street to First Avenue, in haunts old and new, Lize and Darcy cruised, pretending not to see each other but finally obliged to exchange a lipstick, borrow a dime to phone, until their year-long feud was crossed off in mutual loneliness. The chances were they would have another big showdown come September—oh, they'd manage to fix each other's wagon somehow during the summer, as they always did, but for the time being hostilities must go in the deep freeze, for they had plenty in common and good reason to unite.

Just two weeks ago that popular artist named Hugow, the Spur's leading attraction, had been whisked off to Cape Cod by that insatiable lady art dealer Cassie Bender. Brazen kidnaping, Darcy called it. Rescue was Lize's private word. Whichever way you looked at it, Darcy was left out in the cold. Deserted. Double-crossed.

"He never said a word!" Darcy kept saying, for good-by was a word Darcy never heard, as Lize and the Spur regulars knew full well. "It's the awful shock that gets me!"

"But he hadn't showed up at the studio for weeks!" Lize reminded her.

"I knew how to find him," Darcy muttered, for she had the same talent Lize herself had for tracking men; their itineraries lit up like the arteries on an anatomy chart the first time she met them. "But now he's really gone, don't you understand?"

Good thing you understand it at last yourself, old thing, Lize wanted to say, but she was not unkind. Darcy's eyes were puffed and her face swollen from weeping bitter brandied tears. She had chosen the darkest booth in the farthest corner of the Spur to wallow in her grief in private, but since she continued to heave and snuffle there could be no secret about her broken heart. This frank exhibition was what had won over Lize. A stiff upper lip would have challenged her, but for her old rival Darcy to make a public show of her defeat brought out the sportsman in Lize.

"Hell, Hugow was always sleeping with Cassie Bender!" she now offered as soothing consolation. "A guy's got to eat."

"I knew he did when he was living with you, Lize." Darcy sniffled into her handkerchief. "But what you don't seem to understand is that our relationship was different. Hugow was absolutely frank with me about everything, that's what I always liked about him. Most men are such liars. But when he went to Chicago that time with her and I hit the ceiling, he said I must be crazy to think of such a thing. 'Cassie Bender is my dealer, you little dope,' he said. 'You don't go around sleeping with your bread and butter. Sure, I go places with her, take her home and all that—I'd do the same for Kootz or Sidney Janis or Pierre Matisse. It's business. I like to make a buck and Cassie sells me, but as for an affair, you must be kidding.' Oh, he was perfectly honest about it."

Lize blinked.

"You knew Hugow before I did, Lize," Darcy said, "and you've got to admit he never lied. He was always honest."

"Maybe he just lied to himself," Lize suggested, a little dazed.

Darcy nodded emphatically.

"That's just it. He was so honest that if he had to lie he'd lie to himself too, don't you see?"

Lize was silent, a feat that took all her strength. It would have been so easy to say, "Yes, Hugow was always honest, as you say. Only last year when *I* was living with him and accused him of sleeping with *you* he burst out laughing. 'That dumb kid,' he says, 'are you out of your mind? Look here,' he says, 'I'll level with you. I've got my share of male egotism, call it plain vanity, so believe me I don't make passes at any dame that asks me why don't I paint like Grandma Moses. I could learn, she tells me. Listen, Lize,' he says, 'you must know how a crack like that would paralyze a man with my ego.' So we both had a good laugh, and a few months later you moved in and I was wondering what hit me. Old honest Hugow."

Anyhow Hugow didn't ever chase a woman, Lize was forced to admit. He was a softhearted fellow, and if a woman climbed into his bed he didn't kick her out. He made a brave stab at being independent, keeping his studio strictly for himself, but Lize had managed to move in, the same as the other girls, and Darcy after her. Poor guy. The technique was so simple you'd think the sap would have learned some defense tricks.

You got into the sacred old studio first with a crowd, after an opening or to see a new picture he might be feeling good about, and then you managed to hang around, helping clean up after the others left. So you stayed that one night and then if he didn't phone you afterward— which he never did, sober—you went back for something you'd left. This time you brought a toothbrush and an office dress, in case you stayed again. Next time you casually left a suitcase, because you'd just lost your apartment and couldn't find a place to move yet, you told him. So there you were, in. Poor old Hugow, it was so easy, but damn his hide, he did always manage to get away, even though he couldn't get you out.

It was a consolation to know he'd walked out on her successor just as he had on her the year before, Lize told herself.

"You might have guessed what you were in for, seeing how he treated everybody else before you," she said.

"But Lize, with me it was *serious!*" Darcy patiently protested. "I don't know how to explain it, but I *understood* Hugow, and none of you others ever had. I just happen to understand the artistic temperament, and that's where you failed him, you see."

Again Lize exercised stern self-control to keep from reminding Darcy that they'd covered the same artists in their time with about the same scores. And as for "failing" Hugow—she'd blow her top if she listened to Darcy go on about why she, Lize, and the others had never been right for Hugow anyway. With Darcy's little voice quavering on and on, Lize found herself brooding all over again about her own season with Hugow. Maybe she would have lasted longer if she'd realized that he took that crazy painting of his seriously. But how could you guess that a grown man thought it mattered whether he made a green or purple blob on the canvas? You could understand his being pleased when people liked it or when he got a big check for it, but to think the stuff mattered all by itself—as if it were a machine that would work, depending on a line being here instead of there. Crazy! Luckily she'd kept her mouth shut when he was in one of his sunk moods, though heaven knows she'd wanted to say, "Why in God's name do you go on with something that makes you so miserable?" She'd just let him fool around with the stuff while she quietly got the studio fixed up with a kitchen unit, a few rugs and chairs from the Salvation Army Furniture Store. She had just gotten to the point where she was inviting other couples in for hamburgers and beer, and the grocer was calling her Mrs. Hugow, when he simply disappeared.

Somebody mentioned something about a shack he used sometimes up in Rockland County and that maybe he'd gone up there to work. His friends didn't seem worried or even surprised. But days passed, and no word from him. Lize would come home from the office and then hang around The Golden Spur, hoping for some news of him. But nobody told her anything. That's the way Hugow always was—his pals shrugged—maybe he'd turn up tomorrow, maybe next week.

If she'd known more about his work she would have soon suspected that he wasn't coming back—at least not to her. She would have noticed that he or one of his cronies was slipping into the studio whenever she wasn't there and taking out stuff he needed. That his newest canvas was gone should have told her something, but she wasn't sure which was the new one because all his pictures looked alike to Lize. Great lozenges of red and white ("I love blood," he always said), black and gray squares ("I love chess," he'd say), long green spikes ("I love asparagus"). All Lize had learned about art from her life with painters was that the big pictures were for museums and the little ones for art.

Lize remembered that the first inkling of real trouble was when she heard that Darcy Trent, who had been at loose ends ever since Lew Schaffer went back to his wife, was commuting to work from Rockland County.

Well!

Lize never allowed two and two to make four until she was good and ready. So she went on hanging around the empty studio for a couple of weeks more, knowing what was up all right, and having it rubbed in whenever she went to The Golden Spur or The Big Hat or The Barrel. Whoever was Hugow's girl was queen of the crowd, in a way, with all the hangers-on clambering to sit with her. But the minute the grapevine had the word that she'd been bounced, the boys who wanted to paint like Hugow and the ones who just wanted to be around a big shot all faded away when she hailed them. Sometimes the whole bar would clear out—a party somewhere, they didn't dare ask her in case Hugow and the new girl (Darcy) would be there. Lize found herself stuck with a moist-eyed Hugow-worshiper, Percy Wright, whom everybody had been ducking for years, but at least he had money enough for them to close the bars together. The poor mug actually got the idea he was *stealing* Hugow's girl, and Lize let him think so.

Percy wasn't as spooky as the crowd thought, even if he did have money (too much to be a respected artist and too little to be a respected snob). He was in some Wall Street office, but his analyst had set him painting, so he had started hanging around the Spur, trying to pin artists down to depth conversations on Old Masters, when the proper thing was to pop off on galleries, dealers, and critics. Lize was bored by his constant boasting to strangers that she had once been Hugow's girlfriend, as if this meant Hugow's talents would automatically rub off on him now.

Still, his spaniel adoration was consoling. He had inherited his mother's old brownstone house in Brooklyn Heights and lived there alone with two floors rented out. He was flattered when Lize started leaving her things there, a make-up kit, douche-bag, then a suitcase "just while she was looking for an apartment." To please her, he let her persuade him to give a couple of big parties, thinking it would establish him with the artist crowd. But, just as Lize had feared, the good guys didn't show up, knowing Hugow wouldn't be there, and the guests were the dregs of all the Left Banks in the world, North Beach, Truro, Paris, or Rome, all knights of the open house, ready to spring at the pop of a cork, ready to stand by through thick of bourbon to thin of wine. Percy didn't mind the expense of these sodden revels that seemed to drag on for days, for he had learned Brooklyn hosts must always be taxed high for wrenching guests from their beloved dingy Manhattan bars, but he resented having their taxi fares back home extorted from him. Lize reproached him for being mean and stingy, but he retorted sulkily that he was *not* stingy, he just didn't like to spend money on other people, that was all. The parties didn't get him anywhere, Lize saw, and she was Indian-marked by her new escort. No use nagging him into buying drinks for the crowd in their own bailiwick, either, for Percy soon set up a squawk. Cash! Money in general was sacred enough, but *cash!*

In spite of these mistakes in adjusting, Percy bloomed under Lize's bullying, as everyone could see. This must have been the same nagging Hugow himself had gotten, he figured, and that set him up as Hugow's equal. He put on some weight, which made him look almost virile. He took to using a sun lamp, grew a little sprig of mustache, wore black-rimmed glasses, tuned his apologetic voice a few notes lower, walked on the balls of his feet, and all in all acted like a man important enough to be kicked around by an ex-girlfriend of Artist Hugow.

Lize had been regarding her time with Percy Wright as a sabbatical year, doing the things outsiders and tourists did—the theater, good restaurants, driving around week ends in Percy's MG, and getting what she could without wounding him in the wallet directly. If a guy could produce enough background, music, and scenery changes, a girl could stand almost anybody. Her pride was saved, too. Some people even thought that orchestra seats at a good show and The Embers afterward was socially a big step up from Hugow's bed in an East Tenth Street dump. And she had a chance to case the field for somebody better. There were fellows in her office—she worked in a printing outfit near Grand Central—who made passes and asked for lunch dates, but they were mostly commuting husbands, scared to miss more than one train, and likely to shout "Yippee!" when they went to a Village spot. Lize had gone for them when she first started working in New York, but after doing the artist bit you couldn't go back to business types, except maybe once in a while. Percy never suspected, being so faithful to Hugow himself that he couldn't imagine a

Hugow woman would go anywhere but back to Hugow, and Darcy Trent had that situation covered. Percy often said how glad he was that the master had consolation for losing Lize.

Lize had a rangy Southwest style and was at her best in trim slacks and sport coats or tailored suits that hung negligently on her lean frame with a fine Bond Street air. Dolled up for a big evening, freckles lightly dusted (those freckles were as good as any collateral for assuring the simple sophisticates of her sterling honesty!), a fillet of rosebuds or butterflies in her close-cropped sorrel hair, a great pouf of satin ribbon on the sleek hips, a dangle of beads at the ears and over the boyish bosom, Lize drew the interest of men of all sexes, but Darcy Trent managed all right too.

Darcy was a wood violet, not as diminutive as she appeared at first glance, but small-boned, small-nosed, small-faced, and given to tiny gestures and a tiny baby voice. She seemed womanly and practical too, and you thought Darcy must be like those small iron pioneer women in the Conestoga wagons, whipping men and children across the prairies, sewing, building, plowing, cooking, nursing, saving her menfolks from their natural folly and improvidence. The fact was that Darcy had never darned a sock, seldom made her own bed, thought coffee was born in delicatessen containers and all food grew in frozen packages. Her practicality exhibited itself in tender little cries of, "But you'll be sick, honey, if you don't eat something after all that bourbon! You must eat! Here, eat this pretzel." In other crises she could figure out efficiently in her head that four people sharing a taxi wouldn't be much more than four subway fares, and that way they could carry their drinks along. She was very firm too in insisting that a man coming out of a week-end binge still reeking of stale smoke and rye should keep away from his job Monday unless he shaved and changed his shirt.

Darcy was delicate in color, almost fading into background, but strong and gamy like those tiny weed-flowers whose roots push up boulders. A man felt that here was a real woman, an old-fashioned girl with her little footsies firmly on the ground, someone to count on, someone always behind you. Darcy's pretty feet were more likely to be on the wall or tangled up in sheets than on the ground, and as for being behind her man, he found out sooner or later she was really on his back. Alas, little women are as hard to throw out as Amazons, especially a confiding little creature like Darcy who had no place to go until there was another back to jump on. Between backs Darcy had no existence, like a hermit crab caught in a shuttle from one stolen shell to another.

Now that Hugow had vanished with Cassie Bender and her damnable station wagon—it was always transporting some artist and his canvases to some place his true mate couldn't get at him—Darcy, the little pioneer woman, had given up completely. She didn't show up at her job in the portrait photographer's studio on West Fifty-Seventh Street for three days on account of her tendency to cry all the time, and after that she was afraid to go in, having a hunch she was automatically fired. She sat around Hugow's studio, hoping there was some mistake, but knowing better. You would have thought she'd stay away from The Golden Spur, where the ritual of brushing off Hugow's cast-off ladies was as rigorously practiced as suttee, but there she was every day or night, getting what Lize had got the year before.

It was "Hello, Al, how's everything? Anybody sitting

here—oh, you're just leaving? . . . Hello, Lester, have a beer with me—oh, you're joining friends? . . . What's that, waiter, you say this booth is reserved? Don't be silly! Reserved booths in the Spur, ha, ha! . . . Oh, you mean because I'm just one person—but supposing somebody else . . . oh, well . . ."

The crushing blow was when some fellow conspirator of Hugow's (probably Lew Schaffer, her old lover) had gotten into the studio when Darcy was out and cleaned out all Hugow's smaller possessions. The stuff, in a cardboard suitcase, was under the bar of The Golden Spur at this very minute, waiting for somebody on the way to Provincetown to pick it up. Hugow was really not to blame, Darcy had been insisting up to this point, everything was the fault of Cassie Bender and his other false friends. But to be deserted like this, left in that rat-ridden old slummy studio with the improvements she had generously installed for his comfort—the makeshift shower, dressing mirror, the wardrobe for her dresses, the cute make-up table—it was as if he was saying, here, take the works, my dear girl, you were so anxious to move in. Oh, that was cruel of Hugow, and so ungrateful.

"I think it was darned decent of him to leave you the place," Lize observed after some thought. "He could have locked you out and changed the key" (as he finally did to me, Lize added privately). "You'd been telling him all along you couldn't get an apartment, remember, so I think he meant to be nice, giving it up to you. After all, he loved that lousy dump."

Darcy was beginning to be sorry she'd bleated all her woes to Lize if they were going to be thrown right back at her. She recalled with relief that she hadn't confessed that Lew Schaffer had treated her the same way—walked out of his place after she'd fixed it up so pretty, walked right back to his wife. She'd been stuck with the rent until she'd unloaded it on some Vassar girls who wanted to Live. She'd found out that Lew had retrieved the place the minute she'd moved out to Nyack after Hugow. Men were sneaky that way. But twice stuck like that! Well, at least Lize didn't know that part.

"I never meant I wanted to live way over in that slum all alone," Darcy said. "Bowery bums sleeping on the doorstep and juvenile delinquents slinking up and down the fire escapes. And fifty dollars a month! Sure, it's cheap when you're dividing it, but all that by yourself for a dump where you're afraid to be alone."

Lize, smitten with a brilliant inspiration, looked meditatively at Darcy.

"Oh, I know I look a wreck," Darcy said defensively. "You don't need to tell me."

"I was just thinking your hair's cute with that lock falling down," Lize said.

For some time Lize had been trying to figure out a way of getting back with the old crowd on her own without losing Percy altogether. He had a big inferiority, with every right to it, and a mean way of getting even when he was wounded. She didn't want to break off till she was sure what came next. This week Percy's sister's family from Buffalo were visiting the Brooklyn house, which gave Lize a good excuse to stay out of the picture in a Village hotel. Whatever came of this Percy would have to admit was largely his fault.

"I was so hurt when you didn't want your family to meet me," she could say to him when the time came.

"I think this is a good chance to break with Percy," Lize said to Darcy.

"I can't understand how you endured him this long, Lize," Darcy said, absorbed in admiring her hair in her pocket mirror. "Hugow couldn't get over it. He just despised Percy, always sidling up to him—'May I join you people? I do hate to miss a word of Hugow's conversation.' Blah blah blah."

"No more blah blah to Percy than Hugow once he gets going," Lize retorted in a burst of obstinate loyalty.

Hugow, Hugow, Hugow—the way damn fool women carried on about him—sometimes not seeing him for years, too—you would think he was the Great Lover of the Ages, a perfect panther of a man, wonderfully equipped, wonderfully insatiable, every nuance at his command. Well, it just wasn't that way at all, and all his men friends, who were sure that was it, were plain stupid. Ask the women (not that they'd admit the truth). There was the big rush at the outset, while he was on a binge between pictures, a hungry-farm-boy technique, that was all; then you could wait for weeks for another pass, living right with him, too. That was what got you,—the cruel, indifferent, teasing withdrawal, all the worse because he had no idea he was being heartless. He could be lying on the bed right beside you, buck naked, absently flipping your eager hands off his body like so many horseflies, till you got so hurt you had to go off to some corner and bawl, with him lying there staring at the ceiling with nothing on his mind but how blue is sky and how black is night. He got under your skin that way, and damn his hide, he could always get any woman back—fifty years from now he could whistle through his old gums and they would all come flying up from hell to warm up his old bones. Other men—like Lew Schaffer and all the artists Lize and Darcy had run through—became just part of the everyday scenery after an affair was over.

Like Lize or Darcy, who never left any trace of their past love.

Oh yes, there was usually a lipstick and a babushka left by Lize in a drawer. And Darcy's potato. ("There's nothing so beautiful in the whole world as a potato, I don't care what you artists say. A potato has everything," was Darcy's very own stand in all aesthetic arguments.) Darcy's potato crept into one painting or another like a Kilroy-was-here mark. Lew Schaffer had done a saint with potato eyes sprouting all over it, for instance, and Mrs. Schaffer had screamed, "So you've been sleeping with Darcy Trent!"

But Hugow got into your blood, kept you itching for him and hanging on shamelessly long after you knew he was through. Lize wondered how long before Darcy would admit it was hopeless.

"How do you mean this is a good chance to break with Percy?" Darcy suddenly asked. "How could you afford to go on staying at the Albert?"

"I could move into the studio with you," Lize said triumphantly.

Darcy's eyes widened.

"Oh no! What would people say, two girls living together! Oh, Lize, we couldn't, we just wouldn't dare!"

"Don't be so old-fashioned, for God's sake!" Lize said impatiently. There was something in what Darcy said, of course. Lize could already anticipate the snickering around The Golden Spur set when the news got out.

"It splits the rent, and you say you're scared alone. Okay, forget it," Lize said, but she had no intention of giving up the idea.

"I'm sorry, I always think of appearances." Darcy was sniveling again, and Lize could have given her a good slap. She looked toward the bar to see if any fresh company had arrived. The young man who had been reading the bulletin board was still there and, meeting his eye, Lize gave him a warm, friendly smile, which she saw had the proper energizing effect, for he started edging down the bar at once, pleased but hesitant.

"I think we can work something out," Lize murmured to Darcy absently, and waited for the right moment.

Jonathan had been stealing curious glances at the two young women in the back, even while his ears were tuned to the bar talk. He wondered if his mother had had just such a girlfriend who could, if he found her now, tell him all the intimate little confidences he longed to know. It was hard to picture his gentle mother in these surroundings, and surely she had never been as sophisticated as these two girls seemed.

The improbable red of the taller one's hair impressed him as stylish, while the smaller one's bright orange skirt lit up the dark corner like a forest blaze—an inviting touch, he thought. (Lize had been thinking that in that brassy hue little Darcy looked like a rather flashy mouse.) Jonathan was heartened to see that these two clean-cut New Yorkers were not above working over a good old American steak, and after Lize's friendly smile he was sure they were not formidable cosmopolitans after all, but simple, foursquare American girls. Never in the world would he have suspected the scrambled montage of bars, beds, and bushes behind their open, homespun faces. They were modern versions of his mother, Jonathan thought. He was considering a move to take the booth next to theirs when he felt a hand on his arm.

It was his companion of the wrecking scene.

"Come have a drink with me, young man," said the gentleman. "I have a class in precisely fifteen minutes and I defy anyone to face that sea of cretin faces without an anesthetic."

As Jonathan hesitated, his new friend went on confidentially, "I overheard you asking about Alvine Harshawe. It so happens that I recall seeing him here many years ago. He was just coming up then—some powerful stories in *The Sphere* and a play in the experimental theater. People used to point him out, that sort of thing."

"What was he like?" Jonathan asked eagerly.

The professor shrugged.

"Too sure of himself for my taste. Of course I was older and had done some writing of my own, but Harshawe was the comer, and the Spur was the writers' speakeasy."

"I'd like to know all I can about the Spur in those days," Jonathan said.

The professor studied him shrewdly.

"Another thesis on the twenties and thirties, eh?" he said. "Just what my colleague in the English Department has been working on for ten years. The Speakeasy as a Forcing Bed for Literature is her angle, I believe. I'm sure she'd be glad to share the background picture with you, because I'm the one who gave it to her, ha, ha."

He signaled for drinks, which Jonathan regarded uneasily.

"Place was horsy at first because the owner was a retired cowboy, got thrown by a wild horse in the rodeo at the old Madison Square Garden and won the place in a roll of dice. Fixed it all up with these racing prints and used to hobble around on crutches in his tight pants and satin shirts, Western style. Fought with a drunk and got thrown right through his own window, there. The place kept the horsy decor after he left, but then the jazz musicians took over till jazz went uptown; then it got the actors from the little theater upstairs, and finally the artists. Harshawe hasn't been even heard of in this place since the abstract wave took over."

"Did you know people who came here, say, around nineteen twenty-eight?" Jonathan asked.

"A few," said the gentleman." I had just started teaching here in the East then, and I used to come in here with a student occasionally, and they would always point out the characters."

"Phone call, Doctor Kellsey," said the bartender. "What do I tell her this time?"

"Damn it, does a light go on all over the city every time I step into a bar?" cried Dr. Kellsey indignantly. "You told her once, didn't you, that Doctor Kellsey hadn't been in for weeks?"

"This is a different lady, Doctor," said the bartender.

"Ah. My wife. In that case tell her you don't know any Doctor Kellsey." He waited till the bartender hung up. "What did she say?"

"Said I was lucky," said the bartender.

"Damn these female bloodhounds," said the professor. He paid his bill and then fished out a card, which he handed to Jonathan.

"Here's where you can reach me if you'd like to get more information. Always glad to talk over the old days with a fellow researcher. Helpful to both of us."

He gave Jonathan a genial handclasp that warmed his heart and hurried out.

DR. WALTER KELLSEY, KNOWLTON ARMS, GRAMERCY PARK, Jonathan read on the card. He copied it carefully in his little red notebook, glowing with the compliment of being taken for a fellow academician.

"Got a light, Buster?"

Startled, Jonathan looked up to see the tall girl with the pink hair beside him. He lit a match for her.

"Come on back and have a drink with us," she said, taking his arm. "No sense in being lonesome. Darcy and I are back here."

"I ought to be out looking for a room," he said, allowing himself to be led into the dark recesses, "and a job."

"It's too nice a day to be outdoors," protested the girl and nudged him gently into the booth. "Isn't that so, Darcy?"

Jonathan saw that the other girl was none too pleased at his intrusion.

"Really, Lize!" she exclaimed reprovingly.

"Okay, I picked him up, so what?" Lize looked him over with obvious satisfaction. "Doesn't he look like somebody, Darcy?"

"Doesn't everybody?" snapped Darcy.

She knew Lize had been getting bored with her damp sorrow, finagling for the last half-hour to get the eye of the stranger at the bar. Oh, he was good-looking in a clean, strapping Midwest way, and he did stand out in the Spur's galaxy of battered, beat-up gallants, but personally she preferred that battered, beat look on a man. At least you knew what they must have done to get that way, and what they were likely to go on doing. This eager, dewy-eyed Buster was too healthy to trust, apt to invite you for a chase over the moors, or to romp around a dance floor, clapping his hands over his head or swinging you around by the ponytail. Health was all right for women—God knows they needed it!—but a man ought to have something more special, an eyepatch, a broken nose, a battle scar, or a tired gimp like Hugow's. That was Darcy's theory. But Lize was on the prowl again, ready to snatch up the first thing that came along, now that she'd made up her mind to ditch Percy.

"You one of those college creeps?" Darcy asked Jonathan politely. "Is that why you got stuck with that stuffy professor?"

"Kellsey isn't stuffy except when he's on the wagon," Lize said severely. "Personally I like him. He's just a good-natured old slob that hates everybody, that's all. Be fair."

"He was very kind to me," Jonathan said. "He's going to help me on my research."

"I'm not going back to work this afternoon," Lize stated. "I think we should stick around here and get acquainted. Were you looking for a room on the bulletin board?"

Surprised that she had noticed, Jonathan nodded.

"I thought as much," Lize said. "You can relax, because we've got the place for you."

"Me?"

"Darcy needs a man to stay in Hugow's studio," Lize said, at which Darcy's crumpled little face tried to stiffen into an expression of moral outrage.

"Really, Lize!"

"It's all right, I'll be there too," Lize said. "Get it?"

Darcy looked at her with unwilling admiration.

"There's only the couch in the studio and the broken-down Hi-Riser in the back room," she said. "It has mice in it—just baby mice, though."

"He could have the couch," Lize said, who knew the place as well as Darcy did, after all.

"That's awfully good of you," Jonathan said, startled. "Are you sure you really would like to—I mean—"

"Listen to him," Lize said. "With his looks. Isn't he a beauty?"

She smiled at Jonathan meditatively.

"I love his hair," she mused. "I wonder what a real sharp crew-cut would do for him."

"You're always cutting people's hair," complained Darcy. "I had to cut Hugow's all over again to get it the way I liked it."

"Well, Cassie's probably sent him to a real barber by this time," Lize said maliciously; then, relenting, "Okay, Darcy, you can cut it this time. Can't she, Jack?"

"Jonathan," he said, embarrassed, not sure they were serious about anything.

Lize clapped her hand on his knee affectionately.

"Now I call that cute," she said. "Don't you, Darcy?"

Darcy was sulking, as if a new baby brother had put her nose out of joint.

"What's he doing looking for this Harshawe?" she grumbled. "Is he FBI or something?"

"We can help him get the lowdown on everybody once we get settled, eh, Darcy?" Lize chuckled. "Is that all right with you, Jonathan, moving in with us? We'll all save money by it."

It must be a perfectly ordinary New York custom, Jonathan thought.

"Everything's in a mess over there," Darcy said. "There's only some moldy marmalade and stuffed olives and shaving cream, but you're welcome."

She was cheering up under the prospect of company and taking an interest in the list of needed supplies Lize was jotting down. A little alarmed at the speed with which things were moving, Jonathan suggested he had better spend the rest of the afternoon looking around for a job.

"You sit right here, Bud," Lize commanded. "Everybody gets their jobs right here in the Spur, you might as well learn that right now. Why don't you take that café job up there on the bulletin board?"

"Do you think I could do it?" Jonathan asked.

This question struck both girls as irrelevant. If a job was what you wanted, you took whatever came along and found out later whether you could do it or not. If you got fired you still had your week's pay and came back to the Spur to hang around till another job turned up.

Jonathan was speechless with wonder at the amazing kindness of city women. Not only did the two new friends insist on dividing the check in three equal parts when it came, but they gave him explicit directions for getting to the Then-and-Now Café on Bleecker Street to apply for the job, and further information on getting to the new home he was to share with them. Then they left to do their marketing and to pick up Lize's suitcase at the Albert.

Jonathan took out his little red book after they left and wrote down his new address on the flyleaf. Before he gave up the booth, he wrote a note to the Miss Claire Van Orphen mentioned in his mother's letters, asking for an interview.

That's the way you did things in New York, he said to himself. Go right after 'em before you have time to think.

# 3

THE NOTE forwarded to her from the Pen and Brush Club
had given Claire Van Orphen a full morning of reflections
on the past. Some young man—the signature was unknown
to her—would like to call on her on purely personal business connected with Constance Birch. He realized, the
writer said, that a busy author like Miss Van Orphen must
have had a dozen secretaries, and Constance Birch had
worked for her less than a year—1928 it had been. But the
experience had meant so much to his mother (for he was
Constance Birch's son) that he dared to hope Miss Van Orphen might retain some recollections of her. Since his
mother's death years ago he had regretted the lost opportunities for not having known her better, and now that he
was in New York he was trying to enrich his picture of her
by meeting those who had known her during her own New
York period.

Constance Birch, Miss Van Orphen mused, putting down
the note and frowning into space. What in heaven's name
could she remember about her beyond the fact that she'd
been the last secretary she had been able to afford? A pale,
sweet, quiet little creature, Claire recalled, so shy you
thought she'd be afraid to go home at night when she had
to type late. Not at all, the girl had assured her. It was true
that she had to cross that dark block under the El to get to

41

her room, but she had the habit of stopping in a very nice bar for a sandwich and a beer, and there was always some nice fellow there going in her direction.

Well, I certainly can't tell her son about that, Claire reflected. Nor about the literary tea Claire had given—oh, those were the lavish days—in the Brevoort banquet suite, with Connie helping her in her nice unobtrusive way, and the surprising way the child had passed out in Claire's room later, passed out cold, as if there wasn't enough to do after a party.

"I'd never tasted champagne before, Miss Van Orphen," she had explained when she revived, greatly mortified. "And I'd never met so many famous men. Wasn't it awful?"

For the life of her Claire couldn't remember the girl's face or much of anything except that she was so obliging you couldn't fire her for her inexperience, and she didn't get on your nerves like the more hard-boiled efficient ones did, who charged more, besides. She did remember how anxious the girl was to learn city ways and yet how singularly blind she was to them. For instance, she always wore tennis shoes and simple little cotton dresses she made by hand, oblivious to the stylish touches from the *Vogues* she studied. Her pale cheeks would flush with excitement when she had to type a letter to some well-known editor, and she would stare with wide, eager eyes when Claire was on the telephone, then stammer, "M-Miss Van Orphen, excuse me, I couldn't help overhearing—do you really know Susan Glaspell personally? My!" Yes, her candid naïveté had made Claire feel sinfully worldly, she recalled, though there had been curious features about it. Like the time it had struck Claire that the child was available almost any hour of day or night and therefore must be having a friendless sort of life, so she decided to take her to The Black

Knight for dinner, that being a popular speakeasy below the square where Claire had been taken once by an editor. On the way down Claire had felt a few qualms about introducing the little country girl to the kind of Village life she herself did not know or even wholly approve. It puzzled and amused her that, when they entered, several patrons, and the owner himself, cried out, "Hello, Connie."

"I thought you said you'd never been here," Claire said.

"Oh, I didn't know you meant Sam's," Connie said. "We just call it Sam's, you see."

Aside from those little kinks, Claire remembered nothing remarkable about her except that she had typed a serial Claire had sold to the *Delineator,* almost her last success. Well, all she could do for the young man, Claire thought, was to fill him in on the general background of Greenwich Village in the late twenties, the way biographers did when they ran short of personal facts.

Having so little to tell him, she would have the added embarrassment of disillusioning the lad about his mother's fine connections. Obviously the slight contact with Claire had been built up after the girl had gone back home and married the old steady beau. Claire recalled Christmas cards signed "Connie, with appreciation for all your kindnesses my wonderful year in New York." She would certainly have to do something for the boy, have him come to the cocktail lounge for tea—the canapés were free. Sometimes a talented guest played the old grand piano, and there were young people around once in a while, so the place didn't seem such an elderly retreat.

It had been a long time since any stranger had looked her up, and Claire began to brighten. In the old days people they'd met on trips were always telephoning the Van Orphen girls—"You told us in Florence to be sure and

look you up when we got to New York." It used to put
the girls on their mettle, trying to put on a good show at
home for those fascinating worldly strangers. Bea wasn't
on hand for the sister act any more, of course; she had to
manage alone now.

Claire pushed aside the avocado plant she was nursing
in its glass of water on the window sill, and selected a pen
from the glass slipper on her desk. She addressed an envelope to Mr. Jonathan Jaimison at the East Tenth Street
address and began writing her note.

One thing Claire had no worry about was her clothes.
She might be obliged to live in a cell, uncertain of selling
a line she wrote, uncertain of the dear moments she could
be granted with Bea, too modest to cling to successful old
friends, but at least she need never worry about her appearance. She was happy in that knowledge.

Friends and relatives had scolded her years ago for throwing away all her money on clothes. "You'll have to go into
your capital first thing you know," they warned. But in
these difficult years Claire was glad of her wardrobe because good, really good clothes never go out of style, she
said, and she'd rather feel a good three-hundred-dollar
Molyneux dress on her back, even if it was thirty years
old, than a brand-new budget-shop print, which she couldn't
afford anyway. The ever-rising room rent in her modest
hotel took a huge bite out of her vanishing income and
dwindling royalties, but the backlog of fine clothes made
her feel secure.

She had had to give up her original nice little suite for
a bed-sitting-room barely large enough to hold her huge
wardrobe trunk and hatboxes. The file cabinet had had

to go to the cellar, but that was just as well. Instead of its testifying to her long, honorable professional career as a writer, those drawers full of manuscripts with attached lists of rejections and future publishing possibilities (now largely out of business) were rude reminders of a lifetime of misspent hopes. The simple little desk with its six pigeonholes, tiny Swiss typewriter in the drawer, notebook and vase of pencils on top, were equipment enough for her present literary activities. The published pieces, the travel books and Christmas juveniles, were on the closet shelf, wrapped in cellophane. The stories she was always writing —for she could not stop the silly habit any more than she could stop saying Now-I-lay-me every night—she kept hidden in orderly stacks under the bed.

In the always-open trunk, stuffed closet, and bulging dresser drawers there were enough costumes for Claire to appear in different combinations for years to come. Some of the older creations, dating back to Paquin and Worth, remained in almost mint condition or only "slightly foxed," as the booksellers would say, and some of the post-World War I numbers seemed to be coming back in style. It was a pity that social life had deteriorated to the point where formal evening dress was seldom—indeed, where Claire was concerned, never—required any more. She had wistful moments of shaking out the bouffant rainbow tulle *robe de style*, the jewel-encrusted beige satin, the ruby velvet with richly embroidered panniers, the bronze lamé décolleté with flying wisps of gold-dotted net, and she would vow that if she ever got her hands on a good fat sum again it would pay her to go on an ocean cruise—they still dressed for dinner there, she was sure—just to get the good out of these treasures. She thought of the places where the gowns had appeared—the opera houses, the embassy balls, the

garden parties, the state affairs honoring Colonel Van
Orphen. All vanished and forgotten, wiped out, it seemed,
almost in a day.

Every morning around half past ten, having had her
instant coffee and an orange in her room at seven, Claire
went to the Planet Drug Store around the corner and had
an egg sandwich or Danish and a real coffee. This was the
big adventure of the day, for all sorts of people dropped
in at the fountain for a cup of coffee and chat with the
counterman or with one another. They seldom started
conversations with Claire, and although she realized her
careful ensembles with matching hats and gloves intimidated them, she simply could not bring herself, a well-bred
woman of over sixty, to step outdoors without hat and
proper accessories. However, the counterman called her
"baby," as he called all the ladies, and she could listen
to the chatter, sometimes quite strange, and mull it over
in her room later. There was a young man who talked
about Shape Notes and the Fa Sol La Singers, from the
West Virginia hills, and some television actors who talked
about "bennies" and "dexies," and there was talk about
show openings, reducing diets (these were always recited
over chocolate sodas), new jokes, hospital experiences with
explicit details that made Claire wince, and gloomy business talk by neighborhood merchants having a coffee or
seltzer break.

"What do you do for a hangover, Jake?" the battered-
looking haberdasher from next door begged to know.

"I just don't go there any more," said the counterman,
and to his and Claire's amazement this made the gourmets
split their sides laughing and became the great goody to be
revived every day with wild shouts of joy. After this daily
dip into the world, Claire retired to her room to write

until her night meal of beans or spaghetti from the Horn
& Hardart Retail Store, or, for a change, a tin of corned
beef or a chicken leg and a pastry. She allowed herself the
hotel dinner once a week. It was not fair that economizing
on food should make you put on weight, but it was sadly
true, and Claire had the devil's own time squeezing into her
old gowns. The young woman at the hotel news stand was
always gesturing to her that an under-arm seam had popped
or that a top hook wasn't fastened. She further annoyed
Claire with her helpful comments that her rouge or lipstick was crooked or too thick, and had she read that rouge
wasn't fashionable any more? Claire always thanked her
politely and continued making up the same way, placing
a circle of fuchsia rouge in the exact center of each cheek
and working it up toward the eyes as she had been doing
since her first Harriet Hubbard Ayer beauty kit.

Once or twice a week, after she had revised an old love
story or sold a little garden piece to a home magazine, she
celebrated by walking over to a certain bar out of range of
her hotel and treating herself to a Manhattan cocktail,
sometimes two. When the frozen faced bartender or one
of the oldtimers would spot the somewhat formidable lady
in her hat, gloves, and carefully chosen afternoon costume
rounding the corner, he would warn, "Here comes Miss
Manhattan," and the customers would tip to the end of
the bar like the balls on a bagatelle board, leaving one
whole row of stools free for the lady.

"Good afternoon, Frank," Claire always said, assuming
her place on the stool with dignity and speaking in her
clear world-traveler voice, "A Manhattan, if you please.
With cherry, thank you." After she had paid her bill, adjusted her veil, and marched out to the street, bartender
and oldtimers would shake their heads and declare (as if

they were Beau Brummells themselves) that nowhere in the world could there be found any outfits to equal those contrived by Miss Manhattan. In this they were quite wrong.

There was a twin of Claire's trunk in a hotel storage cellar on West Fifty-sixth Street, in which were many duplicates of Claire's collection. This trunk was the long-forgotten property of Mrs. Kingston Ball, née Beatrice Van Orphen, Claire's twin sister. Beatrice and Claire had dressed alike and done everything together until they were twenty-eight, when Bea, always the bolder of the two, declared the end of twinship. They had just lost another lover who, like all his predecessors, couldn't make up his mind which twin he preferred and was intimidated by there being two of everything. If there must be a pair, then he should have both or none; one would only make him feel cheated, as if he'd got only one book-end. Bea prophesied that this vertigo would attack every suitor they ever would get to the end of their days (somehow they got only one beau between them at a time) and they were blocking each other's futures. Claire was shattered and hurt by this proposal, as if she were to be stripped of her very skin, but Beatrice was determined. From now on she would tint her hair lighter and wear it short, and, since Claire loved their former style of dress, she could keep their dressmaker and Bea would buy ready-made. They would begin new, separate lives.

It was a bewildering blow to Claire to realize that this revolt had been simmering in her dear twin's head for years. It embarrassed Claire to think of her fatuous complacency, never dreaming of any divergence in their ideas on any subject. Her sense of humiliation (for she felt she had somehow fallen below Bea's standards) made her accept Bea's program without protest. When Bea burst into con-

trite tears at the final parting, saying, "It'll be much better
for you too, going it alone," Claire gently comforted her
with "Of course, dear, we're just standing in each other's
way."

So Bea moved to a hotel near Carnegie Hall, for she
would concentrate on their musical interests. Claire would
pursue her budding literary career and live downtown as
before. They would have different social engagements,
take trips separately, affect different restaurants. This strat-
egy, murder for poor Claire, worked out well for Bea.
When Claire chose a Scandinavian cruise, Bea took Hawaii
and there met and wed Mr. Ball, a widower. At his death
she returned to her old hotel in New York but never to
active twinship again. By that time the wound had been
assuaged for Claire by her trickle of literary success—
garden and travel articles and love stories for family magazines; she too was content with occasional meetings which
usually did nothing but reveal how far apart they had
drifted.

When Claire, carefully corseted and squeezed into the
plum velvet suit with moleskin toque and scarf, came up
to Bea's gloomy hotel for lunch, Bea hastily whisked her
through the long lobby, past the overstuffed Gothic sofas
where the passé (let's face it) international musical greats
sat all day reviewing the American scene. In the coffee shop
Bea would pounce on the darkest corner table, half ashamed
and half protective, suspecting the quizzical looks from
the amusing young men of her present circle, fervently
hoping that her current pet would not see her and guess
her true age by Claire's costume. She knew that Claire did
not look any more of a period piece than the majestic old
Brunhildes and Isoldes wafting their moth-eaten velvets
through the hotel corridors, but it seemed worse to flaunt

your antiquity as Claire did than to be merely eccentric.

On the other hand, when Bea arrived down at Claire's hotel for the Washington Square summer concerts, wearing a jaunty strapless print sundress, gold barefoot sandals exposing red-painted toes, shoulder bones stabbing out behind like stunted wings, arms bare except for the costume jewelry and short white gloves, flowered ribbon bandeau on the close-cut blond hair, large Caribbean straw handbag swinging from her elbow, Claire led her to the very darkest corner of *her* gloomy dining room, feeling the sour glances of the lobby crones, reading bitchy meanings into the remarks of the nasty desk clerk that Bea was so sure she had beguiled.

"She's my sister, my own twin, and I love her, of course," each lady said after these reunions, "but we have nothing in common—nothing!"

All the same Claire longed for the day when Bea would need her and they could be together again.

# 4

A MAN is lucky if he discovers his true home before it is
too late. True mate and true calling are part of this geographical felicity, but they seem to fall magically into place
once the home is found. Virtues that have been drying up
in the cocoon bloom and flourish, imp becomes saint, oaf
becomes knight errant, Pekingese turns lion.

Jonathan recognized New York as home. His whole
appearance changed overnight, shoulders broadened, apologetic skulk became swagger; he looked strangers in the
eye and found friendship wherever he turned. With the
blight of Jaimison heritage removed, his future became
marvelously incalculable, the city seemed born fresh for
his delight. He took for granted that his mother's little
world, into which he had dropped, was the city's very
heart.

Within a month he knew more of New York than he
had ever known about the whole state of Ohio. True, each
day he learned something that upset whatever he'd learned
the day before, but after all the world went round, didn't
it? He had an address, and he had a job which allowed
him time to pursue his private program. The job was collecting historical tidbits about the neighborhood for a
giveaway news-sheet in the new espresso café called Then-
and-Now. The café was in the basement of a Bleecker

Street real-estate firm that wanted to siphon off excess profits for tax purposes. Jonathan received thirty dollars a week, free sandwiches, cakes, and coffee, a desk, and a percentage of any ads he brought in. His new friend, Dr. Kellsey, adopted the café and furnished him with old Village lore. His other new friend, Earl Turner, was generous with editorial advice too, for he had once edited a glittering magazine called *The Sphere*. Mimeographed copies of *Café News* were stacked on the café's pastry counter, and to make sure the owners would consider it a success Jonathan saw to it that the sheets disappeared with speed.

A safe rule, Jonathan thought, was to assume that whatever would seem amazing in Silver City was the proper thing in New York. In Silver City people fussed over where they lived, the size and number of rooms, the suitable neighborhood, the right furniture. All New Yorkers, however, fell into whatever bed was nearest and called it home. In Silver City you lived with your family. In New York you lived with anybody but your family. The sofa might be full of mice just as the cot was full of rocks and the trundle full of nits, but for all Jonathan cared they could have been jumping with aardvarks. It was New York!

He was fortunate in having as roommates two ladies who were authorities on everything that mattered, and Jonathan listened gratefully to Darcy and Lize. The Golden Spur, they explained, was the cultural and social hub of New York City, which was bounded on the south by the San Remo, on the east by Vasyk's Avenue A bar, on the west by the White Horse, and on the north by Pete's Tavern. Friends who had deserted this area for uptown New York or the suburbs were crossed off as having gone to the bad. All connection with respectable family background had best be kept dark. Anybody with a tube of paint and a board was an artist. But writers were not writers unless decently unpublished or forever muffled by a Foundation placebo. The Word came only through grapevine gossip, never through print. The printed word on any subject was for squares. Although he had not met them, Jonathan felt on intimate terms with all the characters Darcy and Lize discussed, and soon was giving his own opinion on their affairs without hesitation. Hugow, Cassie Bender, Percy, Lew—they were his instant best friends, unseen.

It would take a little time, of course, to get used to living with two girls, having them stumble over his sleeping body in the studio on their way to bed at dawn. He had been gauche enough to propose that he move his bed to the windowless storeroom, a suggestion that brought a look of blank bewilderment to the girls' faces.

"What's the matter with your sleeping right here in the studio?" demanded Lize.

"What's so good about the junkroom?" Darcy pondered, equally baffled.

"I mean I'd be out of your way." Jonathan floundered. "I mean you'd be free to use this room for your dates and if you wanted to cook you could get to the kitchen without falling over me."

"Why would I be bringing a date to *my* place?" Lize asked Darcy in great mystification. "What makes him think we knock ourselves out cooking supper for a date?"

"I think it's kinda sweet of him, Lize," Darcy said tenderly, studying Jonathan with her little head sidewise, like a mother hen. He blushed and wondered whether she was measuring the depths of his naïveté or merely planning a new haircut for him.

"For your information, Buster, and strictly for the records," Lize told him firmly, "any date of mine takes me out, see. Home is for when you don't get a date or want to change your clothes. I've passed the stage where I date a guy just to save him money."

Darcy began to giggle.

"That would be the day," she said.

"Forget moving your bed," Lize said. "What I want to know is whether you can cook."

Jonthan had been used to cooking his own meals at Aunt Tessie's. No trick to it. Put some butter in a pan on the stove, throw in a piece of meat or can of something, and when it starts smoking, eat it.

"Steak? Hamburgers?" Lize asked with a light in her eye.

Especially steak and hamburgers. Ham and eggs.

"Didn't I tell you?" Lize cried triumphantly to Darcy. "I knew he was just the boy for us."

Jonathan was glad they allowed him to prove his helpfulness by fixing hamburgers for them that very night. The kitchen was his, they cried, from now on. Eager as he was to please, it took several days to learn just what was expected of him as cook, since the girls took off for their work before noon and never came home till there was no place else to go. Jonathan could use the kitchen table as a desk with no culinary distractions except at night, or rather at daybreak. The girls, though their programs after office hours seemed identical to him, did not hunt in pairs, but they did come home at approximately the same time, i.e., around four in the morning, after the bars had closed. Jonathan soon adjusted to this schedule, assuming it was typically New York. If he was awake he was glad to fix them bedtime scrambled eggs, but other times they did not disturb him.

Then one night he was roused by a little visitor groping

her way into his bed. In the dim light from the street lamp he saw that it was Darcy, haloed in curlers, garbed in a pajama top, and greased as for the Channel swim, with some pleasant-smelling ointments. Flattered, he made room for her and she snuggled silently into place. The poor girl must be a sleepwalker, he deduced, and he should be ashamed for taking advantage of her infirmity, but, as often happens, his conscience arrived too late. All he could do was mumble, "Darcy, I'm terribly sorry this happened. I promise you I won't let it happen again, if you'll forgive me."

"Now you're waking me up!" wailed Darcy impatiently "Can't you be quiet?"

"I just want to apologize—" But Darcy was fast asleep.

A few nights later he was wakened by Lize's sprawling into bed beside him.

"Just looking for a light," said Lize, extending a cigarette which he drowsily managed to light for her, but it seems she needed other comforts too. Taken off guard, conscience failed to strike, and since Lize had not a stitch on she must have had some dim inkling that the beast might be near. This time Jonathan reflected that an apology was not in order, nor even a thank you, but certain things mystified him. He knew it was his provincialism, and he would soon learn city ways, but—

"Do you always smoke—I mean—in bed?" he asked her cautiously, looking at the cigarette still dangling from her fingers.

"Hell, a girl has to do something." Lize yawned.

He had feared that these episodes, in which he blamed himself for taking advantage of their hospitality, would result in a change of atmosphere, but it finally dawned on him that they were no more important or meaningful than the midnight hamburger. City women were wonderful, he decided, but very strange. He heard them arguing over the comparative merits of their diaphragms and had the good sense to know they were not speaking of singing. In any case he was resolved to dodge further service as diaphragm-tester.

He also had the good sense to keep his private mission a secret from them, hoping they would not ask him about it, but he need not have worried.

The girls never asked questions about a man's private interests or listened when he tried to tell them. For them it was enough that he was a man and that he was there. Who needs a *talking* man?

They were both dear girls, Jonathan thought, looking after his interests and approving of everything he said and did in a way no one in Silver City had ever done. They liked the plaid shirt and moccasins he'd gotten on Eighth Street, just like Earl Turner's, they understood his passion to grow a beard as the flag of his emancipation from Home and Family, and then applauded his change of mind due to the initial itching. It was funny, Jonathan thought, when you considered how constantly these girls disagreed when they were together, how similar their tastes really were when you got one of them alone.

Both girls claimed to be afraid of their Tenth Street slum neighborhood but would spring out at any hour of the night to go any place else fearlessly. Coming *home* was what got them, each said, and maybe this wasn't fear of marauders but a sense of defeat in the evening's operations. In any case, after a while Lize took to dropping into Jonathan's espresso spot before closing time, for his protection going home. As soon as Darcy found this out, she insisted they divide his time equally, night for night. Protecting these young ladies from hoodlums was not just a matter of walking them across town and home, Jonathan discovered. It meant collecting nightcaps along the way, invariably ending up at The Golden Spur to check up on who was there, what they'd missed, and to make sure that home was all there was left of the night.

In spite of their new truce, Darcy was distrustful of Lize. She warned Jonathan of his danger on one of their walks home.

"You've got to watch out for that Lize," Darcy said. "She claims she walked out on Percy, but he told me himself that he's the one that made the break. You can say what you want to about Percy, maybe he is a creep and nobody wants him around, but he's no liar, and he told me she's trying to get him to take her back. Talks about you all the time just to make him jealous. I hate seeing her try to use you the way she does. I try to sleep on the outside so she can't go barging in on you in the night—oh, Lize doesn't stop at anything, you know, where there's a man."

The next night Lize favored him with the same warning about danger from little Darcy, who was really stronger than he guessed. Jonathan thanked them both. He found he could keep them from harping on his danger by introducing Hugow's name, for this was a topic of which they never tired. It was a lesson in female psychology to hear that although Hugow had cruelly deserted each of them they bore him no grudge, for he had more than atoned by treating the other one badly too. The real villain in the case was that gallery woman, Cassie Bender, who was forever swooping down on some unsuspecting artist just as a girl was making out with him. A snob, they pronounced her, forcing Hugow to leave the old bars he loved for great champagne dos uptown with movie stars and Texas millionaires, the sort of thing Hugow detested, downright vulgar really, especially if you weren't invited.

Worse than snob, Lize cried, Cassie Bender was a common whore.

"Slept with every artist she ever handled," affirmed Darcy "They all admit it when you pin them down."

Jonathan noticed that these caddish admissions were "pinned down" in the girls' own beds, but somehow this did not reflect on their own virtue.

"I swear I'm not going to break in any more artists for that old nympho," declared Lize, and both girls looked thoughtfully at Jonathan.

"I guess Hugow is a very fine painter," Jonathan said quickly. "Do you consider him better than Schaffer or the others?"

The girls pondered this for a moment, as if they had not thought of it before. They must have some opinion, he added, since they centered their private lives on painters.

"I don't see that there's much difference." Darcy shrugged. "They just think so because Cassie Bender gives them a line. One is the best one year and another the next. Cassie ruins them."

Jonathan gathered that Cassie Bender's real crime was her connection with that enemy, Art. She created a world of fame for a man and, common whore that she was, could lock other girls out of his life for weeks on end (as she was doing now with Hugow) just to get work out of him! Smart businesswoman, nuts! She'd just been lucky enough to grab a big chunk from some rich old goat years ago. She had started her stable with that and now could buy her own pets.

"Wait till she gets a load of Jonathan here," Lize said.

"Me?" Jonathan was startled.

Darcy clapped her hands and studied him with fresh appreciation.

"Wow," she said. "I never thought of that."

"She'll buy him a box of paints just as an excuse to get her mitts on him too," Lize predicted. "I shouldn't be surprised if she doesn't line him up as a Hugow replacement."

"Wow," Darcy said.

"That's the Bender bitch for you," Lize said. "One of these days we'll come down here and find no pigskin briefcase, no electric razor, no tan raincoat on the hook, no Jonathan, just Cassie Bender's Lincoln streaking up the avenue."

"I'll bet he'd go, too," accused Darcy.

Jonathan wondered wistfully if his ignorance of painting would prevent him from meeting this predatory temptress, but he thanked his friends and said nothing could persuade him to leave his new home.


More important than the finding of a home with experienced guardians was the adoption of The Golden Spur as Jonathan's club. Earl Turner, the world traveler and personal friend of the great Harshawe, was responsible for this move. Before you looked for a job or a home or a girl, Earl instructed Jonathan, you must establish your bar base in a new city, just as you would choose a fraternity on entering a university. Look them all over carefully, he counseled, every bar people mentioned in the Village area—Minetta Tavern, White Horse Inn, San Remo, Leroy, Jumble Shop—all offering their special brands of social security. Compare their advantages and disadvantages. Is this a tourist trap, a "Left Coast" hangout, or is it on the Bird Circuit, a meeting place for queers? Once you've made your choice, you conduct your social and business life there, since your home, mate, and job are bound to switch constantly. Make the owner or bartender your friend, use the place as a mailing and phone address, make your appointments there. Note the hours best suited for confidential talks there, the time for crashing a big party, the days when the roast beef is fresh and when it is hash; learn which barflies to duck.

Even if The Golden Spur had not recommended itself to Jonathan because of his mother's association with it, he would have chosen it. There was, as Earl pointed out, a nice diversity in the patrons. There were the college-faculty types, superior of their kind, for had they been average they would be sucking up to their departmental chiefs over in the Faculty Club or angling for academic advancement and traveling fellowships in stuffier environments. They wouldn't care to be caught bending elbows with the Spur's wild artists. The Spur artists were all "modern" in that they were against the previous generation, though generations in art were not much longer than cat generations.

In season, these individuals flooded the bar Monday nights, flushed down in the preview champagne from the Upper East Side gallery openings, and on Friday nights from the show closings. The star of the occasion, at other times perhaps an inarticulate modest painter, then appeared with his brand-new claque, a tangle of patrons, dealers, and a change of blondes, himself now loud with triumph and ready to lick his weight in wildcats, which often turned out to be necessary. It's a madhouse, everyone cried joyously on these nights, a real madhouse, let's never go home.

Now that it was midsummer, the Spur's daytime character had a more tranquil aspect. Summer bachelors, whose absent wives disapproved of such places, strengthened themselves with a few scotches to face their shrouded rooms in the new luxury apartments nearby. Somber Adult Education students, in town to slurp up enough culture to nourish them through the long dry winter in some Midwest Endsville, sipped beer at the bar and dreamed of a wild Greenwich Village nymphomaniac who would oblige them to forget their careers. Young housewives in pants and sandals, hair in curlers under scarves, dropped in for a beer with their last-minute supermarket purchases and looked wistfully around for the no-good boy friends they'd given up to marry good providers. There were the old-timers, fixed in their own grooves of this drink on this stool at this bar at this time every day, year in, year out, so that they never heeded the changes in patrons from touts and bookies to little-theater people to neighborhood factory- and shop-workers, to whatever there was now.

Since Jonathan had accepted the Spur as the hub of New York life, it was only fitting he should invite Miss Claire Van Orphen to meet him there. It struck him as a favorable omen that chance had made him spend his first night in New York in the Hotel De Long, under the very roof of his mother's old patron. He read encouraging warmth in the note hinting that her memories of his mother were pleasant.

"Claire Van Orphen? Never heard of her," said his literary monitor, Earl Turner. Seeing Jonathan's face fall, Earl added kindly, "She must have been a best-seller in her day, that's why I never knew her."

Claire had dressed herself with care in the rose-spangled chiffon from a 1924 seasonal sale in a Paris boutique. In the hall mirror she saw that the dipping hemline might date it, and she evened it with gold safety pins. In a softly lit tearoom she would pass nicely, she thought, and the beige silk cape would cover any defects.

As with many writers, Claire's powers of observation worked only in unfamiliar territory, being comfortably off-duty on her daily beat. She had passed the Village Barn, Nick's, Ricky's, and a dozen other spots regularly for years without seeing them. The nasty little man at her hotel desk looked surprised when she asked how to get to the Golden Spur, and she thought it must be due to something racy about the place.

"It's right under your nose, Miss Van Orphen," he said with his customary sneer. "Right around the corner next to the auction gallery."

Even so, she would have walked past the place if a young man had not stepped out and called her by name. She could not help smiling back at the engaging face.

"You must be Jonathan," she said. "How did you know me?"

Jonathan could not answer that the regal attire was exactly the costume he expected of a lady author, so he stammered that his mother had described her often. This gave Claire a twinge of uneasiness, for she had so little to tell him about his mother. She could not bear to disappoint him. What a dear young man he was too, with his twinkling brown eyes and quick smile that radiated a warmth uncommon in the world today! The gallant way he urged her to keep on her cape because of the air-conditioning inside moved her almost to tears, so long had it been since any man had been so solicitous.

Gratefully Claire vowed to herself she would do anything to help this dear lad get whatever it was he wanted. He was surprised that she had never been in the Golden Spur, since it was, he understood, the cultural center of Village life. Claire hastily assured him that she had, of course, often heard its praises sung and was happy to be there. She was flattered that he took for granted she would have a cocktail instead of sherry, and when he instructed the waiter to make her Manhattan dry, not sweet, she did not confess that the sweetness and the maraschino were what she liked best in a Manhattan. What a fascinating life she must have led among all the famous characters in this neighborhood, Jonathan said, and Claire nodded and smiled mysteriously into her glass, happier than she had been in years.

But nagging away behind her immense enjoyment of this adventure was the worrisome problem of digging up memories of his mother. For the life of her, Claire could not conjure up any but the palest picture of Connie Birch. A soft voice, yes, a very nice voice, unobtrusive, almost apologetic, she remembered, though the accent was corn-belt with that little bleat over the short "a"s and the resolute pounce on every "r." She must have had something special, though, Claire reflected, or else her mate had had, to produce such a remarkable offspring. It pained Claire to think of how obtuse she had been all her life, never seeing the true nature of those close to her—her own sister, for instance!—and now this boy's mother; granted she had been too much the lady to stare, polite blindness was surely no virtue in a writer. How nice it would be if she could produce a few intimate little vignettes to justify the young man's seeking her out!

Already Claire tingled with possessive pride in him, beaming when other patrons spoke to him, wishing fervently that sister Bea, who had many young men, could witness the way he introduced her, as if she were Edith Wharton. "This is Miss Van Orphen, Claire Van Orphen!"

She laughed at the story of his night in her hotel and of discussing with a porter the funeral of the newly deceased major he'd never known. Claire declared this to be a most amazing coincidence, for this would have been the funeral of her good friend Major Wedburn. Glad to gain time before she must answer questions about his mother, Claire chattered eagerly about the late Major Wedburn, such a distinguished military historian, pompous perhaps, but most impressive. He used to invite her every year to Ladies' Day at the Salmagundi Club and then was so amusingly discreet lest someone gossip about their residing in the same hotel! They exchanged manuscripts for criticism, which was nice, and had other professional contacts.

"Why, Major Wedburn was the one who sent Constance Birch to me for typing!" Claire suddenly interrupted herself, overjoyed to have found one small nugget, and in her relief invented words of admiration the Major had used at the time. Claire was ordinarily truthful, but she did want to prolong the interview. She made a bold decision to invent other little tidbits as coming from the late Major.

"That's the sort of thing I need," Jonathan said gratefully. "Sometimes I have only first names to go by; then my Aunt Tessie remembered others. When a name would be in the news, Mother would tell Aunt Tessie all about meeting the person with you or at your big parties."

Big parties indeed, Claire reflected wistfully, remembering the episode at the Brevoort, almost certain that it was the last time in nearly thirty years that she had entertained over six people at once.

"For instance, she wrote of meeting Alvine Harshawe with you," Jonathan went on, producing his little red notebook, "and there was a famous lawyer, George, who often called on you."

"George?" Claire repeated, her face reddening with embarrassment, for this nice boy's mother had certainly done some exaggerating, to say the least! Alvine Harshawe indeed! Claire found his work much too gamy for her own taste, but she would have been glad to claim his acquaintance. She could not deny knowing the man without calling the lad's mother a liar, so she improvised. "She must have met Harshawe when she was researching for the Major, who knew him well"—it *could* be!—"and the lawyer would have been George Terrence. George handled our family affairs for years."

She saw that the young man had his pencil poised alertly above the little red notebook.

"Of course I don't see much of him nowadays, because we haven't much for him to do any more," Claire said a little uneasily. "And he and Hazel have the place in Stamford, so—"

"Of course that is the George Mother meant!" Jonathan exclaimed. "Terrence, eh? All I knew was that the girl Mother lived with on Horatio Street was named Hazel and that later she married this lawyer named George. How do you spell Terrence?"

Claire spelled it out mechanically for him and gave the address outside Stamford where the Terrences lived. She was thoroughly baffled now. She could have sworn that

Connie Birch had never been around during George's calls. But on the other hand she had not realized that the girl George married had been Connie's roommate. It was hard to believe that stuffy, ambitious Hazel had ever shared bohemian quarters with a colorless little nobody from the Midwest. But, if Connie had lived with Hazel, of course she had met George.

"I will write and ask them for an appointment," Jonathan said, pocketing his book again, beaming. "They're sure to have a lot to tell me."

Thinking of the Terrences' rigidly circumscribed social life of the past fifteen years, Claire wondered, and felt a little sad.

"I'll write them a note too," she said firmly. No matter how stuffy they had become, they surely could not fail to be charmed by Jonathan. Goodness knows, anyone as anxious to play the social game as Hazel Terrence could always use an extra young man, and George had always set himself up as such a liberal (carefully cushioned on a solid old capitalist tradition), which certainly meant being kind to strangers, didn't it? Claire thought, a little ruefully, that, although she was too proud to ask the Terrences any favor for herself, she had no compunction about asking for the young stranger. There was so little she could do for him; she had not really earned a second Manhattan. To deserve it she began improvising compliments that had been paid to Constance Birch. The Major, for instance, often mentioned the girl's outstanding ladylike qualities in a crass age. The Terrences—yes, it must have been the Terrences—often had remarked that little Miss Birch was too fine, her standards too high, for the vulgar struggle of the big city. Indeed—here the dryness of the second Manhattan must have affected Claire's ordinary prudence—she believed it was George Terrence himself who had advised the sweet child to go back to the simple decencies of her Ohio home. " 'Go and marry the boy back home,' " she improvised. "Those were his very words."

"Mr. Terrence advised that!" exclaimed Jonathan. "Then perhaps he was the one—"

"Unless it was Harshawe," Claire amended. "Or someone in the poetry group she attended, I remember—she was so different from the modern girl of the time, you see; we'd gone from the flapper to much worse, and such a plain old-fashioned girl stood out. I do hope you appreciate what a genuine lady your mother was, Jonathan, one of those shy, innocent little creatures everyone tries to protect. We all missed her when she went home, but we were glad for her sake. As George Terrence said—"

She paused, at a loss for more plausible remarks from George, but Jonathan took no notice, for he was consulting his precious notebook.

"Here's what my mother wrote about her friend Hazel's fiancé," he reported. " 'George is practically certain to be a great lawyer, another Clarence Darrow.' "

What a desperately romantic young woman the boy's mother must have been, Claire thought.

"Dear me, George Terrence was much too modest to make a trial lawyer," she corrected him gently. "Very brilliant on briefs, of course, and highly regarded, but—"

"He might be the man!" Jonathan said, pursuing his own thoughts. "He didn't marry Hazel till Mother had gone back to Ohio and gotten married herself, don't you see?"

"No, I don't see," Claire confessed.

"All I have to go on is the fact that my real father was a very famous man," Jonathan explained.

"Mr. Jaimison?"

"No, I mean my *real* father, the man my mother was in love with before she married," Jonathan said. "He might have been a famous lawyer, mightn't he? And George Terrence, as you say, took a great interest in her?"

Claire's mouth fell open.

"You can't mean what you're saying." She choked. "Not that quiet, sweet little girl. My dear boy, you're not going to ask George a question like that!"

"I shan't ask him directly," Jonathan reassured her. "I just want to meet him and find out what he can tell me about my mother, and I can judge from that. If it turns out I'm the heir to a great legal mind, I will know what to expect of myself."

She mustn't spoil this beautiful friendship by behaving in a panicky, spinsterish way, Claire told herself. Be cool, be debonair.

"Of course," she said quite casually. "I felt better about my literary potentialities when I learned a great-grand-father had once published a novel. It's like money in the bank, knowing there are certain genes you can count on."

"I knew you'd understand," Jonathan said. "All my life before this I didn't think I could count on anything but the Jaimison pigheadedness. Now I can be anything. For instance, if my father was a great writer—"

"Like Alvine Harshawe." Claire smiled.

Jonathan blushed, but defensively admitted that it was a possibility. He had taken to keeping an extensive literary journal himself, he said, writing at his espresso shop, which, so far, was pleasantly ignored by the cake-and-ice-and-coffee set.

"I had no idea young people nowadays took anything

but martinis," Claire said. "Do they really go for ice cream?"

"Sometimes they're on 'tea,' or else heroin," Jonathan said. "They keep off alcohol because they don't want to mix their kicks, you see."

Claire nodded approvingly.

"Very sensible, I'm sure," she said, taking a dainty sip of her Manhattan. "I've always felt one gets more out of life by enjoying one pleasure at a time."

There, now! she thought, proud of herself for having smothered her virtuous instinct to warn Jonathan against dope fiends, drunkards, and harlots. But the pitfalls were everywhere, waiting to trip her into some horrid puritanism that would limit the youth's confidence. To be on safe ground she asked about his room and if he found New York lonely.

"I couldn't ever be lonely in this town," Jonathan said dreamily, "even if I lived all alone instead of with these two girls."

"It must be jolly," Claire said, catching her breath. "I mean it must be so much more interesting with two than just living with one."

She was steeled to babble on about the sheer common sense of triangular living or multiple-mistressing, but was saved by a man beckoning to Jonathan from the telephone corner. While Jonathan was gone to confer with his friend, Claire looked about her, filled with the joy of being brought —perhaps shocked—back to life. The hunting prints and racehorse pictures on the wall struck her as masterpieces of art, the flyblown lamps perfect period gems, the stables as booths a most original decorating caprice, and now Jonathan was bringing toward her the stranger with a little goatee and a plaid shirt exactly like Jonathan's.

"This is Earl Turner, Miss Van Orphen," Jonathan said triumphantly, as if he had finally brought the heads of two great nations together. "You're both writers so you must have lots to talk about. Earl tells me I have to go right over to see about a fire in my building—"

"It's all over now," Earl explained. "It's just that Hugow wants Jonathan to let him in and get out some canvases he left in there. Valuable paintings, that sort of thing."

"Earl will look after you," Jonathan assured her. "You've helped me so much, and I'll call you again next week."

He grasped her hand with a radiant, innocent smile, as if illegitimacy, opium-smoking, two mistresses, and a house on fire were all on the good ship *Lollipop*. He dropped a bill on the check. Claire sat back as he hurried out, and his friend in the beret slid into the seat. Claire saw that the friend was a man over fifty, and she knew from experience that there's nothing irks a man over fifty more than being stuck with a woman his own age. Earl's glum expression agreed with her guess.

"It's an interesting little place," she said politely. "Such interesting types, don't you think? Those artists at the bar, for instance."

"They're waiting for their girls to come in from work and buy them a drink," Earl said morosely.

"Interesting!" Claire said firmly, but she felt weak and deserted and knew she should leave.

She could feel the fine self-confidence built up by young Jonathan melting away under the bored expression of her companion. He scarcely glanced at her, classifying her no doubt as a dull family friend of Jonathan's, entitled to the respect due her age but nothing more. He looked beyond her to greet new and young arrivals, drumming on the table as he smoked. Stubbornly Claire took her time finishing her drink.

The Spur was filling up with the pre-dinner crowd now, all races and all costumes, bohemian, white-collar, beach, collegiate, Hollywood. There was an undercurrent of muffled anticipation in the air, and the special timbre in the murmuring voices, the secret knowledge in the gurgling laughter, the searching look in the eyes of everyone seemed faintly sinister to Claire. The revelation of what Jonathan Jaimison was seeking here, his sudden departure, and the letdown after her initial excitement left her frightened and unnerved, as if all this were building up to the real opera, in which there was no part for her. It annoyed her that her hands shook as she drew on her rose-colored gloves and that Jonathan's friend should be watching her now.

"Pretty rough crowd for you, I'm afraid," he said.

"Not for me, Mr. Turner," Claire said with dignity. "I find the people most attractive. The blond girl you bowed to looks fascinating."

"Fascinating indeed!" Earl said. "She just got back from Greece, where she's been living on money she got from selling her baby. Couldn't afford an abortion, you see, so she went ahead and made a nice deal out of the kid, if you call that fascinating. Now she'll make a career out of breeding."

He wanted to shock her, Claire knew, and steeled herself.

"Enterprising, then," she said lightly. "Girls today are so clever. I suppose that nice boy—or is it a girl?—with her is on 'tea.'"

Earl snorted derisively.

"He never made that kind of money," he said. "He's lucky to scrape enough together for Dexedrine and beer."

"A pity," Claire said wildly. "He looks so intelligent, you'd think his habits would be more original."

Earl was looking at her now with puzzled amusement. "You think he ought to live up to that long hair?" he said.

"Why not?" Claire asked and rose to go. She would be the stately literary figure that Jonathan assumed her to be, she told herself defiantly, not the timid spinster. "At least he looks an artist."

"Trust the buckeye boys to play the tourist's dream," Earl said. "Like the drugstore cowboys."

Maybe he wasn't being deliberately rude, Claire decided.

"I'm sorry I don't know your work, Mr. Turner," she said graciously. "Jonathan said you were a writer. I'm sure I've heard the name."

"Probably from the time when I edited *The Sphere*," Earl said, mollified. "Of course that was some time ago."

Some time ago indeed, Claire thought, for the magazine had come and gone a good twenty years ago.

"Such a brilliant magazine!" Claire said. "I was so sorry to see it fail. Well, good night, Mr. Turner."

"Wait," said Earl. "I'll walk you to your hotel."

The polite gesture seemed to surprise Mr. Turner himself as much as it did Claire, but it had been a long time since anyone had remembered *The Sphere*.

"No reason you should know my work," he said as they walked up Fifth Avenue. "I haven't published anything recently."

"Nor have I, Mr. Turner," Claire admitted. "There doesn't seem to be the demand, do you think?"

"Certainly not for me." Earl gave a mirthless laugh. "Frankly I never got back in my own stride after rewriting all the world's leading geniuses for *Sphere*."

"I'm sure you're much too modest," said Claire. "I'm afraid you're being too severe an editor of your own work."

"Well, in a way," Earl conceded, and was moved to tell Claire of his foolish perfectionism that made his stories too good to sell or for that matter even to write. They stood in the lobby of the Hotel De Long, eagerly chattering of literary matters, ignoring the avid eyes and ears of the elderly witches and aging beaux propped along the wall sofas.

"You should make them into a book," Claire advised. "I must remember the name of that editor at Dutton's for you."

The lobby heads swiveled unanimously as the two literary friends moved toward the elevator and were lost, alas. In Miss Van Orphen's tiny room (she was glad her little plants were blooming so nicely) they continued their discussion with great animation over glasses of instant coffee laced with a few drops of Christmas brandy. When Claire reported the delicious recipe the Planet's soda jerk had for hangover ("I just don't go there any more"), Earl declared she had the makings of a perfect little vignette for *The New Yorker.*

Claire promised that she would certainly try to write it, for it had been a long time since she had had any editorial inspiration. Earl acknowledged that it had been a rare pleasure for him, too, to exchange ideas with a fellow writer. They should meet often. As a first step he would call on her this very week and give her his constructive suggestions on whatever manuscripts she had on hand.

A wonderful day, Claire thought, and all due to the invasion of New York by young Jonathan Jaimison. In her gratitude she wrote a note before she went to bed to the George Terrences, urging them to see Connie Birch's son by all means. And then—because it was cruel to have a red-letter day and no one to share it—she had to write a note to sister Bea, imploring her to name a day for lunch, for it had been weeks, months. You just had to have someone, Claire told herself, tears in her eyes. Even when you knew they were bored with you, as Bea was with her, you had to have someone to *tell*.

# 5

Hugow sat on the cracked stone stoop of the brown tenement on East Tenth Street and watched the fire ceremonials
going on across the street. He had been so interested in the
black and gold medieval-looking firemen's uniforms, the
loudspeaker directions from the chief, the beautiful red
engines, and the hose snaking in and out of windows that it
took a minute to penetrate that the fire was in his own
building. It was a small fire, put out almost at once, but he
had panicked, thinking of the canvases he had stored in the
fourth-floor studio. He was shaken, too, with the evidence
that his hunch to rush home had been justified.

Last night, for instance, he had been swigging Tom Col-
linses on the terrace of Cassie Bender's shore house four
hundred miles away when he was suddenly smitten with a
passionate, overwhelming hunger. And for what?

For hunger.

He wanted to throw up the whole scene, the fine yellow
gin, the perfect studio Cassie had fixed for him, the successful authors and actors and art-lovers and Bennington girls
—"the cream of the Cape," as Cassie said—their Good Conversation; Christ, how sick you could get of Good Conversation. "Good Talk." There was no such thing as Good
Talk. Talk was Talk and worse than marijuana for getting
you high and nowhere. Sure, he talked too much when he

was drunk, but he had the sense to be ashamed afterward, ashamed for diluting the pure classic joy of drinking with the cheap vice of yakking. He had wanted to throw up the fine Cape Cod air, the beach, the crystalline sunshine, Cassie's smothering love, and the rooms full of intelligent appreciators, and get back to a slum full of overturned ashcans, Bowery bums sprawling over the doorstep, lousy barflies who insulted him, jerks, Eagle jerks, Cub jerks, people who hated him for himself alone and not just because he was doing all right. He wanted to get back to a studio that had no comforts, just light and nobody in it; he wanted a new girl, someone who didn't understand him and that he couldn't understand, so that they could run through each other fast with no dead vines clinging, as in most of his other affairs. He wanted to *want*, that was it, he wanted to see something far off floating up like a forever-lost kite out of all possible range, something to blind and dazzle him so he could work for it. He wanted dirt, limitless oceans of dirt, so he could have the intense need for clean, he wanted loneliness so he could suffer the old ache of yearning for human contact.

The urge was so overpowering that he had walked past the pretty girl waiting for him to bring her a drink, pushed through the little groups on the terrace, down the sunflower path through the vegetable garden, through the tangle of bayberry bushes down the hill to the highway, the martini glass still in his hand. A butcher's truck stopped for him and turned him over at a gas station to an oil truck headed for Brooklyn. Hugow had to fight carsickness all the way down, but it wasn't the riding or the bumps, it was being fed up with being fed. Fat-cat-sick, that's what it was. Death. He had to get back to the screaming panic of the city. He had to get back to his own Village, to the half-finished canvas he had deserted. He had to find again that green, the wonderful green, the true paint-green, the unearthly sea-bottom moon-green, not the lousy nature-green of trees and grass. He'd almost gotten it once, then Darcy bugged him and he bolted and left everything in the old Tenth Street studio. When he got down there finally and saw the fire, he knew the picture had been calling for him, calling for help, and that had scared him, reminding him once again —as if he needed to be told—that what came from his brush was his own blood.

He could have gotten there earlier, but he had waited to be sure Darcy wouldn't be around, so he could sneak out his canvases without a scene. The crowd collected for the fire had drifted away, the Chinese laundry in the basement had been flooded, Chu Chu was out front, screaming curses at the cops and firemen.

Hugow had rushed up the steps, was putting his key in the lock when a cop's hand closed over it.

"What's your name, bud?"

"Hugow. I want to get into my studio."

"Hugo, eh. So you got a studio here. Funny there ain't no Hugo name here."

"It's the fourth floor rear."

"Fourth floor rear, eh. 'Jaimison, Trent, Britten. Fourth Floor Rear.' No Hugo. Let's have that key, bud, before you go making trouble for yourself."

You can't argue with cops—not when there was a chance of Darcy's popping along to make things worse. Even old Chu's recognizing him did no good, since he shook his fist at Hugow in his crazy-mad way, shouting that those evil artists upstairs must have set the fire in his honest laundry, throwing their turpentine rags around. Hugow had to withdraw, finally having extracted the information that the whole place was under guard until there was no chance that the original blaze would spread upstairs. No one would be admitted without credentials. After a moment's puzzled speculation on what had brought Lize and Darcy under the same roof, Hugow turned his attention to the third name. If he could get hold of this Jaimison he might be able to get in. Somebody at The Golden Spur would know who was staying here with the girls, Hugow was sure—the bartender, Earl Turner, or Lew Schaffer. He went to the candy store on the corner and phoned the Spur. Sure enough, Earl Turner was around and said the fellow Jaimison who was camping out with Lize and Darcy was right there. Earl promised to see that he came over to let Hugow get in and collect his stuff before the girls showed up.

"What goes on here anyway?" Hugow asked as an afterthought. "Is this a design for living?"

"Wasn't it always?" Earl answered.

It had been several weeks since Hugow had been in his old neighborhood, and he walked around Tompkins Square while he waited, dropping into the Czech bar for a beer, buying a bagel at a Polish delicatessen, and thinking that for all its many nationalities and mixed customs it was a mean, thin-spirited, hostile neighborhood. That was the East Side, rich and poor, all the way up till you got to Yorkville. He'd spent three years in the Tenth Street studio and was glad to be out of it, glad he'd lined up a new place way over on the West Side near Houston. The lights coming on around Tompkins Square and the fading daylight gave a romantic glow to the old houses, the "fudge light" that made madonnas out of the fat old shrews yelling out windows for their children or dragging them along the streets with a whack and a cuff; it made kindly peasants out of the suspicious, foxy merchants waiting in the doors of their shops to short-change any crippled blind man, especially if he was a brother. You could live on the East Side all your life and still be a stranger. It must be the Italians who warmed up the West Side, for they laughed and sang and loved their babies: they wore pink shirts and red dresses so their flying clotheslines were really glad rags. The East Side was too near Vermont, maybe that did it, Hugow mused, happy with this fancy, Vermont, where the country itself was always trying to throw off the people, like a beautiful wild horse that will never let itself be conquered by inferior riders.

The bums were the only good thing about the East Side, Hugow thought, getting back to the stoop opposite his studio. At this time of day they had drifted down to the Bowery missions for their handouts, but they'd be back later with their half-pints of muscatel as nightcap before bedding down in the entry halls or stoops along here. The Third Avenue El used to hold them in as much by its safe shadows as by its posts stretched out like a lifeline all the way down to Foley Square. When the structure was torn down, leaving the avenue shorn of shade, bald as the Siberian steppes, the bewildered bums spilled all over to the side streets, rootless and compassless, churning east and west, river to river, still calling the Bowery home, but the Bowery was now an overblown matron without her stays. There was no home except other bums, bottles, empty doorways, a sunny stoop in winter, a shady one in summer. The Bowery was only in the uncaged, prowling, alley-happy heart. Like mine, Hugow thought, always on the prowl for something to louse up his life.

He lit a cigarette and watched for the Jaimison man, wondering if he belonged to Lize or to Darcy. Either one would serve to get himself off the hook. It was a relief to

be free of Cassie too, good old Cassie who was always rescu-
ing him and had sustained him during his last work. Funny
how a woman and a picture got finished for him at the same
time. Funny that, whoever she was, she could never reach
him again, her warmth could do nothing for his chill, the
empty chill of finished work, the chill that he knew was a
piece of dying. For this he could only be revived by a fresh
love, simple and childish, or worldly and artificial, or perhaps a wild, nettlesome, raging affair of action, drama,
brutal encounters without affection or any plane of communication. No one could say he was unfaithful. The word
unfaithful was not for him, nor the word promiscuous, nor
the words irresponsible or ungrateful, because a man who
has never been chaste, faithful, responsible, or grateful
could not become *not* those things. Say he was a person of
prodigious needs, using everything and everybody as his
personal fuel. Only when he was drained, between pictures
as he was now, did he become a human being, simple,
lonesome, and sweet, making the friends and loves then
that would feed him later.

The blond young man hurrying down the street must be
Jaimison, Hugow surmised, and went to meet him. Having
heard of the great Hugow, Jonathan was surprised to find
him no Viking Apollo with a thundering baritone voice,
but a man shorter than himself, with a hesitant apologetic
drawl, an indolent way of walking that partly concealed a
slight limp, long grayish-brown hair that he shook out of
his eyes impatiently, a pointed sort of face, fawnlike when
he focused his intense gray eyes on you, through you, perhaps beyond you. He was in slacks and sport shirt and

needed a shave. After the brief mutual examination, Hugow took Jonathan's arm.

"So you're the replacement," he said. "You paint?"

"I'd like to," Jonathan said politely.

"Either you paint or you don't paint," Hugow said. "Did Earl tell you what I wanted? I've got to get the rest of my pictures out of the place before Darcy shows up and gives me a bad time. The cop thinks I'm a burglar, so you have to sponsor me."

At the entrance there were now only two cops and Chu, who was angrily boarding up his broken window. Jonathan unlocked the door, and they climbed the three flights to the top floor. Jonathan had gotten used to coming home to a hurricane of feminine disorder, realizing after only a few weeks' training that the trim perfection of two young ladies' working appearance could not be achieved without a wild trail of bath towels, shoes, powder, bobby pins, scattered hose, coffee cups, tousled pajamas, empty milk bottles, and basins of soaking lingerie. Now he felt embarrassed and scooped up a tangle of wet nylons.

"I usually throw everything in a closet," he mumbled apologetically. "I'm the last one out in the morning."

Hugow took a look around the room and threw up his hands.

"They've taken over, I see that much. This is what women mean when they say they want to look after you. How do you manage to fit into this picture?"

"We're in and out at different times," Jonathan said. "We don't interfere with each other."

Hugow went to the kitchen. The dishes from a spaghetti supper of two nights before were in the rusty sink, and a half-gallon chianti bottle with an inch of red in the bottom stood on the floor. Hugow opened the closet door, where a shredded broom and a balding floor mop leaned. He reached up to yank a pulley which brought down from mysterious heights a clutch of canvases strapped together. He handed them to Jonathan. He reached up again and triumphantly fetched down a bottle labeled BURKE SPRINGS BOURBON. He noted that it was almost full and nodded with satisfaction.

"First thing you have to learn about a dame is whether to hide your bottles high or low. You have to hide them high for Darcy," he explained. "I'm surprised Lize didn't spot it, though."

He took a drink from the bottle and handed it to Jonathan.

"Lize and Darcy! How do you like that!" He laughed. "Thank God it's you in the middle and not me this time. I guess I owe you something for taking Darcy off my neck. I suppose they're both sore at me now."

"They blame it all on Cassie Bender," Jonathan said.

Hugow frowned.

"I forgot about Cassie," he said. "She's the one that's cursing me out right now, I suppose. I should have sent a wire or phoned collect or— Oh hell, I can't be apologizing to Cassie all my life, can I?"

"Not for the same thing, I guess," Jonathan said, and this seemed to please Hugow for he slapped him on the back approvingly.

"Too bad you aren't an artist or you could take on Cassie too," he said. "Never mind, you've got your work cut out with Lize and Darcy. How'd you happen to get trapped?"

"We thought it would save money," Jonathan said.

"More power to you, man," Hugow said skeptically. "Maybe you can handle those things better than I can. Let's get a move on before they can jump on us. You and I can cart my stuff over to my new studio. They don't know where this one is, that's a break.'

Hugow opened a closet door, peered under the cot, took a last look around the studio, found a tin can of evident value to him, which he handed to Jonathan with the whisky bottle.

"You take these. Let's go."

There seemed no question that Jonathan would come with him, and Jonathan thrust the bottle into his pocket and followed down the stairs. A bearded old bum, pockets overflowing with rags, grinned and pointed urgently at Jonathan's bottle.

"I'm a Harvard man too," he said. "How about it?"

"Get your own brand," Hugow said, flipping a coin at him.

They walked down First Avenue, down toward Houston, where they would get the Houston Street crosstown, Hugow said, which would let them off near his new studio. He was always so glad to get back to Manhattan, he said, that he started walking as soon as he hit the beloved pavements so as to get the empty, clean smell of the country sunshine out of his system and let God's own dirt back in. He stopped at a pushcart and bought a bag of plum tomatoes. In the shadow of a boarded-up tenement building a group of derelicts were quarreling quietly over a bottle. The light from a basement bar next door shone upon a huge figure of a man blocking the street.

"Doesn't anybody want to buy my blood?" he was saying in a tired singsong. "I have very good blood. Doctors give a hundred dollars a pint for my blood. Don't somebody want to buy?"

Outlined by the traffic lights and lamps above and below, he stood motionless, like a wax display figure on sale, one great hand uplifted, commanding Hugow and Jonathan to stop. He had no dangling rags and bags as the other bums did, but his outfit had a mission-neat, mothball, decayed shabbiness, vest, jacket, pants, shoes in the same varying shades of ghoul green as his skin, and the wide-brimmed moldy old Quaker hat. The large bulbous nose, the greenish-gray hair and lashes, the gray-white eyes, all had the deathly color of leather buried for centuries in Davy Jones's locker, and the neatly rolled cloth bundle under his arm seemed a mariner's kit. His complexion was the curious paste of Dutch blondes mixed with blue-black native, with no gold or glow of tropic sun coming through. He must have been drowned a long time, Jonathan thought.

"Do you wish to buy my blood, sir?" the man murmured.

He was still standing there, motionless, as Hugow and Jonathan got on the bus. Hugow looked back out the window, and Jonathan saw that he was smiling radiantly.

"That's what I've been needing," he said. "God, how I love New York. Did you see that green?"

"Mushroom color, I thought," Jonathan said.

Hugow shook his head dreamily.

"The green I love, the green that is everything but green," he murmured. "I should have bought his blood just to see what makes it."

Jonathan said nothing, afraid he might strike the wrong note and cut off this beautiful new friendship at its very birth. This rare creature, this great god who seemed to be the heart of The Golden Spur circle, had taken him in as one of his own kind without hesitation. Jonathan felt as if a wild bird had flown to his shoulder and one false move would frighten it away. Now *he,* like the others, would be one of Hugow's willing slaves. He forgot about Claire Van

Orphen left in the Spur, he forgot what chores were expected of him at the café, he was in the beatific glow of the master's favor.

At Varick Street, Hugow motioned to him to pick up the canvases and get off the bus. They turned a corner and stopped in an alleyway behind an old wooden warehouse. Hugow unlocked the door and they entered a pitch-black hall and fumbled their way up rickety wooden stairs. At the third flight a skylight let in enough light to show the way, and through a tiny half-moon window Jonathan glimpsed the twinkling lights of the North River craft and the Jersey shore beyond. The loose boards clattered underfoot, and a piece of stair rail broke off in his hand and rattled down the steps.

"I figured if I got a place crummy enough, I could keep out dames for a while," Hugow explained. "A guy's got to have a little time to himself, right?"

"They couldn't find their way here," Jonathan said.

"Women find their way any place," Hugow said. "They know where you're going before you've even made up your mind. But I'm safe for a while here, thank God."

Jonathan lit matches while Hugow fiddled with the latch. It turned out a key wasn't necessary, for the door fell open at the first push.

"Damn those kids," said Hugow.

But the burglar was a female and seemed to have made herself at home.

The girl was sprawled over a battered Victorian sofa, her long legs in black leotards flung up over the back. A pair of candle stumps dripped into saucers on an empty packing

crate beside her and cast a glow over a dark face, sullen in
sleep, with a tangle of thick black hair falling over it. She
opened her eyes as they entered the loft.

"Iris!" Hugow exclaimed. "How'd you find it?"

"Asked around the bars," she said. "Mad?"

"Tickled to death. How'd you get in?"

"Beer opener." She sat up, yawning, and looked at them
defiantly. "No use getting excited just because you forgot
to invite me. I can't get into my room because the sublet is
still there."

"What about your tryout?" he asked.

"Flopped. I flopped, especially. I was run out of West-
port."

"So hello," Hugow said and tousled her hair.

She stood up and stretched herself lazily, like an enor-
mous cat. She was taller than Hugow. Jonathan could not
take his eyes away from her, fascinated by the tawny sheen
of her skin and by her voice, which was rough and dark,
with breaks in it like a boy's.

"There's nothing in the icebox but ice," she said.

"Ice is all we need," Hugow said, taking the bottle out
of Jonathan's pocket. "This is my best friend. Better ask
him his name."

"Jonathan Jaimison," said Jonathan.

"You're a writer?"

"Oh yes," Jonathan said, pleased. "Yes, I think so."

"Isn't this place great, Jonathan, boy?" Hugow demanded. "Look at that window. Look at those rafters."

Jonathan nodded but he could not take his eyes off the
girl. Why, this was love at first sight, he thought. It had
something to do with Hugow's adopting him and the man
selling blood and the half-moon glimpse of river lights and
the way the dark girl in the candlelight lit up the room with

her voice and flash of laughter. Did she know it was love too? She was staring at him with her thick black brows drawn together.

"You look like someone," she said.

"Who?" Jonathan asked eagerly.

"Maybe somebody in the news," she said. "I'll remember later."

Hugow found jelly glasses and set them out with a tray of ice and his bag of plum tomatoes. He pulled out a lop-sided brown leather chair, into which he sank happily.

"Beautiful!" he said, and Jonathan agreed enthusiastically. It was a barn of a place, really, floored only in the middle, with the rafters spreading out under low eaves at both sides. Etched on the big window, the West Side highway strung red and green lights into a dark yonder. A folded cot leaned against the long plank table.

"Wonderful to be back." Hugow sighed, fondling his drink. "Cozy nest, fine drink, fine old friends. Then Iris! My hunches are always good. I got the message about the fire in the studio and then the message that Iris was here. Amazing!"

"I knew if I had sent you a real message you would never show up," Iris said.

Hugow winked at Jonathan.

"Iris is a quick study," he said.

"You taught me," said Iris.

Jonathan looked from one to the other, feeling very much left out. They were a thing, no doubt about it. You could feel the current crackling between them, even though they were half the room's length apart and not looking at each other. He felt miserable and suffocated with love for both of them. If they were lovers, he should have the decency to clear out, but he couldn't bear to leave them, or the beauti-

ful room furnished so sumptuously in shadows, distant
lights, and unknown desires.

"Iris is going to be a great actress, Jonathan," Hugow
said.

"I know it," Jonathan said sincerely. "You can tell."

"Can you really?" Iris asked eagerly, fixing her eyes on
Jonathan. They were great dark eyes that seemed to drink
in more darkness, brimming over with night, he thought,
orphan eyes, deserted-wife eyes, slave eyes, beggar eyes.
Even with her white teeth gleaming in a fleeting smile she
seemed utterly dark, only reflecting outside color like the
black river yonder. It was a relief to have Hugow break the
spell.

"Iris is almost twenty-one, so she thinks she knows what
the score is," Hugow said banteringly. "Three years in New
York, what the hell? Wait till you're forty-five and doubt
sets in."

"Hugow never has had any doubts," Iris said.

He should go now, Jonathan thought, forcing himself to
move toward the door. Hugow jumped up and clutched
his arm.

"Stick!" Hugow's lips formed the command.

Jonathan sat down again. Hugow was hungry and talked
of going to either Ticino's or the Bocce place. Jonathan,
mindful that he could get free cakes, sandwiches, and coffee
at his place of employment, tentatively suggested the Then-
and-Now. Iris said nothing for the simple reason that she
had fallen asleep, her dark eyebrows tangled in a frown,
but even with the eyes closed a deep black unhappiness
clouded her face.

"Iris is my one good deed," Hugow confided. "I broke it
up when I saw I was going to louse up her life for her."

"Where does she come from?" Jonathan asked.

Hugow shrugged.

"Middle West, or maybe upstate. Far enough away so she can live her own life. I picked her up when I did a backdrop for a little theater over The Golden Spur. She was in the cast and got some notice. I don't know whether it was because she can really act or because she looks so goddam tragic."

"I'm hungry," Iris said unexpectedly, then sighed. "But I am so tired."

It was agreed that Hugow would run around the corner and bring back pizzas and peperoni and more bourbon.

"You can look after Iris," he said. "Do you mind?"

Mind!

Now he was alone with Iris, here was his opportunity to register, but without Hugow he couldn't think of a word to say. Jonathan could scarcely breathe when she bent forward and put a hand impulsively on his.

"I'm so glad you stayed," she said in an intense whisper. "You see I just did something that scares me terribly and I've got to tell somebody—not Hugow—to make it go away. I mean I came so close to—well, please let me tell you and promise not to mention it again or tell Hugow."

Jonathan could nod at least.

"You see I had this wonderful part, and if the tryout was any good we were to come in to Broadway next month. But I was all wrong for it. Oh, I never dreamed I could be so bad! We flopped and it's my fault. So I got my sleeping pills and came here and—"

"You mean you were going to—" Jonathan choked.

"Please don't tell Hugow," she implored, clasping her hands together. "He's got guts and he thinks I have too.

But I just couldn't stand living if I thought I was no good as an actress. There's just nothing else in life for me."

"Not even—Hugow?" Jonathan ventured.

She smiled at his innocence.

"You mean because he was my first lover. But you see that was all mixed up with my first job in the theater where Hugow was the scene designer, and it was my first year in the Village, and he was my first famous man. Hugow stood for the whole picture, don't you see? That's the way a girl's mind works."

That was the way it must have been with his mother, Jonathan thought.

"Hugow was good for me," Iris acknowledged." I was flattered that the great man liked a kid like me. He thought I was older and when he found out I was just eighteen he panicked. We were shacked up in Rockland County, but he packed me up and sent me back to town. I was so embarrassed to be treated like a child after all. 'Marry some nice guy,' he said, can you imagine? 'Have some kids, live a nice normal life.' "

"Do they always say that?" Jonathan asked, surprised. "That's just what the man said to my mother."

"What man?"

What man, indeed?

"Something like that happened to my mother, that's all," he said. "At least you didn't listen to him. You stuck to your guns."

Forget about his mother, he advised himself sharply, think Iris, Iris, Iris.

"Oh, but do you know what I said to him? You won't believe me!" Iris covered her face with her hands at the memory. "I burst out crying, if you please, and said, 'But

I don't want a normal life. I don't want a nice guy. I just want you!' Oh, I was such a little stupid, Jonathan!"

How in the world could Hugow have resisted such charming naïveté? Jonathan marveled, wishing he had been on hand to console her.

"I thought my heart was broken. Honestly!" Iris's great sooty eyes begged him to forgive her childishness. "I must have been a pest, hanging around the Bender Gallery, phoning Cassie Bender to try to find him, lurking outside the Spur. Wasn't it too silly of me? As if he was Gregory Peck! Not that Hugow isn't a dear, but really!"

"I'm glad you're over it," Jonathan said sincerely.

She flashed him a sad, grateful smile.

"I am too. As soon as I got a job touring in a Chekhov revival I forgot him like that! Awful of me, wasn't it?"

But she was here tonight, Jonathan reflected.

"It might start up again," he suggested.

"You don't know me, Jonathan." She shook her head firmly. "I've grown up. When I close a door I really close it."

He was very pleased to hear this. That was exactly the way he was himself, he said.

"I'm fond of Hugow still," Iris granted. "After all, I admire him as an artist. And we still can laugh over how crazy I was. And I wouldn't hurt him for anything in the world."

"Certainly not," Jonathan said, elated by the faint warning and promise in her voice. "But what about the sleeping pills? Would you have gone through with it?"

"If you hadn't come in?" Iris shook her cloudy hair and considered for an intense moment. "I don't know, Jonathan, I really don't know myself. Maybe if I hadn't fallen asleep first. Then when you said you could tell I would be a great actress I wanted to live, because you made me believe in myself again."

Jonathan glowed with happiness. He had saved this lovely girl without even knowing he was doing so. She was leaning toward him, and he could not keep from kissing her tempestuously. He kissed the tiny mole that finished off the corner of her mouth like a beauty patch, and he looked with delight at the slow smile that transfigured her dark face with light.

"Do you know something, Jonathan?" No, he thought, utterly bemused by the way she murmured his name. "I knew something about you too, the instant we met. I knew you were going to be somebody different and really great. Like me. I could tell."

"You could?"

"I could tell, Jonathan."

It must be the real thing with her as it was with him. But he wouldn't want to hurt Hugow, his new friend. He heard his step on the stairs and went to the door with one of the candles to light the way.

Hugow beckoned him out to the hall and handed him some packages.

"Beer for breakfast too," he said. "Stick around till I get rid of the kid. She's a sweet kid and hasn't many pals, but I don't want to start this up again, you know how it is. Don't want to hurt her, but—"

"She oughtn't to be alone," Jonathan said cautiously. "I shouldn't tell you, but she's got some sleeping pills—"

He was surprised at Hugow's mocking retort.

"Pay no mind to that sleeping-pill bit. She's stagestruck, don't forget. There's always got to be an act."

Unsympathetic, Jonathan thought, but that would make

his own sympathy more welcome to her. Iris made no move to play hostess but lay back regally on the couch, accepting cigarettes and drinks. Jonathan was happier than he'd ever been in his life, he thought, knowing she liked him and that Hugow wanted him there. He suggested warily taking Iris off Hugow's hands by inviting her to the Then-and-Now for a café Saigon.

"Iris thinks that espresso coffee tastes like wet blotters," Hugow said. "You fix us some highballs instead, Jonny-boy."

"Jonny-boy"—just what his mother and Aunt Tessie called him.

Jonathan went into the kitchen, glad to be useful in so many ways. He wondered how he could go about getting Iris to himself, since Hugow had been firm about not wanting her there. Each had made it clear that the last thing they wanted was to reopen their affair. Pondering how to handle the situation, he brought the ice back into the room in time to surprise the two friends locked in a passionate embrace. They sprang apart guiltily, snatching for cigarettes; Hugow lighted them both busily from a candle.

Jonathan stopped in his tracks, baffled. Even though they didn't want to hurt each other—

"I've got the ice," he mumbled idiotically. Then, as neither spoke, he hurried on. "It's a good icebox. Makes a lot, so you don't need to worry about running out of ice. Lots better than the old one over on Tenth Street."

"That so?" said Hugow. He was examining his cigarette intently. So was Iris. They didn't look at him, and he tried not to look at them. He dropped the ice tray on the sofa and backed toward the door.

"I've got to be running along," he said and went on explaining, as if any explaining was needed. "I've got to go to the espresso, see, then it's a long way over to East Tenth—"

"Sure you don't want to stay here?" Hugow murmured absently.

"Couldn't possibly," Jonathan babbled, burning with embarrassment. "Lize and Darcy expecting me, see, and I—see, I wouldn't want to hurt them."

He was out of the door, stumbling down the stairs, paying no mind to the glint of the river lights through the half-moon window, muttering, "Wouldn't want to hurt Lize and Darcy, see, can't go round hurting people. . . ."

Wait till he found out who he was, he thought, and could stand up to any situation. Iris would discover that he was indeed Somebody. A legal wizard, maybe, he thought wildly, if he was the child of George Terrence. A real writer, as big as Hugow in another way, if his father proved to be Alvine Harshawe. He thought of the pile of Harshawe published works in the drawer of his desk at the café, works he was reading carefully in the hope of finding some veiled allusion to his mother or a plausible connection with her life. He thought of the journal he had always kept, as people do who have no one they trust to understand them. Tonight he would write a sardonic bit about Iris and the folly of sudden love.

Jonathan walked hurriedly toward the shop, across Carmine Street, still smarting at being an unwanted third. He was being properly punished for losing sight of his true quest, that was it. Tomorrow he would confer with Earl Turner as to an interview with Harshawe. Miss Van Orphen was arranging a visit with the George Terrences for him too. Before he dared to fall in love he must find his guiding star.

# 6

At first Earl Turner showed only a pessimistic interest in Jonathan's attempts to get a response from Alvine Harshawe.

"That guy wouldn't give five minutes to his own mother if she wasn't photogenic," he said. "Maybe he's in Hollywood, or China. You wrote him at his agent's and at the Cape Cod address and at the town house. Nothing much you can do now."

"The *Times* said Zanuck was coming to New York expressly to see him about their picture," Jonathan said.

This was news to Earl, and apparently very interesting, for he meditated in silence for some time.

"You leave this to me," he said finally. "If Harshawe's in town I'll go see him personally and fix it up."

Jonathan was enormously grateful for this kind offer, having no idea that his good friend was going to "fix it up" for him by first putting the bite on Harshawe for himself. Earl had been beating his brains trying to figure out a way of asking Alvine for money again without having to crawl. It irked him that his recurrent need to beg emphasized the hopelessness of his own career and the triumphant infallibility of Alvine's. No chance of their positions' ever being reversed. Oh no. Fate, that cheap opportunist, never lets a winner down.

"There's a piece about him in *Esquire*," Jonathan said. "It says he misses the old days in the Village when he was in dire straits."

"I miss those old dire straits too," said Earl. "Dire straits, my foot! Better than being broke, I can tell you."

It was a good thing to have Jonathan's interests as an opening wedge to call Alvine, Earl thought; anything to vary the monotony of his usual routine. Every time he made his touch he found himself making grandiose allusions to big deals in the offing and the loan being only for a fortnight. Old Alvine never failed to shrug ironically, foreseeing in his damnably rude way that Earl wouldn't have the nerve to show up again for years, then not to beg but to borrow again, past loans never mentioned as if time had worn away interest and principal.

Galling to admit that Alvine, as always, was his last resort. Earl's system of Paul-Peter financing had caught up with him, as it did periodically, and suddenly there were all Pauls and no Peters. Creditors seemed to be converging on him from all over the world. It must be Earl Turner Festival Year, he thought, and all of these pests were as menacing as if the debts were for hundreds instead of piddling little fives and tens. Whenever a stranger glanced twice at him on the street, he knew he must be a collector. When an old friend crossed a street toward him he knew there was some buck or two he had forgotten to repay. Even the sun coming out was just a promise of tomorrow's rain, a reminder that the very heavens had their own collector. His wretched hotel, the One Three (not to be called Thirteen) had been goading him with ultimatums. So, on our knees again to old Alvine, Earl had thought gloomily.

At least the case of Jonathan Jaimison was a change of

gambit, and there was a chance that Alvine would like the crazy angle.

If he could get through all the flunkies and chichi to Alvine, that is. The great man's stock must be slipping, however, for his agent's secretary readily admitted that he might be reached on the agent's cabin cruiser up at the City Island yacht basin, or else at his own town house. Earl tried the house number, and sure enough, Alvine himself got on the phone. How the hell did Earl know that he was here hiding out?

"Broke?" he asked. "What is it—bail, rent, blackmail?"

"All three, as usual," Earl said. "But that's only incidental. I can put it to you in about fifteen minutes when I see you. It's an episode from your past, fella, that might interest you if you've got the time. Nothing serious—maybe funny."

Alvine was in the mood to be curious. Earl should drop in around twelve and tell him his story. Earl could have been there in five minutes but he passed the time in Central Park feeding the ducks, then strolled slowly eastward, scattering peanut shells and thinking about old times.

His usual daydream was running through his head, the one about Alvine, with the background changed now to East Sixty-fourth Street. The picture was always the same. It was the one where Earl saw himself at the wheel of his Cadillac-Rolls-Jaguar-or-whatever, slowing up to notice workmen busily piling up furniture on the sidewalk. Some officials are standing about, and then Alvine himself comes out of the house, pleading with the officials. Earl sees at once what is up—Alvine is being dispossessed. Hastily he leaps out of the car and rushes up to the scene, bulging wallet in his hand.

"Why didn't you tell me things were bad?" he demands of Alvine kindly, thrusting bills into everyone's hands. "Didn't I tell you I would pay you back someday when you needed it? Now the tables are turned and I'm tickled to death to help you out of the jam, old pal. Come, come, Alvine, no blubbering—good heavens, man, what else would you expect from your oldest friends? Let's be systematic about this, now. Men, put that furniture back where you found it; I'm taking care of everything, spot cash. And you, Alvine, buck up, old chap, men don't cry! No, don't explain! The main thing is I've got everything under control, so let's forget it and go have a drink. Twenty-One okay with you? What do you mean your clothes are too seedy? Hell, man, they know me—a tie is all that's necessary. Okay, hop in, and we'll stop off at Bronzini's and buy a dozen."

Earl knew that the grade of his daydreams had not improved since his Peabody High School days, but he was hooked by them, no matter how cheap, the way he was still hooked by Almond Joy candy bars, sneaking into telephone booths to wolf them down. He absently fumbled in his pocket now to see if he might buy one, knowing that he should be careful of his change. This brought on another dream, the one about finding money in the street, and his eyes darted expertly along the gutter. He had stopped hoping to find bills of any larger denomination than a twenty, reasoning they would be too hard to explain and too hard to change in his circle. You could change an imaginary ten-dollar bill easy enough, but a dream fifty could get you in trouble. Actually he had found coins on several occasions and was always scrounging around in mud puddles and in the teeth of oncoming trucks to pick up dream quarters that turned out to be real bottle caps. Once, spotting a possible dime in a gutter, he had bent over so suddenly his bursitis nipped him in the back and he couldn't straighten up while a Fifth Avenue bus braked to a screeching halt at his very coattails. Since then he had made it a sporting rule not to bend over for anything less than a dream quarter.

The Harshawe house suddenly leaped out of the block at him, and there was no use denying that the imminence of seeing old Alvine again—in a matter of seconds—excited Earl, and he knew a silly grin was on his face as if he were right in the presence of Scott Fitzgerald. He forced himself to stand quietly a moment before the little brownstone house that flaunted its iron balconies and old-fashioned lamp-posts in the teeth of the surrounding modern apartment houses. He reminded himself of Alvine's childish weaknesses—his pose of hating New York for its social demands, his pretense of hating publicity. He wasn't seeing a soul this time, he had assured Earl on the phone, just wallowing in solitude and work, and was only pausing in his intense concentration long enough to see Earl.

Satisfied that his grin had changed from hero-worship to sardonic detachment, Earl was ready to proceed. Following Alvine's instructions, he rang the caretaker's basement apartment and was told to go on up to the third floor, where Mr. Harshawe was still in bed. The living rooms were done up for the summer, the furniture in shrouds, the smell of camphor all over, floors bare, shades all drawn.

"That you, Turner?" Harshawe's voice boomed from behind an open door, and there was Alvine lying in bed, unshaven, bags under his eyes, hair a little grayer than five years ago falling over the crooked black eyebrows, the brown eyes still keenly probing, calculating every flaw in your own appearance. He was a big hunk of man, Earl noted, and all those years of gracious living had left their mark. Earl patted his own flat belly with quiet ostentation, as if it were the result of rigid abstinence.

One thing that never changed about Alvine was the wild disorder of his bedrooms, no matter which wife was in charge. He always had great giant beds, for he wrote, ate, snoozed, read, entertained, did everything in bed. "Alvine's playpen," his present wife, Peggy, called it, and was constantly complaining about the difficulty of making Alvine get out of pajamas. There were stacks of newspapers, every edition, magazines, notebooks, manuscripts, proofsheets, a bathrobe, and a typewriter skidding over the counterpane. A tray with a box of potato chips and a highball glass was on a chair, and a half-opened suitcase on the floor spilled out a tangle of shirts, socks, and ties. No sign of any feminine life, Earl noted, but then in all of Alvine's ménages the female was boxed up out of sight whenever Earl made his calls.

"You old bastard," Alvine greeted him, propping pillows behind his head and sizing up his guest. "I made out a check over there under the ashtray, if that's what you're looking for."

Earl flinched. Same old Alvine. Kick 'em right in the teeth before they can put on their poor little show.

"I was merely looking for wife tracks," Earl said coolly. "Don't tell me you've booted Number Four."

"I left Peg up at Chatham with a houseful of crumbs and waiting for more," Alvine said. "Anything to keep a man from working. 'You're so dull when you work, honey.'" Alvine mimicked his wife's boarding-school accent. "Or 'Really, dear, you're not having brandy before breakfast?'"

"She'll be sore you left," Earl ventured.

"Peg? She'll act sore but she'll really be glad she can sound off about my opinions without me shutting her up," Alvine said sourly. "She won't have to apologize to her pals for my insulting them. Oh, she'll give me hell but she'll be having a ball. Have a drink, or is it too early for a dedicated littérateur like yourself?"

Earl poured himself a short one from the Jack Daniel's bottle on the dresser and noted the empty glasses and overflowing ashtrays on floor and chairs.

"Big night?"

Alvine gave an impatient snort.

"You're as bad as a wife, Turner," he said. "You find somebody in bed an hour or so after you've managed to drag your own can out, and right off you start pointing and yelling big night, big night, aren't you ashamed, it's after ten, Bergdorf's is open, Saks is open, Irving Trust is open, get up, get busy, do something, do your crossword puzzle, tear up your mail, get on all the phones, start apologizing for last night and tomorrow too, while you're at it, get on the ball, don't just lie there minding your own business."

"Well, now, Alvine, really—" Earl protested.

"I should have married you, Turner," Alvine said. "I could have had four wives' worth of nagging without changing mistresses."

"Sorry, old man. I forget I'm day people and you were always night people," Earl said.

"Who says we're people?" Alvine yawned. "There's the check, don't you want it?"

Earl picked up the check and put it in his pocket. The minute he had it there he didn't give a damn what Alvine said. Needle away, boy, he thought, nothing bothers me now. Maybe he'd get around to his Jonathan errand and maybe he wouldn't.

"What happened to that system you used to have of getting advances from publishers?" Alvine asked. "They used to be tickled to death to hand you out advances on a mere idea. They were so sure they wouldn't have to bother reading anything. What spoiled it? Did you turn in a manuscript?"

Earl laughed too, as if it were a great joke instead of being in a small way—two chapters—all too true.

"I haven't had an idea myself in ten years," Alvine admitted graciously. "Sit down and talk, man, fill me in."

You got mad at Alvine, insulted and humiliated by him, but you couldn't resist when he raised his little finger toward you. So Earl sat down on a chair full of *Esquires* and *Trues* and told him what the old ironworker had told him in a Myrtle Avenue bar about his son being a junkie and pinning the stuff on the old man. . . .

"This fellow tells you this for true?" Alvine yawned again, and when Earl nodded, Alvine snorted. "Earl, how many times do I have to tell you that what a simple workman tells you in a low bar in a Brooklyn accent isn't necessarily true? You're safer swiping straight from De Maupassant or O. Henry, somebody out there in good old public domain. These bar confessions are always straight out of *Reader's Digest* or the *Post*, magazines a literary type like yourself wouldn't be reading. No, my friend, I'd be afraid to use that little idyll. And nobody likes a worker hero any more, anyway."

That was good old Alvine for you, first encouraging you to talk, then knocking your wind out.

"Who said anything about that?" Earl said. "The junkie is your hero these days. Where have you been?"

He knew he shouldn't have flared up, trying to take Alvine down, but the damned check in his pocket made him feel like an equal. He was ashamed as soon as he saw Alvine's eyebrow shoot up in its old Clark Gable way. You shouldn't take advantage of your betters, Earl reminded himself savagely, especially a great genius who hasn't had an idea in ten years. The genius had poured himself another drink and Earl held out his glass to the spout, reflecting that the old boy was hitting the bottle but then, with the favorites, the bottle never hit back as it certainly would with himself.

"Otherwise, how's life?" Alvine asked amiably, pushing himself up with another pillow to watch his caller—to count his crow's feet, Earl thought, see the grease spots on his shirt.

"Nothing new. A review now and then—eight bucks for fifteen hundred words of new criticism in a little magazine, or forty for six hundred words of old criticism in the Sunday book sections. A pulp rewrite of a De Maupassant."

"I mean what kind of place do you live, what about dames?" Alvine interrupted.

Material, Earl thought. The sonofabitch was always scratching for material like a dog scratching for fleas.

"I'm in this Hotel One Three, men only," Earl said. "Way over east in what they call the New Village. A real fleabag. Signs in the lobby, NO LOITERING IN THE LOBBY, kind of funny considering that the lobby is only five feet square. Signs in your room, ONLY ONE PERSON AT A TIME IN THIS ROOM. FOOD IN ROOM FORBIDDEN, and all that. I have a little electric plate hidden."

Earl saw that Alvine was amused. Probably already figuring how he could use the stuff. Okay, let him have it.

"A fellow there wrote a song from the signs," he said

obligingly. " 'Won't you loiter in the lobby of my heart.' "

Good. The master was grinning.

"Dames?" Alvine persisted.

"A few favors from old friends, that's all," Earl said. "They throw me out regularly. Damn it, I'm a lonely man."

"Lonely!" shouted Alvine, suddenly coming to life. "What do you know about loneliness! Why, you're not even married!"

Earl had to laugh.

"Let alone four times like me. Oh, it's no laughing matter," Alvine went on bitterly. "You played it smart so you've still got your freedom. But me. There's nothing left of a man after he's parceled himself out to women four ways—five years lost here, five there, eight there, another six here . . . Believe me, that's loneliness! This door of your past to keep shut, that one mustn't touch, this one a booby trap—so what the hell have you got left of your own life? You can't even run around naked in your own mind!"

"You can think about all those front-page reviews of your books," Earl said with what he hoped was a good-natured chuckle. "Or having supper with the royal family after your play opens. Or editors wrastling on your doorstep. Don't get me crying over you, old man. It isn't that tough."

Alvine reached out for the highball glass on the floor and poured himself a drink.

"Write a story about a poor old writing stiff, a very complicated, well-educated, rich old author, perfectly adjusted to his lousy environment. Don't you see that great new Cinderella angle? The poor old slob, when he walks in a restaurant strangers flock to his table, put their drinks on his check; they visit his country home with their picnic hampers, they pick his roses, throw their banana peels around, urge their kids to swim in his pool, and when he shows up—it's his home, after all—they tell him they don't see what's so hot about his books or plays; in fact they don't even know them. They have no intention of leaving until they're chased off, so they can tell how mean he is. They ask if it's true he's 'interracial,' is it true that O'Hara writes all his stuff for him, that his present wife was a call girl in Las Vegas, that his mother spends most of her time in a straitjacket, that his kids are test-tube products, and that he's been living on dope ever since he left the breast—"

Earl had to shout to override Alvine's tirade.

"Stop breaking my heart!" he cried. "Who would read an old story like that? Talk about bar confessions! Where's your sympathetic character? Where's your struggle? Who cares about one man's most embarrassing moment?"

"Oh forget it!" Alvine said, lying back wearily. "Forget I said a word. It was just that I thought with your determination to write and my determination not to, between us we'd make one hell of an author."

Earl knew he shouldn't let Alvine get his goat but it always happened and he hated himself—and Alvine more —for it. He hated that wave of affection Alvine always felt for the person he had just kicked in the face. Good old Earl, he would say, how lovable of him to be a confirmed flop! He might be a nuisance but never a competitor. Other old pals might forge ahead and get stuffy—take old George Terrence, for example!—but you could count on old Earl to be down there at the bottom of the ladder, looking up at you like a dumb old mutt that can never learn the tricks.

What burned Earl was that Alvine no longer made any pretense of believing in his big projects, as if they were windy lies or so unfeasible that only poor gullible Earl would be taken in. He might have pulled off one of his deals, Earl thought, if he hadn't felt Alvine's skeptical eyes on him. Skeptical, hell—absolutely certain of Earl's failure. If others were always so damned sure you'd need the safety net, you usually ended up in it. You did what people expected of you. Look at Alvine. Everybody from high school on had always expected Alvine to make good, so he did. Everything worked out tick-tock. He turned out a play or novel, then sat back for years on his yacht or somebody else's and let the profits roll in—television, Hollywood, road companies, musical adaptations, foreign rights, revivals, with every gossip columnist beating the drum for him. Industrious, they called him, when every little word earned its own living again and again for years without Alvine's turning a hand. Yet people were always saying to Earl, "Why don't you get down to work, Turner, write something?" Sell something, was what they meant. He wished suddenly that Alvine would get sore at him, dignify him with a little decent jealousy, tell him to go to hell, get him off this hook somehow, let him fail in his own way without rubbing in how easy it was for others to succeed.

Well, they were each other's oldest friends. Not that it meant they liked each other. Some old friends went to their graves without learning to like each other, without even getting to know each other.

Earl and Alvine had become friends through geographical necessity at first—graduated from the same Schenectady high school, into the West Side Y, then Greenwich Village, always planning to write, talking endlessly about writing, getting down all those upstate characters and legends, yak-yak-yak. Earl realized he should have got the picture then and there, because while he rolled into bed at daylight, perfectly content with their discussions, Alvine went right to his damned typewriter to get it all down. Next time they'd meet, Alvine would have a fat manuscript to read to him instead of resuming their talk as Earl wanted to do. "Where's your story, Turner? The one you talked about all week?" Alvine would ask. Earl would explain that the material needed more time; he was too much the perfectionist to rush right in and mess up a great idea before he was ripe for it. He never could get over Alvine's reckless plunge from idea to typewriter. Cheating, he thought; not really playing the game. You could have a depth talk about murder, couldn't you, without tearing right out and killing somebody? Earl had a vague feeling of having been robbed, too, he wasn't sure of what. But what had he said that always set off Alvine without starting his own motor?

When Earl got the *Sphere* editorial job they shared an apartment with George Terrence, a rich young lawyer, on Irving Place. By that time Alvine had published some sketches about Schenectady boyhood, things about places and people Earl knew as well as Alvine did. Editing them for *The Sphere,* Earl felt robbed again. They were bits he intended to put in his novel when he got around to it, only now it was too late. They didn't see much of each other after Alvine married his literary agent, Roberta somebody, and don't think she wasn't a big pusher for his success, typing, selling, making him into a big enough shot for his next three wives. Not that Alvine ever gave any of them credit. He could use up their money, their life stories, their profitable connections and then complain they blocked his work.

"Do you mean to tell me you still hang around the Spur?" Alvine asked. "Next you'll be telling me that you still get grain alcohol from the mad druggist and make your own gin in the umbrella stand."

"At least the Spur is still alive," Earl said, remembering not to get sore. He wished he dared remind his chum of those old days when they were tickled to death to gouge the cash out of old George Terrence for a night at the Spur. "How about visiting it one of these nights?"

He was surprised that Alvine didn't laugh at the idea.

"Damned if I wouldn't like to, Turner," he said thoughtfully. "I need to freshen up on that background for the thing I'm working on, but how can I drop in a place like that and get the real picture?"

Conceited bastard.

"You mean you'd be recognized right away so your fans would tear your clothes off," Earl said, oh, very sympathetically.

Alvine nodded.

"Not that bad, but you know how it is. Old has-beens needling me for making it when they never could with their genius. Dames yakking about my mystique and their boyfriends sore and claiming I'm trying to rape them."

"I see your problem," Earl said. "Still, maybe I could handle the stampede. There's a young fellow around there now looking for you, and we could pick him up. He wants to know if you remember his mother. She had some pleasant memories of you."

"Pleasant memories," Alvine mused. "Sounds like a belated paternity suit."

You're not kidding, Earl thought. No reason for that big grin.

"Just the thing for writer's block," Alvine said. "A paternity suit ought to start you thinking. A real blockbuster."

So it was going to be a big joke.

"Her name was Connie Birch," Earl said. "She typed for you. Mean anything?"

"There was a Connie," Alvine recalled. "Sure. I promised to pay for the typing when I sold the piece. Lived way over on Horatio, Connie did. What became of her?"

"Died some twenty years ago. You can cross her off the bill."

"Dead or alive, Connie's got forty bucks coming to her," Alvine stated piously. "I'll settle with her heirs."

"You used to get 'em to type for free if you slept with them," Earl said. He could still get mad remembering how lucky Alvine used to be. "What was the deal with Connie?"

"Don't be a cad, Turner," mocked Alvine.

"You mean you don't remember," diagnosed Earl. "Anyway, this kid, Jonathan Jaimison, is crazy to see you and hear about his mother's New York past. Maybe he wants to write a book."

This was the wrong approach.

"Too many goddam writers already," Alvine said. "Why does anybody want to pick a lousy trade like that?"

"Look who's complaining," Earl said. "Nothing in it for Harshawe, of course. Just a million bucks and a passel of Pulitzers."

"I've never had a Pulitzer," Alvine corrected him with a rather brave, wistful smile. "A drama prize once, never any for my novels. Worst damn play I ever wrote, too."

So you did know that much, Earl thought.

"The picture deal was all loused up, you know."

Now wasn't that just too bad? Earl kept silent.

"Oh sure, I've had a couple of book-club breaks," Alvine granted, getting the message that he needn't expect sympathy. "But I've never gotten the critical reception for my novels that the plays get. That's why it's a challenge to me. I'm thinking of concentrating on novels, get out of this damn Broadway muck, give myself a chance to breathe. Keep to myself."

"Here?"

"Could be. Peg hates New York." He must have been mulling over what Earl had said earlier, for he said, "Say, what does this Jaimison kid you were telling me about, Connie's kid, look like?"

"You, come to think of it," Earl said. "By George, he does!"

Alvine sat up straight, both eyebrows up, incredulous but pleased.

"No kidding," Earl went on with delight. "I've been trying to think who he reminded me of all along. He's blond, and his eyes are different from yours—instead of his looking right through a person as you do, you can look right through him. But the build and profile are straight Harshawe, by George."

"Clean-cut American youth, standard model, that's all." Alvine shrugged, but he was amused. "Maybe I'll look him up at that. I ought to know more about that generation."

"For the new novel," guessed Earl, but Alvine only smiled enigmatically. Okay, make a big secret of it, Earl thought, but then Alvine always claimed it was no good talking about his writing, the way it was no good talking about cooking or dancing or singing—you just did it or you didn't, that was all there was to it. The born genius.

"What about you, Turner?" Alvine asked. "What do you want out of your writing, anyway? Dough? Kicks? Immortality?"

"I just want to be overestimated," Earl shouted, "like everybody else, goddammit."

Alvine burst out laughing. He liked that. He liked other people's hard-bought cynicism, but Earl was embarrassed at having betrayed himself. Now that he was standing up, ready to go, Alvine was suddenly crazy to have him stay. Have another drink—okay, one for the road then, and what have you read of the current trash? "You always read more than I do," Alvine said graciously. "When a book's bad I'm disgusted with the whole trade, and when it's good I wonder how such an oaf could turn out such good stuff. But you've got real critical sense." So Earl was beguiled again into trying to placate the master, telling him all the things wrong with Faulkner, Hemingway, Sartre, and the English crowd, till Alvine was crowing happily.

"We'll have a night going the rounds," he promised. "I'll have a look at this Jonathan kid."

Oh sure. Earl had sense enough to know that Alvine's geniality came over him only when the guest was headed for the door. Now was the time to leave.

He was able to congratulate himself, once outside, that this time he had not stayed too long. He had lived so long in cheap little hotel rooms that whenever he got into a regular home he couldn't bear to leave. He was as sensitive as the next one, but hints that hosts wanted to dine or sleep or go out bounced off Earl's consciousness once he was lost in home-hunger, standing in the door, half in, half out, not sitting down again, mind you, but not gone either. The few times before when he had succeeded in visiting the Harshawe ménage, he knew well enough he had overstayed, and it was funny too, because the minute he got in the door he kept watching Alvine anxiously to see if he looked bored or annoyed, which he did in a very short time. Then Earl got privately enraged and stayed on out of pure stubbornness. He could laugh at himself afterward.

"I know what old Alvine will have put on my gravestone when I go upstairs," he merrily told people. " 'We Thought He'd Never Go.' "

A good visit on the whole, Earl thought, walking down Lexington. Alvine had cheered him up in spite of everything. Suddenly he realized he had not even looked at the check. Maybe Alvine, who thought like a cagey rich man these days, was letting him have a measly fifty. Earl's lip curled. Already he regretted not having given a few straight criticisms of the last masterpiece, instead of buttering him up exactly like the disgusting toadies Alvine always managed to make of everybody around him. He regretted the faint twitch of affection he had felt when Alvine asked if he had time to wait for the restaurant next door to send up a bite of lunch. A real proof of Alvine's friendship, Earl had first thought, wanting to have an intimate little snack right there, just the two of them, instead of taking him out to phony chic spots like the Pavillon or Twenty-One, where his phony success friends would crowd around him. On second thoughts, the hell with this cozy little snack business, why didn't he invite him to those good places where he could meet those phony new pals? If phoniness was what he liked, his old pal Turner could be as phony as they come.

Earl reached in his vest pocket and took out the check. For two cents he'd tear it up and mail the pieces back to the old bastard. Then he peered at the figure written out. Three hundred dollars. Yes, three hundred dollars.

Three hundred cool dollars just like that. He stood still, breathing deep of the wonderful diamond-studded air, looking down beautiful Lexington Avenue, a street paved with gold, saw the little jewelry-store window right beside him and decided instantly he would go in and buy the silver wristwatch on the blue velvet.

It was true that Hotel One Three had promised to lock him out of his room if he did not pay today, but such catastrophes would not happen to a man armored with this beautiful check. A fine sense of accomplishment flooded his being, as if his own honest labor and not Alvine's generosity had brought about this reward.

Then a pang of irritation beset him, and he wondered how in heaven's name this piece of paper could be translated into cash. If he presented it to the hotel they would take out not only what he owed but a month in advance and probably raise the rate besides for such a rich guest. If he tried to get the bartender at The Golden Spur to okay it, then he would have to pay the old tabs he'd been hanging up at the Spur, and, besides paying all the customers from whom he'd borrowed a dollar or two over the years, he'd have to loan them money. He saw a branch of the bank on which Alvine's check had been written and thought of starting an account on the spot, but it would be days before he could draw on it. Passing a Riker's luncheonette, he saw that today there was steak-and-kidney pie, and it reminded him that he hadn't eaten today, and very little yesterday. Visions of great steaks of the past rose before his gaze; he thought of Cavanagh's, old Billy the Oysterman's, and the old Luchow's before it went Hollywood. He realized he was still walking and the great places he thought of were far, far away. Keene's Chop House then, he thought, and his mouth watered at the dream of those fat chops with Old Mustie Ale and a go at George Terrence's pipe always preserved there. But even Thirty-sixth Street was far away. And what good was a three-hundred-dollar check anywhere—no better than his cash treasure of a dollar and sixteen cents.

He was one of those doomed people who simply were not made to have money, he thought indignantly, child of eight generations of solid, substantial, bumbling Americans, born back in their rent—back eight generations with compound interest, the way old George Terrence, for instance, was born on top of eight generations of trust funds, so that he was honored as a success in his career before he'd made a dollar. He and Alvine used to sneer in the old times when their roommate, old George Terrence, would complain of being broke—less than fifty bucks in his wallet, maybe—might have to sell a bond, go into his savings, then after that go into one of his trust funds, and after that into his stocks, and then get an advance on the inheritance from his grandmother, then from his mother or uncle. Men like George honestly thought that to be broke meant just that. No, Earl conceded, George had never experienced the thrill of finding an extra one-dollar bill in his pocket after a week-end party—hell, George probably didn't even know they made one-dollar bills. George never had the exquisite ecstasy of spotting a dime in the gutter—dimes he knew, as any other born rich man does, merely as the coin used in tipping. Poor George had nothing but unlimited credit and could never be made to understand how a man with a big check in one pocket and a dollar sixteen in another could still be financially inconvenienced.

The gourmet lunch would have to be foregone, Earl saw. The sensible thing was to take the bus down, get some provender in that new supermarket near the Spur, stock up on coffee and eggs, and fix up a snack on his electric plate in his room. Once in the market he added a pint of milk and a bun to his eggs and coffee order, but when he offered his coins to the cashier she suddenly took a close squint at them—why hadn't she done this to the other people's money? he wondered—and cried out, "This quarter is no good!" The ladies behind him, who were battering at him with their pushcarts, stared indignantly at him. Crook. Pickpocket. Blackmailer. Forger. It seemed, the cashier stated with growing suspicion, that the coin was offensively Canadian and never mind about its being worth twenty-seven cents in United States money, it was worthless in the supermarket. Earl, goaded by the righteous, scornful eyes of the ladies wheeling about him menacingly, took the milk and bun off his order and skulked out.

He started on the walk back to the Hotel One Three, automatically ducking back and forth across streets, swerving around corners from Sixth to Broadway and east across Fourteenth to avoid passing a certain dry-cleaner's, a certain drugstore, Teddy's Barbershop, Smart Shirts, Inc., a dentist's office, and a few bars, in all of which he owed varying sums. It occurred to him that he had almost worn out his present neighborhood, but where was there left for him to move? He had lived up and down town, East Side, West Side, in furnished rooms and fleabags from Chinatown to Harlem, pushed by creditors from Avenue A to Chelsea and even across the river to Hoboken, where he had holed up in a six-dollar room on River Street, living on beer and free broth from the Clam Broth House, then swung back across and up to Yorkville, Spanish Harlem, down again to the dingier fringes of the East Thirties, then westward ho again, widening his orbit as obliged by his little debts. He needed a helicopter, he thought savagely, to skip his pursuers and land *bingo* right in his own bed. Only a day ago he had been speculating on how long before he maneuvered himself right out of the city into the Atlantic Ocean. Never mind, all this would be changed when he cashed his check, and he should be glad he didn't have to make this simple trip by way of Woodlawn Cemetery.

The walk cleared his mind and he began appreciating the wonder of Alvine's forking over three hundred bucks. He began to figure out little tranquillity pills to various creditors, and he visualized the new suit—almost new, in the window of the Third Avenue Pawn Shop near Twelfth Street. He had promised himself that he would buy it with the first eighteen dollars he laid his hands on. Already he was enjoying the anticipated cries of joy from all those creditors as he passed out tens, and twenties.

"What's all the excitement?" he heard himself saying. "Didn't I tell you I would pay it later?"

Figuring all he had to pay out left him with the sudden desolate realization that a fortune had passed through his hands and nothing was left for Baby. Supposing he did manage by some miracle to cash the damn check, by night he would be as broke and desperate as he had been yesterday. Yes, and hungry too.

Earl did not realize that his feet had frozen into the sidewalk, as if his mind had commanded *Whoa* and they waited like patient old cart horses for a new command. His hand absently groped in his vest pocket, where, surprisingly enough, the check still reposed. As long as it was there, uncashed, he was a rich man. As long as he didn't cash it there was a choice left open. He could, for instance, simply take off for Mexico on a cheap flight and live pleasantly for six months. Write a novel. Like *Under the Volcano,* maybe. Mexico would do it for him. The instant this grandiose idea occurred to him, he knew it had been garaged in the back of his brain all along. His feet seemed to recognize the change of plan, for they automatically turned around and started in the other direction. Earl was not sure where they were taking him, but the knowledge of the uncashed check in his pocket gave him a dizzy glow of unlimited power.

At the corner of Twelfth Street he caught sight of a couple coming toward him, the lady in paisley-trimmed horsehair picture hat, flowered taffeta suit, and purple gloves definitely Claire Van Orphen, the young man Jonathan. In a flash he knew what he would do.

"Friends!" He made a deep bow to her and another to Jonathan. "I was just about to call both of you to say good-by."

"Good-by, Mr. Turner!" Claire exclaimed in dismay. "Where are you going?"

"Acapulco," he said. "Later the interior. I can really write in Mexico."

He would have gone on babbling, for he did feel guilty at having done so well for himself on a mission that was supposed to benefit Jonathan, but while he was casting about for some definite word to give the boy, Claire placed a detaining hand on his arm.

"But you can't go, Mr. Turner," she cried. "I've just been telling Jonathan the good news. You remember your theory about updating my old stories? The switch, you called it. Making the heroine the villain and vice versa? You said they would sell in a minute that way."

"I couldn't have been that definite, come now," Earl said warily. "I only revised them as a little game."

"You said in the old days the career girl who supported the family was the heroine, and the idle wife was the baddie," Claire said gleefully. "And now it's the other way round. In the soap operas, the career girl is the baddie, the wife is the goodie because she's better for *business,* didn't he say that, Jonathan? Well, you were right. CBS has bought the two you fixed, and Hollywood is interested. Jonathan and I have been looking for you all over. Isn't it wonderful?"

Earl drew a pack of cigarettes from his pocket, negligently selected one, and offered the pack to Jonathan. He felt quite faint.

"Not surprising when you know the score as I do," he said. "One does learn a little in twenty-five, thirty years of professional writing."

"You see you can't go away now, with all my other manuscripts for you to revise," Claire said anxiously. "And I have your check right here in my purse, fifty-fifty, just as we said."

"Check?" Earl repeated vaguely.

Mexico vanished. Escape vanished. There was nothing but checks.

"Supposing we stop in here at Longchamps and talk about it over a brandy?" he said, exuberant confidence suddenly overwhelming him. "I've just left Alvine Harshawe and he is delighted at the idea of meeting Jonathan, here. We talked for hours about you, boy. Wants to see you. Any day now you'll be hearing from him."

"Maybe I should telephone him," Jonathan suggested radiantly.

"Wait a bit. I'll be in touch with him again," Earl counseled. "Never fear, I'll fix it up. Come on, now we celebrate."

Claire was already being seated at a sidewalk table.

"You must let me be the hostess, then," she said.

"If we must we must," Earl said with a gallant shrug.

# 7

THE THEN-AND-NOW CAFÉ did so little business that Jonathan worried over its survival. The real-estate man upstairs, who owned the building and half a block of houses beyond, was well pleased, however. A nice little capital loss, he gloated, rubbing his hands happily, just the break he needed. Moreover, he proposed to put more money into it for the same mysterious tax reasons, and since Dr. Kellsey's generous suggestions had not seduced trade so far, he was invited to submit more of his profit-proof ideas.

It was Dr. Kellsey's inspiration to have the walls covered with blown-up photographs of Pfaff's Beer Hall (of the 1850s), O. Henry's hotel on West Eighteenth Street, Henry James's early home on Mercer Street, Stephen Crane looking like a Bowery bum, John Masefield tending bar at Luke O'Connor's saloon, Richard Harding Davis dining on the Brevoort *terrasse,* and other nineteenth-century literary figures of the quarter. These reminders that other writers had been there before them merely annoyed the new crop of poets, subtly hinting that they themselves might end up tomorrow as blown-up "Thens" on these very walls. Dr. Kellsey himself realized this and thought all the better of the idea. Besides, he enjoyed his position as chief and sometimes only customer, with a big table to himself and no wide-eyed apprentice poets to watch him pour cognac into his espresso under the table, a routine that put him into a nostalgic mood for the old Prohibition days.

Jonathan was learning something new about the city every day, but there was no use trying to make today's lesson fit onto yesterday's. Each day the blackboard was erased and you began all over, yesterday's conclusions canceled by today's findings. Darcy, for instance, had confided often in Jonathan that there was something dangerously feebleminded about a girl (Lize) who could hook up with a creep like Percy Wright. But now Darcy went the rounds at night with this very same creep, generously making him spend a couple of dollars at the Then-and-Now sometimes, admonishing Jonathan not to mention this to Lize.

"She'd really flip," Darcy prophesied. "It burns her up that so many men fall for me when she tries to hang on to them. God knows she's been doing her best to get Percy back but she hasn't figured out yet that I'm the reason he's holding out. He's just too nice a guy for Lize, that's all. He's kinda cute, too, the way he hangs onto his budget until you get him gassed enough to forget it. He says we aren't being fair to Lize, when she's so hot for him, but I say let's face it, Lize is just one of those women that can't hold a man, that's all, it's not his fault."

Jonathan obediently wiped Darcy's earlier statements about Percy from his memory and with the same open mind listened to Lize's stories of Percy pursuing her, begging her to come back. Sometimes Percy himself, deserted in some bar when both girls had found better fish to fry, attached himself to Jonathan and confided his own troubles, which were not frustrations in love but anguish that his idol, Hugow, was unmistakably shunning him. It was because Hugow's girls could not keep from falling for his unworthy self, Percy sighed. He told Jonathan it was not all roses having that terrible power over women, always breaking up homes, but what could a man do?

"If Hugow would only let me explain the situation," Percy said wistfully.

Jonathan told him he must not blame himself too much. It occurred to him that there was truth in every lie if you waited long enough, and you might as well believe everything while you waited.

Earl Turner said he was helping Claire Van Orphen "update" her fiction, and Miss Van Orphen's story was that she was helping Earl Turner get back on his feet professionally. Jonathan admired both of these people and felt fortunate in their friendship, just as he did about Dr. Kellsey's. The doctor brought his class papers to correct at a table in the Then-and-Now, enlivening this chore with helpful hints to Jonathan on his newssheet. He summoned his anecdotes of the past by running a beautifully manicured hand through his lordly gray mane, then pressing the hand to his closed eyes, a fascinating gesture that Jonathan could not resist imitating. Sometimes he caught himself performing in unison with the doctor and would peep out through the fingers over his eyes to see if his friend had noticed. Then the doctor would shake his mane (Jonathan would do the same), smile sadly (Jonathan would return the smile), and both would sigh, perhaps over the beauty of the past, perhaps over the folly of youth, perhaps over their shared sensitivity.

Jonathan took pride and comfort in the doctor's remark that he was the only young person who had the gift of curiosity. Students used to have it, oh yes indeed, the doctor said, but not any more. Everybody used that new word "empathy," said the doctor, but actually the word for the present age was "apathy." Apathy was what drove him to drink, said the doctor, apathy laced with either hostility or sheer ignorance in the young, apathy mixed with resentment and moral complacency in his wife, apathy with long-suffering and sulky envy in his lady-friend and departmental associate, Miss Anita Barlowe.

"But you, my dear Jonathan, you are eager to know things!" the doctor had said. "You want to know what I can tell you, what anybody can tell you, and you listen, too, by George. You make me feel alive."

So Jonathan was glad to have the doctor peer over his shoulder the night he was writing his historical items for the week.

"Have you mentioned that Poe wrote "The Raven" over here on Carmine Street?" asked the doctor.

"Last week I said he wrote it on Third Street above Bertolotti's," said Jonathan. "They gave us an ad."

"Ah yes, I keep forgetting that the function of history is to bring in advertising," Dr. Kellsey said. "How about noting that Stokes killed Jim Fisk over Josie Mansfield right in the Broadway Central Hotel just below Third Street? Mention that the hotel was redecorated with the tiles and fixings from the old Waldorf Peacock Alley. And say that poor old Hearstwood, in *Sister Carrie,* spent his last days there—committed suicide there, didn't he?"

"Will they think of that as a plug?" Jonathan debated.

Dr. Kellsey sipped his coffee judiciously.

"Very well, then take the Brevoort. Jenny Lind stayed there, and in Edward Sheldon's play *Romance*—played by Doris Keane, incidentally—her suitors unhitched the horses and drew her carriage right from the theater to the hotel. And it wasn't even air-conditioned then."

"That was the *old* Brevoort," demurred Jonathan.

"Try the Fifth Avenue Hotel, then, across the street from where Mabel Dodge had her peyote party forty years ago."

"No ad in that," Jonathan objected cautiously. "The Narcotics Squad might get after them."

The doctor chuckled.

"By George, you're getting to be a regular public-relations man. Must run in your family, that knack, or maybe it's plain Scotch caution."

Jonathan winced. Any reminder of the Jaimison family virtues sickened him, and it depressed him that his friend could find any trace of them in him. He made up his mind to tell the doctor the circumstances that made him definitely non-Jaimison, though Earl Turner had advised him against confiding in anyone else for fear it would block useful information. He opened his mouth to give a mere hint, but the doctor's delighted interest brought out everything Jonathan could remember from his mother's documents. When the doctor lifted a skeptical eyebrow over a point or two— "Are you sure she meant The Golden Spur and not The Gilded Lantern; that was a gypsy tearoom? And are you sure she took a poetry course at the night school, because I myself was teaching there then?"—Jonathan pounded the desk, ready to offer affidavits.

"Of course I'm sure. What surprises me is that you didn't know her yourself since you were teaching there. Look." Jonathan pulled the snapshot of his mother from his pocket and pressed it on the table before Kellsey. "Doesn't the name Connie Birch mean anything to you?"

The doctor obligingly took out two other pairs of glasses from his briefcase and studied the picture intently. Then he folded up both pairs of spectacles, readjusted his regular glasses, and handed back the picture to Jonathan. He stared at him in solemn silence for a moment.

"My boy," he said impressively, "we have here a most extraordinary coincidence. I did know your mother. She was in my poetry class. It was the braids that reminded me, and the unusual wide eyes. Connie. Yes sir, little Connie Birch. Amazing."

Jonathan felt faint and gripped the desk. Through a whirling mist he saw the doctor's fine hand rumpling through the handsome mane and heard his classroom Barrymore voice echo dimly in his ears.

"The very child who took me first to The Golden Spur, as a matter of fact," he was saying. "I forget names, but I was new here then, and this dear child with braids around her head had cried when I read Alan Seeger's poem, 'I have a rendezvous with death—' "

"Yes, yes," cried Jonathan. "She always cried over that."

"I invited her out after class for a beer and sandwich to comfort her," said the doctor, his rich voice choked with memories. "I found her naïveté refreshing, but it was she who suggested The Golden Spur. Usually I dropped in to Lee Chumley's, maybe the Brevoort or Jumble Shop. It surprised me that she should know such an out-of-bounds place as the Spur. Sporting types, jazz singers, writers looking for color, wandering trollops—yes, I was shocked to see that my naïve little student was devoted to this place."

"And after that—"

"After that I often took her there after class," recalled the doctor, stroking his head rhythmically as if this stimulated a special department of his memory. "She was always affected by love poems, and I'm afraid I got in the way of specializing in them—Sara Teasdale, Millay, Taggard—

just because of the charming way this little student reacted to them. Gave me an excuse to console her, you see."

"You saw her home, then," Jonathan said, beginning to wonder uneasily if he had pressed the wrong button. He admired and respected Dr. Kellsey but he was not sure he wanted a closer connection.

The doctor reflected on this question and then nodded.

"I must have," he said. "It's true I was having some marriage problems at that time—in fact my wife was having me followed, as I recall, and my friend Miss Barlowe was having my wife followed—ha, ha—so little Connie Birch was my only refuge. Yes, she led me to the Spur. Curious, eh?"

"She wanted to meet someone there, perhaps," Jonathan suggested. "She knew Alvine Harshawe, don't forget, and he went there."

Dr. Kellsey shook his head fondly.

"Your mother was far too sensitive a girl for a big extrovert like Harshawe," he said. "Oh yes, she pointed him out to me—strange I remembered the incident without realizing it was Connie Birch—but a delicate child who cries over poetry would never be taken in by your Harshawes."

"But there was someone," Jonathan persisted. "She did meet some man at the Golden Spur—don't you remember any of her friends?"

The doctor twisted his mustache meditatively and stared into the dark street outside.

"I don't remember how I got the impression she was alone in New York and without friends," he mused. "I remember being surprised when Louis, the old waiter at the Brevoort Café, spoke to her by name when I took her there. And I was startled to run into her at a Pagan Ball at

Webster Hall—she'd come all alone, she said, imagine! Strange, come to think of it."

"She must have known someone would be there," Jonathan suggested.

The doctor frowned thoughtfully into space.

"I didn't recognize her because her braids were down, the hair flowing. I knew she didn't realize the type of party it would be. Later I looked around for her to take her home, but she'd disappeared. Frightened, I think, for it was a real brawl."

He stopped short. A sharp suspicion had crossed his mind that he had indeed found Connie that night, must have taken her home, for how else could he account for having been found by police next noon asleep in Abingdon Square in his tattered Hamlet costume? God knows his wife had flung it in his face often enough later so that he couldn't deny it.

Jonathan wondered if his mother had ever been frightened at the idea of anything, especially a wild party. Even in her weakest stage of invalidism she welcomed any excitement. He was sure she was like himself, always ready to accept whatever occurred as the normal.

"Don't you think she went alone to the party and to the Spur because she knew a certain man would be there?" he asked. "She said in her letter that this well-known man would always be there and would walk her home later."

The doctor's eyebrows lifted. He looked pleased.

"I did get some recognition for my reviews in the *New Republic* then," he admitted thoughtfully.

Jonathan choked back an impatient exclamation. He hadn't foreseen this angle and he wished he could keep the doctor from pursuing it.

"It was a long time ago, my boy," said the doctor with a

faintly mysterious smile. "And the whole episode had slipped my mind until now, but I assure you I would certainly have known if your mother was seriously interested in some other man."

Here was the closest he had come to an actual friend of his mother's, and it was leading nowhere, or if it was leading anywhere it was no place Jonathan wanted to look. He knew the doctor was studying him carefully and he became very busy at the typewriter, determined to drop the subject. But the doctor's speculative gaze made him uneasy, and he found himself tousling his hair in the doctor's familiar gesture. Presently the doctor rose and put his papers back in the briefcase.

"Remarkable," he murmured. "Incredible. I must put my mind to it and see what comes up. I'll do my best for you, my boy."

The tender way in which he said "my boy" made Jonathan berate himself for asking the doctor's aid. He rose politely to say good night, and the doctor stepped beside him.

"We seem to be almost exactly the same height," he said. "You have perhaps half an inch in your favor, due probably to all that spinach and orange juice of your generation. Well, good night."

"If she wasn't meeting Harshawe, what about George Terrence, the lawyer?" Jonathan cried after him. "Miss Van Orphen is sure Terrence went to the Spur in those days."

"Claire Van Orphen must be getting on in years now," said Dr. Kellsey. "I used to meet her at little affairs at the New School in the old days. She's probably a little confused about the past. It's hardly possible that a legal eagle of Terrence's standing would have haunted the Spur."

"But my mother knew him well," Jonathan insisted, unwilling to let the older man go without some leading answers.

The doctor raised skeptical shoulders.

"My little Connie? George Terrence? Possibly, possibly."

He gave Jonathan a soothing pat on the shoulder and tossed his hair back. Jonathan was annoyed to find himself tossing his own head again and meeting the doctor's quixotic smile.

"Amazing," murmured the doctor as he strode out.

He was humming, Jonathan noted with misgiving. Earl Turner had been right in advising him to confide in no one. Instead of getting helpful information he had let himself in for some unappealing doubts, for the doctor's suspicions had been quite obvious. Might as well be a Jaimison, Jonathan brooded, as to find his veins coursing with academic ink. He had a lightning vision of himself in future trudging over dreary campuses, briefcase bulging with student papers, growing a mustache like the doctor's, cultivating a rolling classroom voice, goading young Jonathans into becoming future Harshawes who would have all the fun and glory while he poured bourbon whisky over his poor frustrations.

"Can't you shut up the joint now?" a female voice urged, and there was Lize in the doorway. "Come on over to the Spur with me. This place is a morgue, how do you stand it?"

Lize didn't explain how she happened to be wandering in this dead end at one o'clock in the morning. She motioned Jonathan to a waiting cab when he locked the door, and he saw that the seat of the cab was taken up by the sleeping person of Percy Wright.

"Come on, we'll take the jump seats," Lize commanded. She cast a disapproving glance at the third passenger. "I asked him to meet me at Jack Delaney's after work for a talk—I wanted to borrow fifty bucks and I knew I'd have to get him stoned to get it—and the silly thing thought I wanted to come back to him and he got all emotional, blubbering away about not wanting to hurt me and all that, so I kept lining up double grasshoppers for him, and look at him! I had to tear out the lining of his coat to get the dough to pay the check. *I'm* perfectly sober. What's the matter with men?"

The sleeping figure mumbled.

"Don't try to wake up and be a nuisance now," Lize admonished him. "We'll drop off at the Spur and shoot him off to Brooklyn with the cabby."

She gave instructions to the driver and turned to give Jonathan a warm smile and a fond pat on the knee.

"I drove past half a dozen times to get you," Lize said, "but you always have that old goat from the college in there. What on earth do you pal around with him for? He's old enough to be your father."

"How could he be my father?" Jonathan exclaimed, stricken. "You have no right to say so—I mean, he's not as old as he looks."

"Okay, okay," Lize said, quite surprised by his fire. "You don't need to shout or we'll wake Junior here. I'm only asking what the old boy's got on you that you're so nice to him."

She patted him on the knee again.

"Dr. Kellsey hasn't got anything on me," Jonathan said tensely. "He's nothing to me—nothing at all."


Dr. Kellsey, after leaving Jonathan in the Then-and-Now, walked down the midnight streets in a kind of trance, crossing Seventh Avenue with speeding taxis shouting at him, finding an exotic charm in the smell of decaying bananas near a market, oblivious to the moist August heat. Bleecker Street along here had not changed much from the Bleecker Street he had known when he first came out of the West in the twenties. Granted that he had never been a man to observe his surroundings, his mind being taken up with a great file of indignant letters he had never gotten around to writing to deans, editors, women, creditors, anybody. In the early days he was always half-sprinting along Bleecker, he recalled, because he was due at class, or due to meet his wife for a showdown, and all along the way the little magic doors used to send out fragrant invitations to stop in the back room for a bracer.

Tonight, however, he was wafted along on a mysterious dream and he passed the strident bar cries of even the San Remo without turning his head. Jonathan's story, and the amazing discovery that he himself figured in it, had shaken his mind. The misty wraith of Connie Birch befogged everything. He was determined to fetch up a clearer picture and a proper sequence of memories, but so far he had experienced only the lightning flash of recognition at her photograph and name, a fleeting echo of a soft, apologetic twang, a hint of unexpectedly eager lips in a dark vestibule with sweet words lost in the roar of passing El trains. There was more, oh, there surely was more to it, but when he tried to force his memory through the door and up the stairs he lost the Connie image and the lips. He had been drunk at the time, that could always be guaranteed for episodes of this nature at that period, or else he had drowned guilt later in a healing binge. But this episode was special, Dr. Kellsey moaned, pleading with himself to produce clearer proof. The possibilities in Jonathan's story seemed to have transformed the world for him, and in his vague new rapture he walked across Washington Square and all the way up Broadway across Union Square and Gramercy Park to the Knowlton Arms.

There was an untapped quart of Old Taylor in his closet, and the idea had struck Kellsey that he might induce the proper memory chain by repeating the conditions of the original scene—plunge himself, say, into an alcoholic haze. He accepted the phone slips the desk clerk handed him, two calls from his wife and two, of course, from Anita, but he crumpled them into the wastebasket without noting the messages they'd left, only musing on how infallibly the two ladies kept neck and neck in their race to brand their own-ership on him, almost as if—he did not know how right he was—they were partners against him instead of rivals *for*. Certainly their taunts at him were similar. "Too selfish to raise a family like any decent, normal man . . . too neurotic to live a proper married life. . . . No wonder he disliked children—probably couldn't have any himself." He grinned, thinking of their combined wrath when they found out about Connie Birch.

Tonight Dr. Kellsey entered his pleasant large bed-sitting-room with a purposeful air. Instead of getting into pajamas as he usually did, he pulled the serape over the open bed and rearranged the cushions. He turned on the pretty little lights over the unusable fireplace, hummed the march motif from *The Love for Three Oranges* (his favorite opera) as he tested the effect of the three-way floor-lamp—should all three speeds glare down on the rather shabby Chinese rug, or should just one muted bulb gently spotlight the big easy chair with the table of Vichy, cigarettes, and glasses hospitably beside it? He adjusted his prized *shogi* screen around the refrigerator with the electric plate and toaster

on top, carefully closed the bathroom door, and then removed his tan cord coat, damp with perspiration from his
brisk walk, hung it over the "gentleman," and put on his
best black Chinese silk robe, quite as if he were expecting
a lady of distinction.

Gratified that the ice was plentiful, he planted a bowl of
it with his bottle and giant glass on the table, poured himself a generous sampling, and sank down into the chair,
ready to entertain as many dreams of the past as Old Taylor
could induce. Old Taylor would, sooner or later, get rid
of his damnable monitor, the fear of losing his job, fear of
scandal, fear of commitments, fear of failure, the com-
posite bogey that had made his sober existence so disgustingly continent and had blacked out the bold Rabelaisian
adventures that he would have liked to brighten his memories if they had not threatened his position. Yes, he had
to admit that half the time the monitor, with its blessed
anesthesia, had been an ally against his accusing wife and
angry mistress, enabling him to shout, "How can I be
blamed for something I did not know I was doing?" When
he was braced alcoholically for his classes, there was never
a passable female student that he had not considered hungrily and, properly loaded, approached. Even complaisant
girls, however, either froze or fled at their professor's greedy
but classical advances. An unexpected goose or pinch on the
bottom as they were mounting the stairs ahead of him, a
sudden nip at the earlobe as they bent over the book he
offered, a wild clutch at thigh, or a Marxian (Harpo)
dive at bosom, a trousered male leg thrust between theirs
as they passed his seat to make them fall in his lap, where
he tickled their ribs—all these abrupt overtures sent them
flying in terror. Brought to his senses by their screams,
Kellsey retreated hastily. Some of the more experienced

girls, after adjusting their skirts, blouses, coiffures, and maidenly nerves, realized that this was only a hungry man's form of courtship. They reminded themselves that old, famous, and rich men played very funny games, and they prepared themselves for the next move. But Kellsey, repulsed, became at once the haughty, sardonic, woman-hating pedant, leaving the poor dears with a confused impression that they were the ones who had behaved badly, and sometimes, baffled by his subsequent hostility and bad grades, they even apologized.

Deborah was his wife, Anita was his mistress, but Amnesia had been his true friend, the doctor reflected candidly, permitting him to stare straight through some little sophomore trollop who thought she had something on him after his passes of the previous evening. Amnesia gave him back his arrogance and dignity, the proper contempt for students and fellow men that was necessary to a teacher. But alas, Amnesia had also taken away the love of his life—little Connie Birch. If, as he was determined to believe, a child had come of that dim encounter, then he was romantic enough to be convinced it was true love. He assured himself there was proof in the mere fact that he had been drawn toward young Jonathan from the moment of their first meeting, and he detected family resemblances now. He took a long drag of his drink and forced his mind into the period when he had taught Connie. He knew well enough he would have turned the case over to Amnesia if it were not that his true love was conveniently dead.

"The biggest thing in my whole life, and I can't remember it." He sighed, and he thought that poor forgotten little Connie was the only woman who had ever given him anything.

There was Deborah, still his legal wife, though long since living apart from him. She had been a blind date when he had been teaching out in UCLA in 1926. He had drowned his distaste for her in corn whisky, and next thing he knew she'd accused him of getting her in a family way and he must marry her. A plain, smug little party, morally convinced that "sex" itself, let alone her groom's idea of honeymoon pranks, was woman's cross, Deborah had later confessed that the pregnancy was a lie to win his hand in wedlock. Walter was so burned over this trick that it was all he could do to put up a polite husbandly front for his job's sake. Deborah was perfectly satisfied to be let alone, now that she was a missus, and they managed to work out a successful façade. Deborah did his secretarial work, as well as working for other faculty members, so she was on the inside track of academic promotions and finaglings. Presently she became secretary to a rich foundation whose board members were too busy to attend meetings, and powerful decisions were left to mousy little Mrs. Kellsey.

Deborah's *sub rosa* importance enraged Walter except in his periods of pious sobriety, when he was allowed to share it and flaunt it in the faces of his colleagues. Her grapevine information got him a fellowship at the right time, and got him the New York job when she was promoted to the foundation's New York office. Drunk and in his right mind he hated and feared her, but in his nightmares of remorse, financial catastrophes, or professional embarrassments, he turned to her. These were their happiest times, he wallowing in shame and she wallowing in virtue. If his reform lasted as long as his binge, then the doctor became fully as smug as Deborah. They dressed up to attend banquets and foundation affairs together, where

Deborah's undercover power was lost in her official insignificance. She was glad, then, of her extra status as faculty wife, and the doctor was equally glad of his temporary edge over her. Penance done and complacency soon exploded, he went back to his other doghouse, the one kept in constant readiness for him by Anita Barlowe, an assistant professor in his department with whom he had conducted an affair for several years.

This was a curiously spasmodic romance, grounded regularly whenever Anita insisted he divorce Deborah and marry her, and sparked again by their common jealousy of some associate's triumph. Anita took a spiteful comfort in keeping him away from his foundation-superior wife, and Kellsey took a manly satisfaction in having one woman clever enough to catch his subtle gibes at her. They usually went to bed together quite happily and got up infuriated, physically appeased but psychologically defeated.

The greatest thing they had together was a permanent fight subject (i.e., divorce), money in the bank, you might say, when they were bored and their love needed a neat whip. Of course he was bound to Deborah too by a perpetual fight subject, i.e., she had tricked him into marriage, yes. But hadn't he got along better career-wise through her wifely conniving? Yes. Hadn't she pulled the right wires many a time to save his ungrateful hide? Yes. What would he have done without her? Plenty, the doctor thought to himself, but he knew none of it would have been good, which was unforgivable of her.

What burned both women everlastingly was the memory of the time Anita had pounced on Deborah and demanded she give a divorce because Walter had never loved her anyway and why did she go on refusing him his freedom? Because he never asked for it, Deborah had replied with one of her smug smiles. Never even mentioned such a thing, she repeated, how very, very strange for Miss Barlowe to ask. Hysterical and humiliated, Anita had tried to pin down the doctor, who was properly enraged that she should have approached his wife. He had never loved Deborah, true. But did he want to marry Anita? No. After this climactic scene Deborah deliberately started calling herself Mrs. Walter Kellsey instead of plain Deborah Kellsey, Anita went into analysis with a Dr. Jasper who looked like a caricature of Kellsey (that helped a lot), and Kellsey resumed his secret binges and blackouts.

Trying to concentrate on his long-ago student romances, Dr. Kellsey was plagued by reminders of the two women who dogged his career. Everything he ever did seemed for the purpose of spiting or appeasing one or the other, and he wondered if there was anything left in him of untainted personal feeling. His surprising burst of joy at the mere hint he might be a father, for instance. Was this an example of a long-mocked philoprogenitive instinct, evidence that he had more of the simple average male in him than he'd ever suspected? Or was it malicious glee at turning the tables on Deborah for that unforgivable old lie about her pregnancy? Or was it a delicious slap at Anita for her bitchy taunts that he feared a "normal married relationship" with a "normal female" like herself because he knew he was sterile? Old Taylor blinked consolingly at him in the lamp glow, calling him back to that magic long ago when something or other had happened.

The Spur had been a speakeasy then, yes. He hadn't gotten mixed up with Anita yet—that didn't start till World War II—but he was still tangled with Deborah, yes. And he used the excuse of his weekly night class to make a night of it, yes. And he had split-second images of that pale sweet girl and himself in a booth, in a dark vestibule, in a kitchen making drinks (the doctor took another gulp of his kindly potion, for now he was on the right track), trying to dance to a squeaky record from *The Vagabond King,* and falling down in a laughing huddle, with the girl and the record whirring round and round and round, and the ruff getting in his way when he tried to kiss—yes, he was in the Hamlet costume still. . . .

Each time he got to the record part the curtain descended. Doggedly the doctor went back from the Spur to the class-room, to Alan Seeger, to blond braids, carried the story along faster, upstairs, kitchen, gramophone, *Vagabond King,* giggling, sprawl—but the blackout always stopped him there. Just once he got past it to a third shadowy image, another man, an objectionably sneering presence, and a wave of poignant indignation swept over Kellsey that there was always some last-minute intruder, the triumph was always being snatched from under his nose, he was always too late. . . .

The telephone rang. Only Anita would telephone him this late, and it meant she had been phoning around for him all evening. He must have forgotten a date with her. He listened to the ring, clutching his glass, blaming Anita for spoiling his dream continuity, finally snatched the receiver and heard her whimpering reproaches you-said-you-said, you-always-you-always-, you-never-you-never—

"Anita," he interrupted sternly, "you sound as if you'd been drinking."

He grinned with evil satisfaction at the outraged sputter-ing this accusation brought forth and when it died down he spoke with pious kindliness. "If you're in condition by

Friday, then, my dear, I'll meet you to talk over all these problems you find in our relationship. I have certain things to tell you."

There! If she will break in upon a man's private dream life, let her stew over the consequences.

# 8

JONATHAN'S NOTE to Mrs. George Terrence at Green Glades, Stamford, arrived in the same mail as a certain letter in green ink to Mr. Terrence. George recognized the ominous green ink, for it was the third such letter he had received, and he fervently hoped his wife and daughter would have mail of their own to distract their attention.

"Who in the world writes you in green ink, George?" his wife inquired, but he was glad she was preoccupied with her own letter.

"I'll read it later," he said, stuffing it into his pocket. "Nothing of any importance comes on Saturday, you know. Why are you scowling over your own letter, my dear?"

"Someone is bothering me again about an old roommate," Hazel said crossly. "I do think it's a nuisance to be expected to keep up with everyone you've ever known."

"That's not like you, dear," George remonstrated severely, glad to have the subject of green ink sidetracked. "As I recall your stories, you had some very happy times at college."

Both George and Hazel were excessively loyal, as a rule, to any demands from their alma maters, though George had been miserably lost at Yale and Hazel had barely finished one semester at Sweetbriar.

"This wasn't a college friend," Hazel said. "This is concerned with a girl I lived with when I was studying the theater. You wouldn't remember her."

Their daughter Amy, who had been patiently staring at the *Stamford Times* society page while her parents loitered over their coffee and mail, looked up.

"I never knew you were interested in the theater, Mother," she said. "I've never heard you mention it."

"I never mentioned it because I forgot all about it. I was young and foolish, like most girls," Hazel said impatiently. "There were all sorts of little drama groups starting up then. Naturally I would never have seriously considered going on the stage."

"I do recall your having a few lines in some little production on Cherry Lane," her husband said, knowing well enough the lasting wound a newspaper criticism of the performance had made on Hazel. "Some of my best clients make their fortune in the theater."

"I can't see why they should write you in green ink," Hazel said, goaded.

"I see no reason why they shouldn't," said George.

Daughter Amy observed the grimly set smiles on each parent's face and sighed, recognizing the signs. Father and Mother were about to engage in one of their obscure duels, flailing delicately at each other with lace-edged kerchiefs that concealed from the observer the weapon and the wound. She had never understood what hidden taunt started the hostilities, but she really couldn't care less. She wondered again how they had endured each other all these years, or did they have some normal human feelings invisible to outsiders? In the tense silence she applied herself dutifully to the newspaper items her mother had marked—MISS ALLIMAN'S PLANS, ETHEL FEIST A BRIDE, JO-

HANNA TRUE TO WED, and other careful hints that Daughter
Amy was being left at the post.

"How nice about Ethel," Amy murmured sweetly.

"About this old friend you lived with, my dear," George
said to his wife. "It wouldn't have been that nice child
from the West, little Connie Whatsername?"

A petulant frown came to Hazel's fair brow.

"Now, why in the world did that come into your head?"
she cried. "I thought it was strange that Claire Van Orphen should be writing me about her after all these years,
but after all, Connie did do some work for Claire. Then
this son writes me, as if I were a blood relation instead of
a chance connection of his mother's. But you barely met
her. I cannot understand how you should remember her at
all."

His wife's irritation soothed George's own uneasiness,
and he pushed his chair back from the table with an in-
dulgent laugh.

"I see I need a lawyer for my answer to that," he said.
His wife and daughter fetched a dutiful laugh. "What I
need is a good lawyer" had been George's joke for years,
but the laughers, aware only of George's highly successful
legal career, never realized how true it was.

In his entire life George Terrence had never been able
to present his own case in any matter, seeing the vulnera-
bility of his own side more clearly than any other, his fine
professional mind cruelly operating as prosecutor against
G. Terrence, defendant. He took a dour, rueful satisfaction in arguing himself out of the good spots in any situation, sternly denying himself jubilation over triumphs,
complacency over good fortune. Detaching himself from
his person, he had watched people exploit his money,
name, and abilities with ironical amusement. In time he

acquired a monumental complacency over his brilliant victory over complacency, and his lengthy sardonic stories of defeats and minor mistakes were more boringly egotistical than other men's boasting.

As a precocious only child of a rich, cultured old family, he conceded (intellectually) that he had no more rights to the pet pony, the toy railroad, the privileges and spending money than the sturdy playmates who were constantly appropriating them. It seemed to him that the superior man degraded himself by fighting over material possessions and proved himself by gracefully conceding. He acquired a defensive ironic bluster and a haughty sulkiness that consoled his pride but did not protect him. At Yale other boys got girls and popularity using George's expensive clothes, cars, credit, and family contacts. They bragged of their rich society pal George Terrence, without letting George share the luster. He stood on street corners in New Haven, watching classmates he hardly knew race by in his Packard, wearing his sport jackets, their arms around lovely girls who would, he knew, rebuff him. (A rumor had gotten around that George Terrence kissed with his mouth closed!)

When he started his career in a distinguished firm on William Street in New York, he took a modest apartment on Irving Place and soon found that, through the pressuring of friends, he was sharing the place with two agreeable younger men interested in literature. At least he wouldn't be lonesome, George was told. It was true he did not suffer in that respect. The young men kept the apartment lively with their girlfriends and all-night gab-fests, and when one or the other was conducting a big love affair, George was likely to find himself locked out. They were as strange to New York City as he was, but they were not handicapped by conscience over privilege as was George. They crashed debutante parties, barged in on good people's dinners, borrowed money from him cheerfully, passed his bootleg gin around, and laughed heartily over his occasionally ironic outbursts.

It had comforted George to know, as he used to sit in his hall room preparing his brief while the living room rang with merry voices, that fun might be fun, but he was the one with the money, the background, and the industry to succeed. Harshawe, a tall, quiet, arrogant fellow, had had a novel accepted for publication, which gave him the edge over Turner, his friend. Harshawe was too tall to wear George's suits, but shirts, sporty vests, ties, socks, and jackets were acceptable. Turner confided in George rather bitterly that the reason Harshawe slaved so hard at his writing was his inferiority about not being a college man. Neither man could understand George's unwillingness to use his Yale Club privileges, where a man could have his liquor in the locker, swim, lounge about, and finally they bullied George into taking them there. It was embarrassing for George, since both interlopers knew all the routine of getting in better than he did, and nobody there knew him or, if anyone did, had a warm greeting that would set up his stock. He felt like an impostor and inwardly vowed never to put himself through such a miserable trial again.

Three months later, however, coming out of Grand Central Station on a Sunday and needing cash, he braved the club. He half expected to be refused entrance, actually. Once inside he saw a familiar pair of long legs stretched out in a big chair, showing Argyle socks made most positively by Mrs. Terrence, Sr., a newspaper obscuring the face, a highball glass nearby, with the arm reaching for it encased in a familiar Terrence tweed. It was Harshawe, who greeted him with lazy good humor.

"How did you manage to get in?" George asked, mystified.

Harshawe shrugged and nodded toward his glass.

"Sit down and have a drink, Terrence," he said hospitably. "Oh, I like the place. I drop in every day to read the papers and have a smoke or a drink."

George wouldn't have known how to manage this himself, so he said, "But how do they let you in?"

"I use your name," Harshawe said. And at that moment a boy came up to him and said, "Your call is ready, Mr. Terrence."

"Thanks, Joey," Harshawe said and rose to stroll over to the telephone, leaving George frozen with outrage, staring after him. In a burst of courage he snatched the *Wall Street Journal,* of all things, which Harshawe had been reading, and resolutely plumped himself down in Harshawe's chair. There was a touch on his arm.

"Pardon me, sir," the boy said firmly, "that's Mr. Terrence's chair, and I don't believe he's quite finished with his paper."

By this time George Terrence was madder than he'd ever been in his life, but, being unaccustomed to shabby shows of temper or pettishness, he could think of no way of handling the situation. All he could do was to gulp down Harshawe's drink and stalk out, forgetting to cash his check. He went straight to the apartment, packed up his things, and moved to the Hotel Lafayette. His anger appeased, his conscience bothered him about allowing a poor underprivileged, undereducated chap of inferior breeding to upset him. He sent a check for the quarter's rent on the apartment, said he had decided the Hotel Lafayette was more convenient for him, and graciously urged both Harshawe and Turner to be his guests at the Yale Club whenever they chose. The gesture restored George's *amour propre*, though it was periodically shaken whenever the three dined at the club and many members slapped Harshawe and Turner on the back, waiters beamed at them, but no one remembered George. The others did the ordering, made the suggestions, sent dishes back as they chose, and in all made George deeply relieved to get back to the Lafayette, where he could enjoy the pale eminence of being the youngest man in the café.

He was doing well in his profession, but when George did well nobody seemed to know it. Other, bolder members of the firm took entire credit in court for George's briefs. George tried to tell himself that the office and people who counted knew it was he who had done the real work, just as the important people at the Yale Club knew he was the real George Terrence, didn't they? But he ought to have learned that people believed whomever shouted the loudest and pushed the hardest. Crushed between his office pals and his old roommates, George appealed to psychoanalysis, a process that occupied two years and afforded that eager healer named Dr. Jasper a good living and some much-needed experience. In the nick of time Hazel Browne flung herself upon George and married him, remaining awed and grateful for this triumph, insisting on being bullied and masterminded, so that there was nothing for George to do but oblige her.

When people praised the powerful change in his character, George declared it was all due to his superb analysis. Hazel dutifully agreed, never realizing how colossal her own part had been in the transformation. She forgave George for his wild playboy youth, ruthless philandering, fascinating mistresses, and mythical past until George had the pleased conviction that he'd really had all that. Hazel

must be right. It was the facts that erred. He allowed Hazel
to worship him as a man of the world and dropped an occasional allusion that kept her ever fearful that she might
lose him yet to the sexpots surely clamoring for him.

It was a good marriage for these twenty-odd years, with
Hazel putting her whole soul into living up to the Terrence
tradition of unimpeachable respectability and George always hoping to live it down. When their opposite views
might have led to bickering they used their daughter as a
buffer, and had grown so accustomed to speaking to each
other through her that they hardly thought of her as a
person but as an intercom.

"Your mother had a charming habit of being late for
appointments when I was courting her." George now addressed his daughter. "While I waited in her living room
her roommate very graciously entertained me. Naturally I
remembered her kindness."

"I'm sure she was trying to get herself invited," Hazel
said to her daughter. "Poor Connie didn't have many beaux
as I recall her. At any rate I cannot understand why I
should have to give out interviews to her relatives after
all these years. Why should Claire Van Orphen suggest it?
What could I possibly have to say about her?"

"What do you think Mother should do about it?" Amy
obligingly passed the query to her father.

"If I were your mother I should write a nice little note
inviting the party to come in for tea if he is in the neighborhood," George said judiciously, feeling for the offensive
green-inked envelope in his pocket. "I gather that little
Connie has passed on and they merely want to patch up
some memories about her. No harm."

Hazel bit her lip.

"I still don't see why she should have mentioned me.

You can tell your father, Amy, that I did write a polite note saying that we didn't get into the city often and that I didn't see how I could tell him anything about his mother. But he wants to see your father too. I think it's very strange. And he suggested coming out today."

A stranger asking to take up his own valuable time was a different matter entirely, and George was on the verge of protesting that the intruder must certainly be put off, but Hazel took the words out of his mouth.

"It's all very well to say I should have him here, but when we only see our daughter once a month and when your father prizes his reading time at home above every other consideration—"

"Not above an old friendship," George said, perverse as usual. "If it's Connie's son, of course I will see him, whether your mother cares to or not, Amy, my dear. It's certainly too late to put him off now, anyway."

Both Hazel and George were getting red in the face, the only outward indication that they were having what would be in other families a knockdown fight. Amy looked from one to the other parent with languid curiosity. This was a game her parents had been playing as long as she could remember, a game which excluded her, but it afforded her privacy and freedom.

Many was the time they conducted a polite discussion through Amy regarding the suitability of a school, a dress, a companion for her, both their faces getting redder and redder but their voices never rising in their careful "your father"ing and "your mother"ing. Amy could have gone off to the wrong college with the wrong people in the wrong clothes without her absence's being noticed. She knew that her meticulously coiffured, massaged, and prim-mannered mother lived in awe of her trim, neatly turned-out father, quite as if his possible disapproval meant violence or excommunication instead of a delicately sardonic comment or a mere cough. Amy had given up puzzling over what their hold was on each other, devoting herself to the fulltime job of concealing her life from them. If they were flaring up now, the cause was certainly more trivial than usual, a silly matter of receiving or not receiving somebody's son.

Mrs. Terrence, always the first to surrender, beckoned the Chinese houseman, Lee, who had been popping his head in the door every few minutes.

"Lee's in a hurry to clear up because he's going to the ballgame," she said. "Do you want to come with me to the Flower Show, Amy?"

"That sounds very nice, Mother," Amy said obediently.

"Mustn't let your mother tire you out," George Terrence admonished. "I'm sure you have lots of studying to do. Sometimes these special summer courses are tougher than the regular ones. Get back in time for a little rest before you leave, my child."

"Thank you, Father, I will," Amy said.

"She'll have all day Sunday," her mother said, "since she has to go back tonight."

George waited till the two ladies had left the table and Lee had started brushing up before he went into the library to his desk. He had to think, but he could never put his mind to anything properly if there was a chance that Hazel would interrupt. She had been remarkably suspicious today about his dreadful mail, he thought, and what with her twittering about little Connie Birch's son, she'd gone out of her way to be irritating. After a few moments he heard her calling, "George, we're off now. Tell your father we're leaving, Amy, dear." At the moment George felt like snarling, "So you're going, then for God's sake be off," but he controlled himself.

He wished fervently that something, anything, would keep his womenfolk away till he could collect his thoughts. He hoped he had remembered to ask where they were going, that was all, and if they were walking to be sure they wore the right shoes. He didn't care if they went barefooted, really, but he did care about showing interest. At any rate they were gone, and the next minute he heard Lee taking out the station-wagon, putting off toward the highway. Thank God.

George fumbled in his desk drawer for a minute before he remembered that he had destroyed the other two letters. He had kept them for a few weeks, intending to give them a completely detached legal study, but there had never come a moment when he could even think about them without panic. Their destruction had seemed to relieve his mind for a while, but the worry had only gone underground, and sprang up at sight of this last communication.

George spread the note on the desk before him, then covered his eyes with his hand. It was childish. He needed a brandy. Standing at the french windows, shot glass of brandy in hand, he looked out at the lush garden, the espaliered pear trees against the stone wall, the purple-blossomed Empress of China trees fringing the rock pool, the heliotrope-bordered paths, the twin fig trees by the gate. What would *you* do? he asked each one of them in turn and went back to his desk, forcing himself to read the letter.

"Dear Terrence: You know damn well I'll keep writing until I get some action or an answer. As a matter of fact, I

like to write you. It gives me a chance to unload some old
burns and a private laugh or two, like the laugh of you
always calling yourself Roger Mills of Toronto. I knew
who you were the first time you picked me up at the King
Cole Bar but I went along with the Roger bit for laughs.
I never could figure out why you picked me, when the
other boys were so much prettier, but I suppose a closet
queen has to pick the mutt type like yours truly to keep
off suspicion.

"I wasn't planning to keep at the trade, really, not having
your problem of being too afraid of dames to lay them. I
could say you made me what I am today if I wanted to
be real mean, doll, but you saved me financially that summer and I thank you. I know I saved you too, for you confessed you couldn't go for a dame that wanted you until
you'd gotten excited over me. (I thought I'd mention that
bit if I have to write to your wife, who, I guess, was the
only one you ever made out with.) You taught me to like
nice things, though, and Roger-George-baby I've got to have
them now for an amusing little punk of my own that I've
got on the hook just the way you got me.

"I'm a lousy actor, as any critic will tell you, so I can always get a job, but I can't make enough to keep this little
punk in the luxuries I taught him to need. I'm laying it on
the line, Rogie-Podgie, I'm nuts about this boy and it's
driving me crazy when he has to screw some old woman for
his bar tab. Love and honor are at stake when I repeat I've
got to have $5000 to square things or I write Mrs. T. about
that little summer's idyll. Daughter Amy—yes, I know you
did make it once, anyway—will be grateful that she owes
her existence to your great good friend and pupil.

"I'll be waiting, let's say till the first."

George looked at the writing again, commanding his

mind to detach itself from his panic and take charge as it
would do for a frightened client. The green letters curled
around one another like snakes, y's and g's and f's had
corkscrew tails, capitals writhed through loops before identifying themselves, even the letter T managed to spiral on
its cross. You didn't need any legal training to deduce that
the writer was abnormal, even criminal. How simple it
would be if this were a client's problem instead of his own!

"Send the chap to me," George could hear himself loftily
advising the worried client. "I'll get him to show exactly
what he has on you and in that way get a line on his own
record. You'll find we can scare him off, lucky to get away
without a prison sentence. Leave it to me."

Hah. Leave it to me. Not when he was his own client,
George thought morosely.

If only he dared consult Doctor Jasper . . . But it had
been Dr. Jasper, after all, who'd gotten him into this mess.
He'd been an eager young psychiatrist in those days, all
hopped up over the new science, and George was his first
paying customer. He'd believed in the doctor implicitly,
George thought with a sigh, probably because it was all
new and exciting and he was as eager to be a guinea pig
as Jasper was to have one. If you're so afraid to sleep with
a girl, said the doctor, then try it out with your own sex,
maybe that's the answer, let's have everything out in the
open. Once you know, then we can handle the problem.
Jasper never expected he would be taken seriously, then,
by anybody. Lucky Hazel appeared on the scene about then
and simplified everything; no further dealings with old
Jasper.

George picked up the note and tore it up carefully, made
a little snake nest in the ashtray of the pieces, and set a
match to them. A slight sound outside made him look up

from this operation. Someone was coming up the garden path, the pebbles crackling underfoot. George stayed motionless, smitten by the dread that the green-ink writer himself might have cornered him. He realized he could be seen from the garden and, from the sound of the footsteps pausing, knew the intruder must be directly outside the window, no doubt staring at him. George forced himself to walk toward the window. He saw with almost a sob of relief that the young man was a stranger with only warm friendliness on the fair, smiling face. He pushed open the french windows, half locked by rose vines.

"The bus driver told me this was the Terrence place," the stranger said.

"I am George Terrence," George said.

"I wrote Mrs. Terrence I would pay a call today. I'm Jonathan Jaimison. My mother—"

George felt a wave of deep affection for this young man, unexpected savior of his peace.

"Connie's boy!" he exclaimed, holding out both hands with an enthusasm that would have astounded his family. "What a splendid surprise. Do come in—no, no, right this way, never mind those tulips, just step over them."

As it had never occurred to Jonathan that he would not be welcome, he was pleased but not surprised at the warmth of his reception. He sat back in the elaborately comfortable red leather chair George had directed him to, accepted a cigarette and a stout highball, refused George's urgent offer of a sandwich, coffee, cake, icewater, protesting that he had breakfasted late. He would not stay long; all he wished was information about his mother's New York life from those who must have known her best. Miss Van Orphen had suggested—

"Splendid!" George Terrence exclaimed happily. "Yes,

a splendid idea of Claire's. I must get in touch with her one of these days, it's been so long. A pity Hazel, Mrs. Terrence, isn't here, since she was such a dear friend of your mother's."

"Perhaps I'd better come back some day when Mrs. Terrence is in," Jonathan suggested tentatively.

Indeed he must not think of leaving, George insisted. After all he too had known the young man's mother, perhaps in some ways even better than his wife had. There had been times Connie Birch had confided in him, for instance, while he waited for Hazel to dress or come home for an appointment.

"You mean she confided in you about her—love life, say?" Jonathan leaned forward eagerly. "About the men she knew?"

George realized that, in his anxiety to detain his caller, he had gone too far. He had only the vaguest memory of Connie; all he remembered was his disappointment when the door used to open on Hazel's roommate instead of Hazel herself.

"No, no, nothing like that," he said hastily. "Surely you never thought your mother was not circumspect in every way. No, we discussed her work with my firm's clients, the Misses Van Orphen, and music, books—"

"But she did know several men," Jonathan persisted, and then asked doubtfully, "You don't mean to say she was not—attractive to men?"

George saw he was on the wrong tack.

"My dear boy, she was charming! Utterly charming," he declared. "You must see that in her pictures." He wished the boy would produce a photograph to nudge his memory. "As a matter of fact, if my wife had been late a few more times I cannot guarantee what might have happened."

"She wrote my aunt that you—or the man her roommate was engaged to was tremendously clever," Jonathan told him. "She seemed to feel as you did, that if you had not been already committed—well, you know how those things are. You were a man of the world, she said, and had so much to teach a girl."

"She said that?" George was touched.

"You explained Marx to her," Jonathan said, "and Freud and that sort of thing."

Those had been courting subjects in that day, George recollected with some embarrassment. Now he did have a sudden picture of sitting on a sofa with the sweet girl, reading aloud from Freud while she consoled him with bootleg gin and orange juice till Hazel came home. He could almost swear there had been a slight hassle, a furtive embrace, a scurrying when Hazel's key sounded in the lock.

"I do want to find out the man in her life then," Jonathan said. "It wasn't you, sir, that winter of nineteen twenty-eight?"

"Nineteen twenty-eight," George repeated, and his eyes fell on the ashtray, where he fully expected to see green ashes. "Why do you ask?"

"I'm looking for my father," Jonathan confessed. "I was hoping it might be you, now that we've met."

The ashes were gray like any other ashes, George saw. A sweet sense of relief was surging through him, and an excitement was beginning in the back of his brain that meant a subtle, hidden point was about to be flushed out into service. He carried the ashtray to the window and poured the contents over the rosebush with great precision.

"Ashes are splendid for the soil, you know," George said. Hazel Terrence would have been astonished at the behavior of her husband that Saturday afternoon. He had always professed a manly aversion to the details of the home, he disliked all social encounters that demanded small talk, and he particularly avoided contact with the younger generation.

Yet here he was showing Jonathan Jaimison over the grounds, pointing out the foundations of the old mill, leading him through the grape arbors and confessing his ambition to have a real vineyard (Hazel would have been surprised to hear this), explaining the herb garden with great pride: *this* was what you did with the *Waldmeister* in May-wine making, this was tarragon, this was rosemary, delicious with roast lamb, this was mint—by Jove, they'd have a julep!

"Next time you come up we must take you for a swim in the brook," George said, as if this was only the beginning of a deep intimacy. Hazel would never have dreamed he knew or cared so much about the flowers she and Lee nursed so tenderly. Her firm, dimpled jaw would have dropped to hear her husband's deferential interest in this young man's opinions on the state of the world and his benign advice on futures for talented lads. She would not have believed her ears had she heard the many times George exclaimed, "Splendid! How right you are!" to the stranger's shyly offered remarks.

Hazel had given up trying to break into her husband's moody silence at dinner with her harmless little anecdotes of town scandals, a tiff with the butcher, a pleasant encounter with an old neighbor, a report on a new supermarket's advantages. George had a way of smiling at her across the carefully chosen table flowers and shutting her up with "My dear, must we clutter up our minds with all this trivia? Isn't it hard enough to manage our own major patterns without dragging in the inconsequentials? We are not curious about others' private lives."

But here was her same George eagerly asking young Jaimison for more and more trivia, listening with deep absorption to a description of the Then-and-Now Café, nodding approvingly at Jonathan's praise of Claire Van Orphen.

"A splendid soul," said George. "I was fortunate enough to handle their father's estate and got to know the two sisters very well, particularly Claire, a most talented woman. And this writer friend you mention, Earl Turner, was an old friend of mine, too. We shared an apartment once with Harshawe, the now famous Harshawe, of course, and frankly I always felt Turner had the better brains. I've often thought of looking him up sometime, but since my semi-retirement we spend very little time in New York—my wife hates it."

Me hate New York! Hazel would have exclaimed, had she heard this statement—as if I had any choice about it! And "looking up" any old friend of his past was the last thing in the world George Terrence would ever want to do.

Whenever Jonathan suggested leaving, George Terrence thought of something else to detain him. So The Golden Spur was still going. Amazing. Jonathan must tell him more. Mrs. Terrence would be heartbroken to have missed him, and she should certainly be back before four. Living in the wilderness as he did, George warmly assured his guest, he found news of the great artistic world a godsend. It was seldom, moreover, that he found a young man who had so many of the same interests and reactions to life that he himself had had at that age. He was only surprised that Jonathan, with the acute perceptiveness he displayed on all subjects, had not taken up law.

"You really think so?" Jonathan asked, highly pleased. "As a matter of fact I did think of law at one time. My mother talked about it when I was still in primary school. Perhaps she was thinking of you."

Another wave of tenderness for his wife's long-lost room-mate came over George. In the course of their talk a far clearer memory of Connie had emerged, and he had fleeting pictures of himself and Hazel, all dressed up for some fancy social affair (it was Hazel who had started him on accepting these invitations), while little Connie lonesomely bade them have fun. Connie had been shy, just as he was, and he should have noticed more things—her interest in him, for instance. But Hazel had rushed him through to the altar so fast he hadn't had time to be even polite. Connie had written him a little verse on his birthday, though, by Jove, he suddenly remembered.

"Your mother was a very fine person, very sensitive," George said broodingly. "Too bad you're not a lawyer. I could be of some use to you now in getting started in New York."

Jonathan had the impulse to declare that he would plunge at once into the study of law if it would please this kind gentleman. He stole furtive glances at him, telling himself that in spite of his being a good four inches taller than Mr. Terrence, and blonder and blue of eye, there was a suspicious resemblance in the set of the ears, the shape of the brow, even in the timbre of their voices, though this might have been because his host's academic style of de-livery was contagious. Jonathan was always susceptible to other people's mannerisms and he was already handling his cigarette in the same way George did, waving it like a baton to illustrate some remark, then plunging it up to his lips as if to stop an emergency hole in the dike. George, suddenly

glancing over, caught Jonathan in the very act of synchron-
izing the gesture with his, and smiled.

"A daughter is all very well," George went on confidentially, "but a man who has worked his way to the top
in his profession, learned a lot along the way, has a lot to
give, needs a son to carry on, don't you see? For instance, if
you were my boy—"

But I am, I am, Jonathan wanted to cry out, quite carried
away as George paused to light another cigarette, I could
be! He did not speak, but he had a feeling that George
Terrence had the same thought. Under the circumstances
they could not come out openly with the idea. But they
would know, and that was the main thing.

"I think I am only being realistic when I admit to you
that my daughter is not a clever girl," George said suddenly.
"Her mother and I have had to make all her decisions, and
we are grateful that she is a good, obedient child. She has
had the best upbringing and every opportunity, but she
has no ambition such as I always had, very little interest in
society even, clings to her home so much she did not want
to go further off to college than New York. I dare say in our
old age this sort of clinging will be a comfort. And yet . . ."

He sighed and stroked his chin. Jonathan stroked his
own chin in sympathy.

Suddenly his host banged his fist down.

"By Jove, it's not too late even now!" he exclaimed. "I'll
put you in our office as a starter, send you to school nights,
no reason you shouldn't make the most of a good legal
mind such as yours. Not necessarily in the courts of law precisely, but there are other angles. How about that?"

"That's too good of you, sir," was all Jonathan could say.

George Terrence wrote something on a card, which he
handed to Jonathan.

"This may be a day you'll remember all your life," he said. "I'll be making arrangements for you, and you come to the office a week from Wednesday. I'll come in myself!"

Behind him on the mantelpiece a cuckoo flew out of a clock, and Jonathan jumped up at the stroke of four, remembering he should take the four-thirty train back to the city. Mr. Terrence leaped up at the same time as a pair of black cocker spaniels tumbled through the french windows.

"Good heavens, the girls must be back!" he said. "Wait while I tell them you're here."

Jonathan stared blissfully at the card in his hand as George left. Incredible that his future should be solved so simply and suddenly. He wandered around the library, studying the family portraits with new interest, measuring his resemblance to them. It occurred to him that if George Terrence was really his father, then it would be awkward meeting his wife. She might even see the resemblance and feel bitterly toward the old girl friend who had betrayed her. Perhaps she already knew. Jonathan found himself weighing all angles of the situation with the shrewd legal slant of which he felt suddenly possessed. Naturally she would be considering the danger of financial claims. Jonathan was smitten with embarrassment. That his desire to claim a parent might be construed as a raid on the family fortune had not occurred to him before, and he fixed his gaze broodingly on the garden, stroking his chin just as George Terrence did when pondering a problem.

He heard a feminine voice enunciate softly but firmly, "I'm sorry, my dear, but you'll simply have to explain that my head is killing me and I must lie down. I'm going straight up to bed. Amy can speak to him."

There was a patient sigh from George, a soothing murmur from another feminine voice, and then the library door opened again to admit George, smiling rather grimly, followed by a young woman.

"This is my daughter Amy, Jonathan," George said. "You must meet this young man, my dear, child of one of your mother's and my very old friends. Will you excuse me, Jonathan, while I go upstairs and see what I can do to relieve my wife?"

"I'm afraid I'll have to say good-by now, Mr. Terrence," Jonathan said nervously, stretching out his hand. "The station bus will be along any minute."

He stopped short. Mechanically he went on shaking the hand of the young lady, dropped it, and grasped George's outstretched hand.

"Amy can drive you to the station, can't you, my dear? Take the Volkswagen, and Lee can pick it up at the station later," George urged. "Amy has to take the same train back, don't you, my dear?"

"I'll be glad to look after Mr. Jaimison, Father," Amy said, and then their eyes met.

Jonathan stared at her incredulously. He barely noticed George Terrence clasping his hand again in farewell.

"We'll be seeing each other, of course, Jonathan," George Terrence called out from the door. "This has been most interesting. Sorry Mrs. Terrence is under the weather. Ah well, the ladies—you understand!"

Jonathan did not hear. Amy stared back at him defiantly.

"There—there must be some mistake," he stammered. "I had no idea you were—I mean—"

"Hush!" She seized his arm petulantly and pulled him toward the garden door. "Come along, they know we have to make that train. They'll be arguing for hours. Why did you have to come here? What have you told him about me?"

"But I came to see him about my own problems! I never even dreamed—"

"I knew it would happen sometime," Amy said, leading him across the terrace to the lower gate where the Volkswagen stood. He got in while she waited to wave dutifully toward the house. Jonathan took the cue and waved too.

"Oh, they can't see us," she said, taking the wheel. "I was just waving good-by to Amy Terrence like I always do."

"I'm confused," Jonathan said, once they were on the highway. "You are Iris Angel, aren't you?"

"Now I am. I thought you'd come out to tell Father, for a bad minute."

"But I didn't know—I still don't understand."

"Anyway, you didn't goof when you saw me, so I forgive you," she said. "I absolutely shook when I saw you there!"

"But which are you, Amy or Iris?" Jonathan asked, mystified. "Aren't they your real parents?"

"Of course they are, when I'm with them," Amy said with an obvious effort to be patient with childish questions. "I'm Amy Terrence for them. You don't think they'd ever let me be anything else, do you? But the minute I'm out of their sight I'm Iris Angel."

Jonathan thought it strange that to his own daughter a great lawyer like George Terrence should be as unsympathetic as a Jaimison.

"But he understands ambition so well," he said. "You could have explained to him."

"Explain!" Iris mocked him. "There's no explaining to your family. You can waste your whole life fighting them, if you're a fighter. But I'm no fighter, and how can you fight when they make you doubt yourself? I'm an actress and the only way I can survive is to play the part called for.

They want their Amy, so I play Amy Terrence for them, and everybody's happy with no argument. See?"

"We're in the same spot," he confessed. "I couldn't start being myself till I'd blanked out the Jaimisons."

He started to blurt out his own story but had the good sense to reserve the vital facts. Iris was fascinated with the hints he gave, and they agreed it was small wonder they had been drawn to each other at first meeting. They were still congratulating each other on the coincidence when they got off the train. At daybreak they were learning even more about each other, lying on Iris's floor on Waverly Place.

Amy Terrence had had secret names for herself all during her childhood, but "Iris Angel" was the one she stuck to after her fifteenth birthday. By that time she took for granted that the girl Amy was a dummy daughter invented by her parents, a proper doll wound up by them for family performances, while the real creature, Iris Angel, used the dummy as armor to hide her private self.

To all appearances Amy had been a quiet little girl, approved but scarcely noticed by teachers in the convent school, later practicing her piano, ballet, skating, and languages at home exactly as required, showing neither unseemly aptitude nor more apathy than was stylish. It had been a mighty feat of silent diplomacy for her to make her father feel it was his inspiration to allow her to live in New York for special courses instead of going to Vassar. A colleague in George Terrence's office had a daughter doing this very thing. The two men agreed that their daughters were too timid and overbred for modern times, and girls' schools would make them worse. The thing to do—if the girls were ever to hold their own in the race for husbands—

was to push them out of the nest, put them on their own (suitably protected, of course) to prepare them for the day when no more spoon-feeding was possible.

The colleague's nice little daughter was persuaded to take Amy into her nice little flat in a nice little made-over house in nice little Turtle Bay. All four parents congratulated themselves on their liberal point of view, and they chuckled at the paradox of their own modernity and their daughters' shy Victorianism. They reminded one another of what mature men and women they had been at that age and what irony to have hatched these tender doves.

Amy dutifully followed her parents' suggestions in registering for secretarial courses, art and cooking classes. She had membership cards at the Museum of Modern Art and the Metropolitan, season tickets for the Philharmonic, charge accounts at suitable stores. She then proceeded to ignore the whole plan and quietly set about getting into the theater, visiting producers and agents with a doggedness that would have amazed her parents. She got a part as a bawd in a *Merry Wives of Windsor* production that played only two weeks but established her, in her own mind at least. She took a basement apartment on Waverly Place as Iris Angel, but arranged with her roommate to keep the Amy Terrence name on the Turtle Bay apartment. For three years she had managed to conceal her true activities, rushing up to her proper apartment when her roommate alerted her that a parent was imminent, appearing at the Connecticut parental home on alternate week ends in the guise of docile student-daughter.

A number of things had happened to Amy during that time. She had taken her turn at falling in love with the painter Hugow, dogged his footsteps through Village bars, phoned him at least twice a day, managed to be seduced by him, had the usual agonies of an abortion, and then was rescued by a summer stock job in Canada. For her parents' information she was on a painting trip with an art class. She then followed him to Haiti and spent three blissful months with him while her roommate dispatched prefabricated notes from Europe, where she and Amy were supposed to be on a tour of the château country.

After her first few panics Amy had become so expert in conducting her two lives that she switched from Iris to Amy as easily as she played her other stage roles. She was helped in the masquerade by two factors. One was the fact that her shy girl friend was in an equally dangerous spot, having a serious affair with a married university teacher and needing reciprocal protection, and the second was the convenient blindness induced by the imperturbable complacency and complete self-absorption of George and Hazel Terrence. Devoted parents as they were, they had never taken their responsibilities easily but had worried and consulted and nagged over every tooth, every mouthful, every sneeze, every freckle of their little girl, smothering her with their anxieties till they lost sight of the girl herself. Secretly she was their weapon against each other. Such a good child, such an obedient daughter, such a treasure! But what heaven to have her being good and obedient some place else, leaving them to their mature, well-organized selfishness!

Amy must have sensed her position the day she was born and seen the advantage it gave her for her own selfish ends. She could have been plotting like a trusty in prison, building complete confidence in good little Amy all those years, while grooming Iris Angel for the escape. She had seldom uttered a thought in the company of her parents, always listening obsequiously, receiving their admonitions with a prim "Yes, Father," "I shall certainly think about that, Father." "Thank you very much, Mother, I am sure you are right."

Fortunately neither George nor Hazel liked the theater, certainly not in its new off-Broadway aspects, so Amy did not feel her Iris Angel identity was imperiled. At first she had feared not disapproval of her stage ambitions but interference in them. There would have been formal discussions, Mother would have escorted her to auditions arranged through suitable social channels, Father would insist on a program of plays to be studied, private tutors would be chosen from distinguished old stars of their own day who would teach her how to beat her breast and nibble the scenery. She knew they would explain to their circle that they had chosen theatrical training for her as invaluable for a future hostess, not really as a career.

If her parents had been able to forget themselves long enough to really observe their little girl, they would have noted that her manners became glibber every year, her Yes, Fathers, and Thank you, Mothers popped out mechanically, while Amy stared into space, increasingly bored by her daughterly role. Hugow and her stage and Village pals never once doubted her Iris Angel personality. Amy would have died of shame had they discovered her bourgeois background, but luckily they were too self-centered to be curious.

Now that Jonathan had found her out, she was surprised that it was a great relief to tell him everything. She had never thought of her double life as wrong; it was merely complicated at times, and inconvenient. Sometimes she was Amy, and sometimes she was Iris, she explained to Jonathan, never both at once, any more than a two-timing husband plays both his roles at once. Besides, it was absolutely necessary if she was to get what she wanted from life.

"I just do what other girls do, only they don't use two names," she said. "They just keep fighting it out with their families, but with parents like mine, I wouldn't have had a chance. I had to play it like a stage part."

Jonathan was such an admiring audience that she played up the part, describing narrow escapes from discovery both by her family and by her Iris Angel set. Now that she was Iris Angel again, her black hair fell loosely out of its prim arrangement, her arms and legs swung freely, she seemed bigger, as if even her flesh had been compressed in her Amy role. The voice changed from the colorless precision to the appealing huskiness that had first attracted him.

Funny, Jonathan kept remarking, that she should have to throw off her family mark to find her own identity, whereas his own problem was the opposite. It made the reasons for liking each other all the stronger, they told each other solemnly. Presently Iris bethought herself of danger and implored Jonathan not to betray her confidences. He was shocked at the idea.

"I am only wondering what would happen if your parents found out the extent of your Iris Angel life," he said. "As an actress, of course, you may have another name. But your union card, your contracts and lease here, and the false Iris Angel background you've given out . . . Can they stop you from appearing in a play, let's say?"

Iris had raised herself on one elbow on the rug where they lay and she was staring at him curiously.

"Or you find yourself unjustly accused in an accident," Jonathan went on, "and your double identity comes out. What is your legal position—"

He stopped when Iris put a hand over his mouth.

"You're just like Father!" she cried. "I can't stand it if you're turning out to get legal about everything. Jonathan, you scare me! Stop looking like Father."

"Do I really?"

"You do! You put your fingers together when you say the word 'legal' as if you were praying, just the way he does, and I can't stand it! It makes me afraid of you. You even say 'splendid' just the way he does."

Jonathan trembled.

"You know I wouldn't tell your father—" he started to assure her, but she interrupted him.

"What I don't understand is why you should have called on my parents," Iris said. "Mother never mentioned having lived in the Village or studying the theater. Until that note of yours came I never heard her mention your mother's name. And I simply can't believe she had all those beaux and dates as your mother said. Oh no. You've no idea how stuffy she is. Even worse than Father."

Curious that Iris had caught the resemblance in him to her father. If he couldn't make any headway with his wishful thinking about Alvine Harshawe, he would be content to be the byblow of a distinguished legal brain, Jonathan decided. Iris's long arms drew him closer, and joy filled him that he had found father and true love at the same time.

"Do you really want to go in Father's office as he said, and study law, Jonathan?" Iris said dreamily. "It will take years and years, darling, and there are so many other wonderful things we might be doing together. Why should he pick on you to be his successor?"

"Don't you see, it's because—" Jonathan started and then froze. Good God!

If he'd found a father in George Terrence, then he'd found not his true love but a sister!

"What is it, darling? If you're worrying about Hugow, you mustn't," Iris whispered. "The past is the past."

Jonathan forced himself to draw away from the warm golden cheek against his, and untangled his legs from the long brown ones. It was an effort to get to his feet.

The past was the past all right, and he should never have stirred it up.

"I've got to go," he said. "I mean we mustn't—I shouldn't —it's a mistake—oh, Iris, I do love you. Good-by."

He dashed out before she could speak, which was well, because any word from her would have brought him back. The faster he walked, the more frightened he was by the wheels he had set in motion which he must now brake as best he could.

Obviously he could not explain to Iris, and he dared not see her. His only hope was to get proof somehow that George Terrence was not his father. Until then he would hide.

For the first time he wished he had left an escape hole, even if it led back to Jaimison, Sr.

# 9

Ever since Jonathan Jaimison had brought magic into Claire Van Orphen's life she had been fervently longing for her twin sister, Bea. It was no use reminding herself that Bea felt no reciprocal yearning, and had never kept an engagement with her without postponing it at least twice. Bea was perfectly sweet about gossiping over the phone for an hour, but all Claire needed to do was say, "It's such fun talking, let's have lunch," and Bea was ready to hang up, almost as if she felt her good nature was being taken advantage of. Then Claire would pick up her poor pride and remember not to phone for weeks, because it was too obvious that Bea used the phone not to keep in touch with her but to keep her away.

Earl Turner doesn't find me such a bore, Claire told herself, and if I know Bea she would be mighty flattered to have an ex-*Sphere* editor like Earl call on her the way he does on me. And Jonathan is the sort of attractive young man she is always making a fool of herself over. And if she could just see me having my Manhattans at The Golden Spur with those two men, she would do her damnedest to make them like her best, the way she always used to do.

But Bea hardly listened to Claire's reports of her new life, or if she did hear she put her own interpretation on Claire's news. Maybe her little books on gardening, travel, careers, or kiddy life, and the occasional nice little love stories in nice women's magazines, weren't great literary triumphs, Claire conceded, but my word, it did mean something to do a job well enough to have it sold at a counter, and it wouldn't have hurt Bea to throw her a compliment. Oh, Bea tried to be kind, but her compliments were always laced with insults.

"I do think you're amazing to go on and on writing those little things you do, Claire," Bea would say. "I must send you that little avant-garde magazine my friend writes for. I'm sure you could catch on to the modern manner. It's such a shame to waste your talents on this other sort of thing. You really should catch up with the times, dear."

Well, what about those sales to TV of the old stories Earl had revamped? What about the old one he'd turned upside down and sold to the *Post*? Even Bea wouldn't dare call TV old hat. Claire didn't want to risk having the joy of her new triumphs crushed, and didn't confide them at first. Not over the phone, she said to herself. But how she ached for the old blind loyalty of their younger days! What good was happiness if you couldn't tell it to a loved one, share it and double the joy?

She herself, at least, tried to put on an act of being interested in Bea's obsession with the music world, all the green-room tattle about the Met and Balanchine and Bing and Lenny Bernstein, all the inside chatter that the ladies around Carnegie Hall feasted on. She may have worked too hard at feigning interest, Claire reflected, for Bea usually shut up abruptly after some comment from her sister. Once she had been downright angry, Claire recalled, after telling stories about Bing all during lunch so that Claire innocently asked how long she'd known Mr. Bing. It turned out Bea had never even met him and was annoyed when Claire expressed surprise at such passionate interest in a man she did not even know.

As Earl says, I probably bug her more than she bugs me, Claire sorrowfully admitted.

In the night the new loneliness for someone to share her success, the ache for Bea, the sister of long ago was unbearably painful. Maybe they could take a cruise together, the way they did when they were girls. They could talk over the family history, go over memories of Father and that dreadful second wife of his (still alive in a nursing home in Baltimore, determined to hang on till every penny was gone). They could fill in the gaps of old stories they had forgotten. They might even live together again.

The idea of suggesting this to Bea was too bold for Claire to entertain at first, but it grew on her more and more. She had a vague suspicion that Bea's money must be running out. Bea had never mentioned what sort of financial conditions her husband had left, but there had been astonishingly little insurance, and once she had told Claire she was lucky not to have had a smart businessman husband like hers to lose half her capital by "shrewd" investments. Claire had confessed that her own ignorance of money matters was all that saved her from the poorhouse. She had stubbornly rejected all expert advice on reinvestments, and therefore still had her small income, which sufficed, with her intermittent royalties. But Bea had always lived on a much higher scale, joking about her creditors and about Claire's naïve terror of bills. It struck Claire that perhaps Bea had been avoiding her lately because she didn't want Claire to guess that the game was up and that the bills were closing in.

Bea had not seemed impressed or even curious when Claire hinted at her new fortune, probably thinking it was only a matter of a few hundred dollars instead of dizzy thousands, with more to come. If Bea would only meet her halfway, a quarter of the way—no, if she would only open the door and let Claire come all the way alone, Claire would offer her a choice of Paris or Rome for a year or two. Claire could hear her heart thumping in terror at the thought of leaving her dear little closet of a room and the new friendships Jonathan had brought to her. But if that was the only way to win back her twinship . . .

She began to speculate on how she could get around Bea without that proud beauty flaring up at any implication she wasn't on top of the world as always. Maybe she would have to make all the arrangements before she even put it up to Bea. Maybe she would have to buy a cooperative apartment in Bea's own neighborhood, the West Fifties or Central Park South, and simply announce to her that a home was waiting just a few doors away, with no troublesome change of habits involved.

But *what about me?* Claire shuddered. At the thought of giving up her breakfasts at the Planet Drugstore, her two-Manhattan binge at Mac's Bar and Grill, her little book gossip with Jo and Lois at the Washington Square Book Store, the Sunday twilight walk through Washington Square, with the young people clustered around the fountain, plunking their banjos and chanting their hillbilly songs, the Good-morning-Miss-Van-Orphen all down the street, in Henry's delicatessen, where she bought her staples, in Schwarz's stationery shop, where she bought her *Times,* Claire felt a childish panic. Childish, oh, definitely. If she was going to win her way back to twinship she would have to grow up as Bea had and face change fearlessly—yes, even enthusiastically. Bea would see that they were indeed sisters.

Claire's twin, Mrs. Kingston Ball, was having her hair
done in her hotel room by Madame Orloff-Gaby. Madame
Orloff was another hotel widow, picking up a living by tint-
ing other tenants' hair, doing their nails, walking their dogs,
feeding their birds, or reading to them in her Russian accent, all her services costing only half the standard charge.
Bea was given to claiming that it was not the cheapness that
made her loyal to Madame but the marvelous musical background gladly shared with her clientele. In her Odessa
youth Madame had been a singer, a true mezzo, as she would
tell you, but a great career was nipped in the bud by a
stupid coach who tried to make her into a lyric soprano.
It was a miracle, she said, that the creature had left her
with even a speaking voice. It was indeed a lovely voice,
Beatrice felt, chocolate-rich, rumbling around in dark baritone cellars and exuding confidence and consolation. You
could tell Madame Orloff absolutely anything, for she'd
been everywhere and seen everything. Nothing surprised
her, yet she was always interested, always deeply sympathetic, supporting you in any folly, or even crime, if that
was your mood. Today had been an unusually quiet session,
Bea silent and brooding, and Madame gracefully taking the
cue. Finally, however, as she took the pins out of her customer's hair, she ventured gently, "Mrs. Ball is troubled
about something today."

"Do I seem cross?" Bea asked apologetically. "I'm sorry.
Yes, I am bothered. It's about my sister, you know, the one
who lives down in Greenwich Village."

"I've seen her with you in the hotel," Madame said. "She
is in trouble and has come to you?"

"No, Claire's all right. It's just that she's suddenly gotten the idea we should live together," Bea said. "We did when we were young, and had to do everything together till I flipped and got out. But now here we are, getting on in years, both of us alone, and Claire's idea is that the time has come for us to close ranks, so to speak. Go to the grave together, I guess."

Madame Orloff's smooth plump hands deftly arranged the other's locks, then patted the top of the head as a kind of sign-off. She took a cigarette pack from her apron pocket, offered one to Bea, and lit them both before she leaned back in the low slipper chair behind Bea, who continued to sit frowning at the mirror. Although bright sunshine leaked through the window, the heavy rose-embroidered curtains were drawn and the electric lights were on. ("There is nothing the matter with my complexion," Bea always said ruefully, "except daylight.")

"We got a very nice tint today, dear," Madame said, eying the image in the mirror. "I added just a dash more of the silver to soften the gold. Very softening. Points up the eyes. So you may live with your sister, then. It would save expenses, eh?"

Bea gave a preoccupied nod.

"It makes perfectly good sense, of course," she said. "I don't know why I'm so bitchy about it. Poor Claire. I almost snapped her head off when she first suggested it. Now why should I blaze up and be so damn nasty when Claire is so patient and amiable?"

"Being twins, you are opposites, that's all."

Bea shook her new crop of silvery blond softly curled locks.

"I don't think so at all. I think we're just two lefts or two rights and we don't complement each other at all. I'm not sure I don't understand Claire because I don't understand myself or whether I understand both of us too damn well."

"It looks so gay, being twins," said Madame.

"I suppose we got a kick when we were little with Mama always showing us off and everybody taking second looks." Bea tried an Oriental effect with her gray eye pencil. "Then I took to having tantrums when Mama would say, 'The twins want this' or 'The twins say that,' as if I personally had no identity at all. Claire loved it because she was shyer and felt that being two was a protection. But I hated seeing my own weaknesses doubled. I was stubborn— you know how stubborn I can be, Madame! No matter what I liked, I was bound to do the exact opposite of what my twin did: Half the time I never knew what I wanted because this mean streak made me automatically take the track contrary to Claire."

"Perhaps you are more alike than you wish." Madame smiled understandingly.

"Sure we are." Bea sighed and rubbed out the experiment in gray shadows around the eyes. "We're probably just one fat case of schizophrenia between us."

"She wants you to leave the hotel?" Madame tried to keep the fear of losing a steady sixty dollars a month out of her voice.

"She sold some film rights and thought of investing in a cooperative apartment right near the Hotel des Artistes— yes, I grant you, it sounds good. She has it worked out even to having a Japanese couple keep house for us, but then I hit the ceiling. It's her money and she means it so well and goodness knows I need money these days, but I said I wouldn't dream of leaving this hotel; then I was ashamed and said I'd think it over, but she was so hurt. She just can't see—"

"You don't get on at all," Madame deduced.

Bea took a comb and began carefully to rearrange her hair in less formal style. Madame subdued the disapproval in her eyes.

"It would mean being clamped back into the grave," Bea went on intensely. "Breakfast and dinner and over our nightcaps remembering anecdotes about Grandpa Sterling's Panhard, and do I remember Father getting ossified at our coming-out dance at Sherry's, and can I still do my imitation of Laurette Taylor in *Peg o' My Heart,* and what fun those tango lessons were at the Castles'. My God, Sonia, I like to watch life while it's going on, be in it if I can, but Claire won't let you. She's got to drag you back fifty years to those good old days when I'm damned sure I didn't have any fun, watched and chaperoned and shadowed every minute. It's as if she has to have a transfusion from the past every day in order to get through the present, and it makes you feel so old and sunk and hopeless, as if everything's over, the game is up, good-by, world!"

Madame Orloff listened to Bea's outburst with a thoughtful smile.

"I live in the past too, Mrs. Ball," she admitted. "Perhaps I bore you too, talking about old days in Paris and Moscow."

"Never!" Bea assured her. "You see I don't know your past, so it seems alive, but my own past and Claire's is dead. I can't have her burying me in it—I really can't. You must see how interested I am in young ideas."

Madame chuckled.

"No one could say Mrs. Ball lives in the past, certainly," she said. "Indeed not. But you say she will pay all expenses?"

"She says she's making pots of money now," Bea said

moodily. "I can't believe it's by her writing, but on the other hand Claire is not one to lie. Neither of us ever cared anything about money"—she gave a dry laugh—"that is, so long as we always had it. But now, with everything hocked and all my bills piling up . . . It would be heaven not to have those worries. And when I have my frightful headaches or rheumatic spells, believe me, I whimper around for some of my own kin just as much as Claire does. The thought of being left alone to die . . ."

"Don't tell me you have such morbid thoughts." Madame laughed incredulously. "You who are always so gay and full of life."

"I don't give in to them, that's all," Bea said. "But if I took on Claire it would be giving in. Not only that, but I'd have to give up my private life."

Madame stumped out her cigarette and studied her hands. Bea, holding the hand mirror, examined a wrinkle in her neck and impatiently turned out the dresser lamps.

"Luis," Madame said quietly.

Bea flung her cigarette into the bowl already filled with barely touched cigarette stubs and lit another one.

"It would be good-by, Luis," Madame murmured. "Good-by, those charming Sunday lunches."

Bea blew a smoke ring jauntily. It was amusing the way she maintained those little flapper mannerisms, Madame thought, blowing bangs out of her eyes, pouting, tossing her head, shrugging her shoulders, ishkabibble. Was it Clara Bow?

"That can't go on forever, anyway," Bea said. "You don't need to tell me."

"What *can* go on forever?" Madame said. "I always say, So far, so good. A family motto. You have gotten some entertainment and some consolation from Luis, as you have from other young men in the past. And the sister would not understand."

"It would be utterly out of the question," Bea said. "Claire's no fool. She's read everything, even if she hasn't lived it. I wouldn't even dare sneak any *chéris* into the set-up, so I'd be furious with Claire for making me give up Luis, and I'll never forgive Luis if I give up Claire's money for him. Maybe if Luis wasn't such a rude little beast—"

"He resents having to have his love bought," Madame said.

"The way I feel about Claire buying me, I guess," Bea said.

"You could give him the money to go back to the island," Madame suggested. "You say he's homesick."

"He says they'd make fun of him if he went back," Bea said morosely. "All he ever wanted in his life was to get to Miami. When he was a kid diving for pennies when the ships docked he'd follow the women tourists and say, 'Take me to Miami, mama, take me to Miami!' He was still saying it when I found him in that inn back in the hills, and I promised I'd take him."

"And you did." Madame chuckled. "Only it turned out to be New York."

"Everybody on the island was mocking him by that time, calling him Mr. Miami," Bea went on, brooding. "I bought him clothes, and he was just too grateful, that was all, so I brought him here, afraid I'd lose him in Miami. Now he says if he ever goes back, they will follow him down the streets yelling, 'Mr. Miami, Mr. Miami.' I suppose I made him the little monster he's turned out to be."

"You were a very unhappy, lonely woman when you met

him," Madame reminded her. "Rushing off to Rome or
Rio or London, packing and unpacking to keep from
thinking."

"I missed my husband dreadfully," Bea said. "It got
worse every year instead of better. Claire wanted me to live
with her then, but how could a pious virgin comfort a
haunted widow? Not that the trips did any good either.
Wherever I'd go I'd say, 'How K. would have loved this,'
and it didn't seem right to enjoy myself."

"K. loved travel?" encouraged Madame.

Bea laughed as a thought struck her.

"That was the funny part of it. If K. had been alive
he wouldn't even have gone, because he hated going any
place. If I'd bullied him into it he would only have loused
it up for me. I'd have been in a rage all the time with him
lying in bed in the hotel refusing to budge, or roaring
around the ship's bar about women dragging their men
away from home and making them change their bartenders.
I don't know why on God's earth I missed him after he
was dead, because I missed him more when he was alive."

Both ladies burst out laughing.

"We miss the man we wish he had been." Madame sighed
pensively. "We never quite believe he is really what he is."

Bea, pleased at the way Madame articulated her thoughts
with such understanding, reached for her purse, and Madame withheld a faint breath of relief. Instead of losing this
steady income, perhaps she could double it, was the thought
that hopped into her head.

"Perhaps your twin is not such a pious virgin after all,"
she said seductively. "Now that she is successful, as you say,
perhaps she would like to be rejuvenated too—a nice rinse,
the proper make-up, an introduction to an amusing man,
eh?"

Bea considered this, then shook her head.

"I doubt it. The only man she went out with in the last twenty years, so far as I know, was our friend Major Wedburn, who lived in her hotel. That couldn't have been anything. No, I'm afraid it would be me joining Claire's life instead of her joining mine."

She leafed through her checkbook, frowning and clucking softly at the stubs. Then, with a deep sigh, she wrote out the check for Madame, fanning it idly for a moment while Madame's eyes followed its flutter. Bea was thinking that once she'd given Claire a definite no she could scarcely dare ask for the small loan she desperately needed. She gave her pretty reconstructed coiffure an impatient shake, as if she could shake off her utterly selfish, unfair attitude about poor Claire. She hadn't even asked for details of Claire's new success, she had been so stunned by the decision that was being forced upon her. Instead of being mad at Claire she should be mad at Luis for making her into such a silly old fool, really. But she didn't dare get mad at Luis. She was darned lucky to have him at any price, at his own good time, and they both knew it.

"Does Luis still live with that old actor?" Madame asked.

"Luis shares Gordon's apartment, yes," Bea said haughtily, knowing exactly what Madame was driving at.

"I was thinking your sister might like the old actor," said Madame soothingly. "Being on TV, you know."

"If you mean we could start double-dating again, no," said Bea. "Thank you, no."

Madame lifted her majestic figure out of the chair, collected the tools of her operations into a large green leather bag, folded her green working smock, and zipped it inside the bag. Bea was still fluttering the check with a vague feeling that while it was in motion it could not be substracted from her slender balance. Madame regarded her indulgently.

"Maybe it would be a good thing to get used to your sister again little by little," she suggested.

"I hate getting used to anything," Bea said. "I hate the very words. I don't think you're alive if you let yourself get used to things."

"Think of it as a test curl before the permanent," Madame said. "Start doing little things together again—going to movies, the theater. Go see her in this new life she says she is having. What would it be to you—only a few hours a week while you postpone the decision."

"I suppose it would help me stall for time." Bea reflected. "I could stay with her for a week or two."

"Twice I went back to my husband and got used to him all over again," Madame said. "I still did not like what I had to get used to, but it was a sensible thing to do. When he died, my conscience was clear and I could dislike him with justice. He left me his collection of military buttons of great sentimental value. I was able to trade it for passage to America."

Bea wasn't listening. There were tears in her eyes as she thought of how horrid Claire's importunings were obliging her to be, and how unfair it was of her dear twin to make her face her foolish weaknesses. Good people forced you to use them, betray them, hate yourself. . . . Bea dabbed at her eyes angrily and handed Madame her well-earned check.

# 10

Earl Turner would have been mightily surprised to know the effect that his visit had upon Alvine Harshawe.

Alvine himself was surprised. At first there was his usual impatience at having his day shot full of holes by a morning caller. But then he was obliged to concede, in all fairness, that he couldn't hold this against old Earl. For the last five —no, ten—years he'd been holding out his day like a live target for anybody to shoot full of holes. He could not claim that his precious train of thought had been wrecked by that ghost from the past, for the simple reason that his thoughts didn't come in trains any more, or, if they did, they stood loaded on the siding, like a freightful of lumber waiting for a powerful engine to shove it to port. Mostly ideas came to him somewhat like office memos, stamped and questioned by the higher-ups before they reached him, the idea and its dismissal in the same message. "Why bother? Chekhov did this once and for all in *Three Sisters*." "You're sticking your neck out with this stale Steinbeck." "Why try to top Graham Greene?"

Why try? That was the hook to get each idea out of the way before he even tackled it. He was as bad as those conceited old stage stars rich enough to float through society for years, protesting that they just couldn't find a play that was good enough. In the same way he was always telling himself it was no use starting work before lunch or before Peg got out of the house, so then it was always too late. God knows it was no use trying to retrieve an inspiration after he'd mentioned it to Peg and she'd made her usual comment, "Do you really think people are interested in that sort of thing?" He didn't kid himself that anything or anybody was deliberately blocking his work; he didn't permit himself that alibi. On the other hand a man who'd worked as hard as he had at other times didn't just stop out of laziness. It wasn't all his own fault. What he really could say was his own fault was the easy way he deferred to Peg's plans, which never had anything to do with his work. That was why he'd been nursing the notion of skipping out, getting off Peg's social leash and holing up in the place where he'd done his best work.

That meant, of course, the New York house, which was closed most of the time and which Peg loathed. Maybe the old magic would start flowing again, he had figured, and even though he'd be lonesome and uncomfortable, used as he was to having Peg around, it was all the better for his work that she wouldn't be there.

One reason Peg wasn't keen on the place was that it was a holdover from Kay, his third wife, who had lived there with him for three tempestuous years. Kay he always regarded with a certain admiration as his emotional wife, always ready to throw a vase (cheap) or glass (empty), choking and panting in her rage, howling and abject in her penitence. The emotions all had to do with property, he had discovered. No bereft mother or betrayed virgin could storm as Kay did over his refusal to give her control of his finances. How childishly happy she was over the first book he dedicated to her, and what a tantrum when she discovered this did not entitle her to all the royalties! He'd managed to get out of that marriage with his shirt—in fact more shirts than she realized. He had been forced to give her this house as part of the divorce settlement—"My first real home since I left Sweden as a tiny little girl," she had pleaded sentimentally, then put it on sale that very same day. Alvine had foxed her by buying it back himself. The couple Kay had hired still lived in the basement, looking after things in return for their rent, and available for extra domestic service when he and Peg came to town.

Well, he supposed Peg couldn't be expected to like the house any more than she could be asked to like old Earl Turner, who wasn't in the *Social Register* or even in the telephone book. But Earl, like the house, belonged to the good old time when inspiration was flowing, and for that reason Alvine had rather welcomed his visit.

Looking back, he reflected that Earl was probably the closest friend that he'd ever had—that is, they'd been around the same places at the same time with the same ambition. Then Alvine had gotten married and later famous—two conditions that forbade a man to have a best friend. Best friends from that time on were his agent, his producer, his director, his leading man, his editor, his broker, plug them in and out of the switchboard as the deals changed. You lost one set of friends with each marriage, another when it dissolved, gaining smaller and smaller batches each time you traded in a wife. Mostly now his friends belonged to Peg, had to be okayed by Peg. Peg liked "amusing" people. By amusing she meant rich or titled or European social, certainly no literary clowns.

Alvine thought when it came right down to it he liked old Earl a damn sight better than he liked Peg. All day long he kept wishing he'd gone along with him, wherever the hell he was headed. Some crummy joint, probably the ideal setting for the new novel. Earl knew the spots all right. Lucky Earl! But let Alvine Harshawe try to get that kind of background! Let him try to pick up a conversation in a waterfront bar. Somebody was sure to spot him. Alvine Harshawe of all people! Was he there snooping for a story or was he really on the skids, as so many would love to hear?

He envied Earl, who could roam all over the city, from arty Park Avenue salon to Bowery mission, talk to strangers, do and go as he pleased, pack away enough juicy human material for a dozen Zolas. Not that he'd ever make use of it, bless his lazy old heart, except conversationally. The more he thought about Earl's opportunities and his own prison of fame, the more drab his present life with Peg seemed. (Wasn't this sterile period Peg's fault?) For years he'd been wanting to write about an ordinary young man involved in an ordinary situation with some ordinary everyday people. The Harshawe trademark, of course, was taut high drama in strange colorful backgrounds, and it was Alvine's plan to apply the same kind of swashbuckle to an everyday plot. But what did he know about everyday? Earl knew, because he wasn't hamstrung by a social dame like Peg.

The idea of envying poor old Earl set Alvine to sulking all day, and he was not cheered by his agent's good news of foreign royalties nor by viewing photographs of his agent's three sons, all great guys and a credit to the father. He began thinking of the son old Earl had found for him and by bedtime, after a few nightcaps, his head was bursting with the possibilities of the case. Could be, could be, he muttered dreamily over and over, and wished now he had gotten more particulars from Earl. He couldn't sleep as the situation began to branch out like a brand-new comedy plot.

What does a man do when he finds he has a ready-made son, twenty-six years old, mind you, by a female he scarcely remembers? Alvine found himself chortling out loud every few minutes. It was great, really great, he thought. In the first place he needed to find out for his comedy what a young man today was like, and here was one handed to him on a platter. By George, he'd announce him as his son, too. What would people say? he wondered.

It was characteristic of Alvine that he thought first of his public and only afterward of his wife. His earlier wives would have taken such news of a mystery son in their stride, he thought—Roberta would have been noble and modern, Ad would have cried a little, Kay would have seen it as a threat to her financial security—but what would Peg do? Alvine sat up and lit a cigarette, grinning. He had been with Peg longer than with the others, eight years—too goddam long, really—and the one thing he knew about her was that Peg didn't care what he did so long as he was in proper evening clothes. He could insult his host, rape the guest of honor, fall on his face with blind staggers, but by George, let him be dressed, black or white tie! All her complaints had to do with his being in a dirty old sweater or T shirt when he did whatever he did wrong—maybe was late or loud or lecherous. No matter how they'd quarreled over something, he could always win her over by dressing up for some fat nothing of a little party. She was prouder of him for having kept his waistline, he reflected, than for keeping his reputation.

What would really make her burn would be the embarrassment, Alvine realized. Peg embarrassed easy, God knew, and here was a real first-rate embarrasser in any family. She would think of all the little trivial social things before the big major thing hit her—like would this son move in with them and would they have to take him places with them and was he going to call her Mummy and all that. Or she might surprise him by throwing a real fit. Alvine figured, with an increasing glow of pleasure, that it might be the means of chickening out of this marriage. He hadn't written —or at least finished—any work since the wedding day. All his other women had kept at him in one way or other to get-to-work, write-write-write—you're-such-a-genius, or we-need-the-dough-for-that-cabin-cruiser or you-owe-it-to-your-public so get down on that typewriter and DO something. They stopped him in his tracks with their helpful yakking. He had thought, when he married Peg, it was going to be an inspiration just to be left alone. It had been amusing, at first, to see people's faces when Peg would say, "My goodness, how do I know what he's writing? I hope it's a space book because that's all I read." The other wives had always been ready to explain him and his work. It had amused him too that Peg, herself a much-admired beauty, was never jealous of the fuss women made over him. Indeed she never saw anything, wherever they went, but women's clothes, men's clothes, and interior decorations. She was always so absorbed in these subjects that when he described some brawl or contretemps that had occurred she would say, "Why, Ally Harshawe, you're making that up! I was right there."

It seemed to Alvine he could do nicely without ever having to hear "Why, Ally, you're making that up!" at the end of every one of his anecdotes. He could stand not hearing her brag of never reading her husband's works, too. His taunt of "illiteracy" only made her preen herself with a yawning, "Darling, you always said I was just a fine big animal." So he was stuck with a fine big animal who took all one winter to read just one of the space novels she often mentioned! He had gone back to separate bedrooms after being kept awake by paperback Ray Bradburys slithering off the bed all night.

He couldn't honestly say he'd lost anything by not writing these last few years. Peg often pointed out to him how much more famous he was now than when she'd married him. There hadn't been any new Harshawe, just revivals of the first two hit plays and all the usual anthologies and reprints of his stories. They'd traveled a lot, been interviewed all over the world, visited maharajahs and accepted decorations or honors. Damn it, you didn't have time to write if you wanted to keep your fame in good condition. Peg was disgustingly right in that, but that didn't stop him from wishing to God he could just sit down and knock something off like he used to. He could do it, too, if he could get Peg, that fine animal, off his neck. How these fine animals hung on, he marveled—he couldn't kid himself she loved him too much, but she loved the life he offered, and she wouldn't give that up.

Hell, he liked the life too, that was the trouble. He liked it best in those rare periods when he was left alone, though. He liked sleeping alone, and best of all staying awake alone, enjoying his insomnia, thinking his own crazy thoughts that Peg could never understand, listening to the all-night programs on the radio, reading a paragraph here and there about the secret of lobster gumbo or Gregory Peck's love life, figuring out what came next in his own life. The finding of a long-lost son would certainly shake things up.

"Peg, my dear, I'd like you to meet an old son of mine, Jonathan. . . ."

The thought tickled Alvine and he dozed off on it, the bedside radio gently clucking away, piping its program straight into his dream about Son Jonathan who was zooming around on a space-ship chased by his agent's three husky oafs in their space-helmets. This blurred into a Long John program about UFOs. The flying-saucer people, it said, particularly the Venusians (a pair of Venusian visitors having been interviewed by a reliable Hightstown, New Jersey, expert; absolutely a fact, affidavits right there in black and white) have a real brotherly interest in our civilization and will not do anything hostile to Earth until we're in a position to threaten them. A Mrs. Ethel Holm, ordinary housewife of Dingman's Ferry, Pennsylvania, also testified she found a very friendly attitude in the two Martians who landed their saucer in her back yard, and she testified in a signed statement right there in black and white so you knew it was God's truth that neither one had lifted a hand to her when she accepted their gentlemanly offer to take her for a ride around Clarion, a small sort of summer-resort planet behind the moon. Drowsily Alvine tried to fish the Jonathan image out of the planetarium ceiling.

Son Jonathan, a cross between a funny-paper space-man and a musical-comedy angel, materialized from a foam-rubber cloud, but just as he was changing into the Creature from the Black Lagoon Alvine woke himself up enough to reach out and switch the dial to Big Joe's all-night show, where more earthly experts discussed alcoholism. One man declared he was not alcoholic, just allergic to alcohol. A mere bite of rum-cake would set him off, stirring his allergy so hard he didn't show up for work for three weeks, you wouldn't believe what an allergy. Glad to have his new son driven out of outer space, Alvine sat up and poured himself a stout highball. He switched to a West

Virginia station where a gentleman farmer was describing how he bored holes in his prize beefsteak tomatoes, filled them with vodka, let them age in the icebox, then ate them for breakfast. The Built-in-Snapper. Delicious. Alvine was about to yell out to Peg to fetch him some beefsteak tomatoes, when he remembered she wasn't there, that he was alone with his darling insomnia.

If he did get rid of Peg, chasing her out with a secret son, he'd probably get somebody else, he reflected, sitting up wide awake now. He didn't want a helpmeet or inspiration or even a bed-broken round-the-clock lay, but he did like to yell out to somebody, say around four a.m., and get a response. If Peg were here and had stumbled, yawning, into the room at his cry, dragging her blanket behind her like Linus, the kid in the *Peanuts* strip, she would have slipped sleepily in the bed beside him, taking a sip of his nightcap, but then she would have complained, "I don't see why you kick about my space books when you listen to the stuff all night on the radio." And then they would have heckled each other back to separate beds again. So why pretend he was missing Peg? He switched back to Long John on WOR and poured himself some more allergy.

Now some very sincere fellows on the air were talking about the darrows, not outer-space people but the ones that live in the bowels of the earth. A scientific fact! It seems the way the experts discovered the existence of these darrows was that an ordinary everyday steel-worker took an elevator from the tower of an unfinished building—this was in Chicago a while back, affidavits in black and white on request—down to the basement. Down there the car slid sidewise—the fellow was sort of surprised—and started plunging down another shaft for almost two miles. Then the cage door opened and the darrows, these little fellows with big pointed heads, started talking to him, and they couldn't have been decenter if he'd worn his lodge pin. They had nothing against the Earth—naturally, they lived in it—and they intended no mischief; they were just out to get Chicago. Similar elevator adventures had occurred in Providence, Rhode Island, and in West Yonkers, all absolutely bona fide, sworn to in black and white by ordinary people. The darrows were, if anything, even friendlier than the Venusians, though of course not so personable. All they asked was to destroy Chicago, the wickedest city in the world. An Elizabeth, New Jersey, cop, a guest of Long John, added that these darrows often surfaced to take night jobs, naturally in work involving extreme heat. Many people reported seeing them working away after midnight in that little bakery near the station in Perth Amboy.

Now there was a tranquilizing thought, Alvine mused. When Peg asked him if they would have to take the new son around to parties, he would tell her to go ahead by herself, he and the boy were going to look up some darrows over in Perth Amboy. Or they might hunt for some of their own, up around the Con-Ed diggings in Columbus Circle, say. Take an elevator down to the basement of the St. Moritz after dinner . . .

"Be sure and dress, then," Peg would say.

Alvine, awake, leafed indolently through the magazine sprawling open on the bed. Dr. Norman Vincent Peale's face smiled benignantly out at him, advising a young man unhappily engaged to a selfish beauty to give up looking for beauty and get himself a girl who had something on the ball spiritually. That's the ticket, Alvine thought. He closed his eyes, wondering if his life would have been richer had he settled down with Jonathan's mother, dear long-ago Connie, instead of skittering around from wife to wife, Venusians to darrows, jumping from flying saucers in Massachusetts Bay to instant sons in Greenwich Village. The more he thought about it the more repugnant the thought of going back to the Cape became, and the more intrigued he was by the idea of the kid, Jonathan. He would stick around town for a while longer, he resolved. He would go downtown and hunt out the boy.

My son Jonathan. It couldn't be. And yet— One thing was sure, he wouldn't pass up the opportunity of announcing to Peg that the boy was his. If the idea of a long-ago love coming to light made her holler, then he would simply say it all happened when he was in his white tie and Meyer Davis's orchestra was playing.

"That makes it legitimate." Alvine chuckled.

The people were the same, the places were the same, but suddenly there was a difference. It seemed to Jonathan that the city had been coquetting with him, persuading him it belonged to him until he was confident, then mocking him for his complacency.

It took all his will-power to keep from calling Iris, and he spent hours trying to write an explanation of his flight the other night that would not reveal the true dilemma. He was so sure she was hurt and unhappy that the note from her was a grievous shock to his pride.

"Jonathan, dear, I know you've wondered why I haven't been in to see you at the Espresso after our heavenly night —I longed to see you—but a part has come up for me in the new Jeff Abbott play and I am studying every minute

for the audition next week. I'm not daring to see a soul—
not even Hugow—because this means so much to me. So
here I am, shut up like a nun as we have to be when the
big chance comes along. Please don't be hurt because you
do understand your Iris is first of all an actress. Love, love,
love."

There, Jonathan told himself, that makes it easier, but
it was disconcerting to have his own role switched. In the
same way he felt betrayed by Miss Van Orphen when he
called up to apologize for not keeping in touch with her
lately and had to listen to her own apologies.

"I've been meaning to invite you for cocktails soon to
meet my sister Beatrice," Claire said. "I've told her about
you, and she wants to meet you. But Earl Turner is working with me over my old stories for this wonderful TV
producer, and I haven't had a minute. I owe it all to you,
Jonathan, because you brought Earl into my life and it's
been so lucky! Please don't think I'm ungrateful, you dear
boy. We'll get in touch with you the first possible minute."

He went to The Golden Spur, hoping to chance on Earl
there and find out if he had heard from Alvine Harshawe,
but he was pounced on by Percy Wright instead, which
meant that he was quarantined for the evening. Even
Hugow failed him, but then, as the bartender and everybody else in the Spur realized, Hugow was deep in preparations for a great new show.

Dr. Kellsey alone was loyal, relaxing at the café table
with his espresso and flask of brandy. But this was no longer
any comfort to Jonathan. Instead he found the friendship
increasingly oppressive. There seemed a new note of pos-
sessiveness in the doctor. His invitations to a midnight
steak at Delaney's or a nightcap at Luchow's had a note of
command. He spoke of having Jonathan dine with a lady

friend of his, an assistant in the English department who worked with him occasionally.

"I'd just like to see her face when I introduce you," said the doctor, and when Jonathan looked perplexed he explained mysteriously, "You see she never knew me when I was your age."

The doctor spoke of moving to a larger apartment in his building, a place ideal for two bachelors. He wanted to know if Jonathan didn't think it was a capital idea. When Jonathan, taken off guard, agreed, the doctor nodded with satisfaction.

"I thought you'd get tired of shacking up with those two little harpies." He gave him a knowing wink. "I dare say you have to sleep with both of them."

The doctor gave a roar at Jonathan's embarrassment and patted him fondly on the back.

"Confidentially, I wouldn't mind it myself," he admitted, chuckling and wiping tears of laughter from his eyes. "I must say I can't see myself turning down a nice piece of cake like that, even though I was just as shy as you are, when I was your age."

"It's nothing like that," Jonathan protested, but the doctor brushed him aside.

"Nothing to be ashamed of, boy, we've got to have it. Only thing is the living with women! Always tidying up your papers so you can't work, or hiding the liquor, and their own junk all over the place. How can you write your novel there?"

"But I'm not writing a nov—"

"Nonsense, you don't have to keep it a secret from me. I know the signs. My guess has been right along that you're writing a novel about The Golden Spur, and I'm all for it, boy, because I always wanted to write it myself. So you've got to have privacy, not women. Women are forever washing either their hair or their stockings. No wonder you're looking worried lately."

There was no use trying to persuade the doctor that he was perfectly satisfied with his living arrangements, and since the doctor had not openly stated that he expected Jonathan to move in with him, Jonathan could not risk offending him by a premature refusal. He decided to simplify his position by finding a room of his own some place else, maybe in Earl Turner's old hotel.

But before he could make any move, trouble started in the Tenth Street studio. Lize, after a fight with Darcy, took off for a printers' convention in Atlantic City. Darcy was going to stay home from work, she said, because she had a "virus," and wasn't it lucky she had Jonathan to look after her? This meant that she had time to wash her hair and launder her stockings and lingerie constantly, draping them over his books and shelves, using his shirts as housegowns, his socks as house-slippers, his writing table as ironing board. She implored him to come home early, bringing a sandwich, and exclaimed what a relief it was to have Lize out of the way so they could really get acquainted. When Jonathan found his books dumped on the floor to make room for gallon jugs of wine, Darcy explained that it was because she had decided to go on the wagon and that always required a stock of wine on hand.

"Everybody else goes on the wagon, why shouldn't I, just for spite?" she said in answer to Jonathan's baffled query. "It always makes people so mad. They think you're on the wagon so you can put something over on them. Lize will be furious. It does give you an edge in a fight, you know." Later she added dreamily, "Anyway I like the way everything looks so crazy when you aren't drinking."

Too kindhearted to desert under these circumstances Jonathan found Darcy waiting up for him at night, and often sitting on a stool watching him like a cat while he pretended to sleep. Too ashamed to confess his fear of living alone with a female, he developed a prodigious snore to protect himself.

"You have the nicest snore of any man I know," Darcy told him. "I really mean that sincerely. It makes me want to cuddle right up."

He tried to spend as little time as possible at the café to avoid Dr. Kellsey. He would move out of his apartment that very night, he vowed, but when he got home there was Darcy, waiting to confide in him, over a chianti nightcap, the fruits of her serious meditations.


"A couple has the most fun," Darcy said. "A person by themselves has to keep thinking up things to do."

She held out her glass, and Jonathan obediently poured more wine into it. It struck him that Darcy drank more when she was "on the wagon" than she did when she was drinking.

"I think we shouldn't pour it out from the jug like this," she said, looking at the gallon jug of chianti on the table with sudden displeasure." I think we should pour some off into a vase or something. It looks nicer."

Jonathan found a milk bottle and carefully decanted a portion.

"Oh, fill it up," ordered Darcy.

Jonathan did. It left the jug almost empty.

"I mean when you're a couple you can do things together," she said and waved at the kitchen table where they sat. "Like this. When a girl gets home she wants somebody to have a nightcap with. And they can do other things together, like—oh, like going to auctions or double features and doing crossword puzzles, I don't know.

"One of the reasons I broke off with Hugow," Darcy went on, ignoring Jonathan's blink of surprise, "was that he never liked doing things together. Half the time he never even told me where the party was till it was all over. I guess I'm just an old-fashioned girl but I don't think it looks nice for a girl to go to a party alone, especially if she hasn't been asked."

"Don't you have to be asked?" Jonathan inquired.

Darcy gave him a pitying look and patiently explained that in New York City people didn't get invitations to parties, you just found out where they were. Oh some uptown women like Cassie Bender passed out invitations, but it wasn't to have people come, it was just a mean way of trying to keep people out. Hugow, for instance, never liked invitation parties or jigger measures or blue-white hair or avocados.

"Too mushy, he said," Darcy explained, holding out her glass. "You see what I mean about a couple having fun, don't you?"

"Like you and Percy," Jonathan said.

"Oh, Percy drags me," Darcy said impatiently. "I can't go a step without him tagging along. It's all right for an hour or two, we talk about Hugow and all that, but I guess I just don't like rich men. A person like Lize would think a girl was crazy to say that, but that's the way I am. Is that the end of the chianti?"

It was, Jonathan said hopefully, but Darcy recalled there was a spot of rum in the kitchen, and one real drink would not seriously affect her wagon, and it was such fun talking things over.

"You take a rich man and what have you got?" she said, holding out her hands and ticking off her points on her fingers. "You've got dinner in some dingy little Armenian dive or Chinatown where there's no bar to run up the tab, you've got a neighborhood movie rerun, you've got waiters hiding from you once the place knows the kind of tipper he is, you've got pink plastic pop beads instead of pearls and cologne instead of perfume for your birthday, and the only reason you get taxis instead of subways is that he gets that thing claustrophobia in subways. That's your rich man for you."

"Was he that bad with Lize?" Jonathan murmured.

"Of course not." Darcy blazed. "Lize is big enough to clobber him into expensive places like the Stork Club and she can get him blotto and carry him home, but I don't think that looks nice and besides I'm not big enough."

Her eye traveled from her empty glass to the empty milk bottle to the empty jug and to the alarm clock on the icebox. It was after two. Jonathan, reading her mind, said that the liquor store had closed hours ago.

"I don't have to drink," Darcy said. "A little wine, that's all, especially lately, now that I've been thinking over things. Living with a girl like Lize makes you see how you could waste your life with the wrong men. Hugow, for instance, was all wrong for me, that's why I walked out. Not so much his being an artist as his being so much older. Of course my folks always hoped I would marry a real-estate man or car dealer, somebody solid."

Jonathan took the glasses to the sink and washed them. Darcy stabbed a cigarette into her lips and waited for him to light it, nodding approvingly as he emptied the ashtray.

"That's what I mean, a younger man takes more interest in the home, washing dishes and straightening things up, not just chasing after women all the time. All the time Hugow lived here he never made the bed once, honestly it was embarrassing. I could always tell he'd had some new woman in when I'd come home and find the bed all made up. I knew he hadn't done it himself. Older men just don't care about nice things, they can't seem to take their mind off sex. That's why you and I get on, Jonathan, don't you think? Take Lize, she doesn't care if the place is a dump, but I mind terribly. Look at that lumpy old couch! Cracked old plaster walls, beat-up old chairs, dirty old curtains! It's all right for a girl like Lize, but for nice people like you and me, Jonathan, I mean, I could just cry."

If Darcy was going to cry, and she was, it meant another all-night session of confessions, and Jonathan had no consolations to offer, even to himself.

"I thought you liked the place when Hugow had it," he said.

"I wouldn't take Hugow back if he was the last man on earth." Darcy sniffled, dabbing at her eyes with a handy dishtowel. "I saw him in the Spur with that Angel girl the other night and I walked right past without speaking, that's the way I feel."

"With—" Jonathan came to attention suddenly.

"That dopey kid that's been following him around for years, says she's on the stage, but she's really just on the prowl for Hugow, that's all, following him around till he's too tired to go anywhere but bed."

Moral indignation was drying Darcy's tears. Jonathan wanted to ask questions but then he would have to listen to cruel answers. So Iris wasn't seeing Hugow any more, so she was absorbed in preparing for an audition next week and was simply so concentrated on this big chance that she forgot everything else. Dedicated! "Like a nun"!

Bad enough to have to renounce the girl you loved because she might be your sister. Bad enough to renounce a possible father because you'd rather make him a father-in-law. But to have your misery compounded by having the girl indifferent to your show of will-power, busy as she was claiming credit for her own, then lying to him!

Was the whole city out to betray his blind confidence?

"I can understand his going back to Cassie Bender"— Darcy was stroking her infinitely well-known wounds— "because she's just like a mother, that's why I was never, no never, the least bit jealous of her like Lize used to be, but what does he see in that big goony-eyed kid? Why we all used to laugh the way she'd come into the Spur and just sit and moon at him, never talking, just watching like she was hypnotized or something. That was three years ago, and now she's at it again, all goofy-eyed. Goodness knows you'd think she'd have learned she wasn't his type by this time."

Yes, you'd think so, Jonathan said to himself, but you couldn't learn when you didn't like the lesson. He ought to learn that Iris was carrying a torch for Hugow just like all the other girls, just as he had suspected at the very first. He ought to be angry now at hearing Darcy's news, but he wasn't mad at Iris, he was mad at Darcy for telling. It meant he had been foolishly trusting in Hugow too, so sure Hugow had no more interest in Iris and was a real friend, even though he no longer came to the espresso café to see him. Earl Turner too busy, Miss Van Orphen occupied, Iris gone, Dr. Kellsey a vague menace—there was no one left but Darcy, and Darcy without Lize to balance things was almost intolerable.

"Don't you think that's a good idea?" He heard Darcy's voice babbling urgently. She had found a miniature bottle of Southern Comfort and was sipping it. "After all, that awful little dive where you work can't make any money for you."

"It's not a dive," Jonathan said.

"Of course it's a dive, dopey," Darcy said. "Nobody goes there but your old goat professor and some funny-looking eggheads and social workers. It's a front for something, pushers or spies or bookies—just like the Metropolitan Museum and that Eighth Avenue subway station—and you ought to get out before you get caught. I mean you should get a job with the real-estate people right in their office, because you'd be wonderful in real estate, Jonathan."

She had her head cocked, with that pouting smile that meant she was feeling cuddly and would wiggle onto his lap in a minute if he didn't stand up, which he did, pretending to want a drink of water.

"You'd make a lot of money and wouldn't have to be spending your savings and you'd have first crack at some nice little apartment in the West Village, over on Horatio or Bank, maybe. We could live there. Let Lize keep this place, if she won't get out."

"We," Darcy had said.

"We could have a big housewarming and invite Hugow and the whole Spur crowd and everybody would bring a bottle," Darcy went on dreamily, still holding out her hand as if it encircled a wineglass, though this had fallen on the floor and was rolling about with a life of its own. "We'd make friends with the cop so we could make noise all night if we wanted, and we'd always have room for company to stay, that's the thing I like about being a couple, don't you? If we had to we could get married, too."

"Percy would want to live in Brooklyn, though," Jonathan said cautiously.

"Now Jonathan, you know perfectly well I'm not talking about Percy," Darcy said impatiently, then relented and flung her arms around his waist exuberantly. "You know I mean us. I'm surprised I didn't think of it before, but then Lize was all over the place."

Jonathan winced, marveling that such a tiny girl could have such a powerful hug.

"I don't think I'd be good at real estate," he quibbled, but this only brought more reassuring hugs from Darcy. Her curlered little head was strategically thrust against his breastbone and was butting him into retreat toward the living room. He remembered his magic words just in time.

"Scrambled eggs!" he cried, pushing her aside. "I'll make scrambled eggs, and maybe there's bacon left."

It worked, as it always did after his first error. Darcy was detoured by the flurry of cooking but not entirely appeased. She watched his operations pensively, ate her share, and handed him her plate to wash. He was able to get into bed and turn off the lights without further personal talk, and pretended to be fast asleep when he heard her call out plaintively from the bedroom, "All men ever think about is cooking."

There was no more time to be lost. As soon as the coast was clear, Jonathan escaped.

It should have but certainly would not have consoled Cassie Bender's shattered vanity to know that Hugow's flight from her magnificent summer party brought happiness to many vacationists now drifting back to the city. There were all the artists whose work she had rejected, all the ladies whose artist boy friends she had snatched, all the

Cape summer people who were not important enough to be invited to her Big Do, and then the anonymous strangers who loved any story about an honest, poor artist putting a rich, snobbish, overaged lady dealer on the spot.

"What I like best is the idea of old Bender being stranded on the Cape with no man of her own"—Cape oldtimers chuckled—"like everybody else."

For there is no place on earth a man is so rare and so prized as Cape Cod. A clever woman plotted for months ahead to round one up for summer, so that instead of being one of the ravening packs of Extra Women she could qualify socially as a "couple," a couple on the Cape meaning one man and at least four women—wife, mother, sister, girl friend, and possible house guest.

"I'll bet she's still burning," gloated Darcy Trent. "She stole him from me and thought she could show him off as her private property and she got what was coming to her. I *knew* he had something like that in his mind when he left me!"

"But what about the big show she's supposed to give him in the fall?" Lize said. "Maybe she'll get even with him by calling it off."

This was exactly the reprisal urged on Mrs. Bender by her faithful maid and confidante, Beulah.

"You done too much for that Hugow," Beulah said. "You gotta lay it on the line now, kick him right out of our gallery."

God, how she'd like to be able to do it, Cassie thought, but there was no point in telling Beulah why she couldn't.

"He's been kicking you around long enough," Beulah said. "It ain't gonna get any better, and what's more you ain't gonna get any younger. That's not saying you look your age."

Beulah was understanding, too damned understanding, Cassie often felt. She knew too much. She could never be fired, certainly.

"You don't act your age either, that's the trouble," said the sage, dusting the knickknacks on her mistress's dressing table as Cassie lay in bed. "Time you settled down. Have the same man to breakfast two days running, take your make-up off when you go to bed, and all like that."

"My own fault for letting friendship louse up a good sex deal." Cassie whimpered. "I get to liking a guy and trying to help him out of jams, and first thing I've lost myself a good lover. If you want to know something, Beulah, the older I get the more I love that stuff."

"What else you going to do with men?" Beulah said. "That's all they're good for, so you got to make the most of it. You ain't going to get anything else out of 'em."

"After all I've done for him he makes me the laughing-stock of the whole Cape." Cassie's tears began to gush again as they had been doing for weeks. "Then all of New York hears about it and men wonder what I did to make him skip. I'll be lucky to find any more lovers. In another ten years—damn it, Beulah, all a hotblooded woman can get in her fifties is a choice of drunks. A drunk who snivels about the good old days, or one that breaks up the joint getting into the mood, or else one that falls asleep before he even begins."

Beulah gave her mistress a comforting smack on the bottom as she passed the bed where Cassie sprawled. Cassie was large, fair, and showy, handsomer in her forties than she had been in her eager, shrill, and scrawny youth, before her hair had turned to gold. Nobody knew what had happened to her husbands or where she had found the mysterious millionaire who had set her up in her own gallery. Beulah had heard that Mrs. Bender had gone into the art racket as an excuse to raid the art quarters of cities all over the world for lovers, but Beulah declared that was just the mother in her. She was the same way herself, just couldn't stand seeing a good man lonesome and starved for love when there was a good bed in her room going to waste.

Cassie was forty-three—well, all right, forty-eight, if you're going to count every lost week end—and Hugow's betrayal had happened at birthday time, when she was frightened enough by the half-century mark reaching out for her before she'd even begun to have her proper quota of love. She was making more and more passes at the wrong men, then trying to recoup with stately cultural pronouncements in her refined Carolina accent, which she kept polished up like her grandfather's shotgun, ready to bring recalcitrant suitors into line. In this crucial period she wavered between her passionate need to be thought of as a splendid roll in the hay and her other urge—a good retreat position really—to be recognized as a Lady.

One trouble, which Cassie refused to admit, was that she forgot to adjust her courting technique to her encroaching avoirdupois. It was one thing for an impulsive, jolly girl to jump on an attractive stranger's lap, crying out that she just loved that Down East accent, but a hundred and sixty pounds of solid female doing the same thing was likely to cause buckling in the property before it was even sold. Gay solo dances, skirts flung overhead to stereophonic cha-cha in bohemian cellar parties might have incited men to lust at one time but now only brought on the janitor complaining of loosened plaster, or an astonished exclamation from younger fry: "Good God, Cassie doesn't wear pants!"

I mustn't ever go to those artists' dives downtown again, Cassie reminded herself over and over. It's all right whooping around in the country places with the old ones, the ones that have it made, like Sandy Calder and that set —even Eleanor Roosevelt or Emily Post couldn't lose anything by that—but it's these young, jealous little bastards that can ruin you, blabbing and getting things in the papers. The trouble is when the party gets wild I forget I have my professional name and dignity. Instead of going home, I go wild too.

Loving men and love as she did, Cassie had a constant struggle to maintain a proper aloofness. Those handsome, fleshy arms were ever ready to be flung around the nearest animate object while she nuzzled its head in her banquet-style decolletage. It was no feather-bed embrace, however, but more a bruising hug from a statue, for Cassie's flesh had no nonsense about it, a nose could be broken on those marble breasts, and young men, touched by the demonstration of warmth, were surprised to find no cuddle comfort here, but more the implacable rejection of a good unyielding mattress. No soft little-boy cosseting, no waste of affection, there was work to be done. With their heads butting into inhospitable crannies and curves of Cassie's neck and torso, they would hear her voice, a Charleston-lady coo to the last, rising above them, as far off and seductive as a steamship whistle inviting them to tropic islands. "This darling man must see me home." Cassie would be third-personing him fondly, and sometimes, it was said, he was never seen again, and only Cassie could tell whether he had escaped or been broken on the wheel.

Beulah's set in Harlem knew much more about Cassie's prodigious appetite for love than Cassie's artist set did. They followed her affairs as they did TV's *Brighter Day,* pleased with her triumphs, shedding tears over her failures. Beulah declared herself as one who believed in minding her own business: she was not like some, noseying in and blabbing one madam's business to the other. This was the pious prologue to each installment of Cassie Bender's Loves, absolving the narrator of all guilt, enabling her to enjoy it the more comfortably, just as confession perfumes the sin. In Beulah's accounts she herself had the leading part, giving full details on all the advice and general theosophizing which guided a grateful Mrs. Bender to success in love and business.

"No sir," Beulah reported herself as saying to Mrs. Bender only a few days before, "you do plenty enough for those paint men without giving them the run of your bed. You do for them and do and do, like this Mr. Hugow, and they takes what they wants when they wants it and then walks out, leaving you bawling. Then you kick some fine rich customer out of your bed the minute Mr. Hugow feels like coming back, and that ain't right. 'I knows all that, Beulah,' she says (here Beulah imitated the whining ofay lady voice), 'but these rich buyers of mine is too old and anyway by the time I've poured enough scotch into us to close the deal I'm so punched up I want to get in the hay with a real man, somebody where I don't have to do all the work. When that damn Hugow shows up I forget I'm mad at him, and there goes the ballgame.' 'Don't you be a fool,' I tells her, 'you hang on to those old men or they'll take away your gallery and you won't have those painters to lay around with.' "

That turned out to be one of Beulah's soundest warnings, though it came much too late, even if Cassie had ever been in the mood to heed it. Right now Cassie had no intention of letting Beulah crow over her good guessing but allowed the girl to believe her weeping was caused by a mere broken heart. She was out of pocket plenty too, since her tender solicitude for Hugow's comfort, the redecorating and repairing of the cottage for his studio, and his own casual treatment of cash, had nicked her bank account. Her grandiose plans for his fall exhibition, too, went far beyond the expenses allowed for business, but she had been excited and, let's face it, hopeful that she and Hugow could make a permanent team. Broken heart, wasted generosity, wounded pride—all these Beulah understood, but if she had any inkling that the Bender business was in imminent danger of collapsing, the tenderhearted girl would have demanded her two weeks' pay, cash, and flown out the door, for, as she herself would say, a person's got theyself to think of.

So Cassie, after her first stormy declaration that she wanted no part of Hugow's work, now saw that she could not afford the luxury of pride or revenge. The boom had been lowered from another direction. She should have seen it coming and insured against it. After all, the once doting gentleman who had put her in business was well on in years and had been due to pass on any minute in the last decade. But he had no family to interfere with his private expenditures; he had kept his interest in Mrs. Bender and their financial arrangements a secret through all the years, spreading his beneficences through several banks. Asking no questions had been one of Cassie's virtues, but it was only because she thought she knew the answers. Of course he would pop off one day, but of course arrangements, in his discreet, thorough way, would have been made for the continuance of the Bender Gallery.

But the gentleman had absconded, just as Hugow had, and it was no excuse that his flight had been through the pearly gates. Cassie had waited, after the newspaper reports of his passing, to hear from the estate manager, his lawyer, or his bank, but weeks passed and nothing happened. In the hysteria of the Hugow business she had found time to ask her own bank to look into the gentleman's last papers to see how her inheritance was to be handled. The bank reported there was no provision made. The gentleman, cautious to the very end, had left nothing to indicate any connection with the Bender Gallery or with Mrs. Cassie Bender. His bequests in other directions had been infuriatingly generous, according to the report, the largest going to a completely unknown woman.

"Why, the old goat!" Cassie raged when she heard of this from her lawyer. All those years—her best years, at that—she had been the old man's darling, graciously accepting his largesse in return for assembling a masterly collection of horns for him, and the monster had been unfaithful to her! When he had taken her to the Lafayette for lunch—yes, it was that long ago—and told her he could not see her again as he was on the threshold of sixty and could not do her justice, he must have been already starting something new! It was a sentimental lunch, Cassie recalled savagely, accompanied by her tears and the final affectionate clasp of some nice bonds and his word that the gallery would be supported indefinitely.

Instead of throwing out Hugow, she would have to beg him to stay, Cassie saw. She would make money on him, for he was on the way up, but she had to make it a big plunge, double his prices, build up the show as if he were another Pollock, which God knows he was not likely to be. And then what? Why, he would drop her for a bigger dealer, naturally.

So Cassie wept and raged and cursed, partly at the dead

gentleman who had been no gentleman and at the lover who had decamped and now must be wheedled back and rewarded with the greatest show of his life. It was a gamble, but she had to do it, even if she had to close shop later on. So here she was, knocking herself out buttering up Texas tycoons and museum heads, hiring the most expensive public-relations firm, planning the most de luxe preview party, playing with her credit, and running after Hugow in all his wretched dives where she knew they jeered at her importunations.

If she hadn't been desperate, and if he hadn't become her most profitable talent, Cassie would have loved to play a vengeful game with him, letting him make all the moves, not committing herself to a show until she was good and ready, letting him realize how necessary she was. But she was in too precarious a spot.

Her lawyer was the one who gave her hope. "Perhaps the fortunate lady who got the quarter-million you expected to get is interested in art," he suggested. "It may be she knew the gentleman's taste and may even have discussed continuing with the investment on her own."

It was not much of a hope but it was worth a try, and after some preliminary investigation Cassie managed to write a discreet note to the heiress hinting that a partnership might be arranged that would be not only just but profitable. While she waited for this barely possible rescue she was obliged further to humble herself with pleasant, even merry, little notes to Hugow as if nothing in the world had happened between them but the exhibition plans.

"If this show is a sell-out," Cassie declared to Beulah, "I'm going to take my cut and buy myself the best-looking lover you ever saw."

"What if it's a flop?" Beulah chuckled.

If it's a flop, we're out of business, Cassie could have answered, but instead she said, "Then I'll start looking around for that first husband of mine, if I can remember his name."

Hugow was immensely relieved that Cassie showed no bitterness toward him. He was lazy about business and a coward about making enemies by switching dealers, framers, even waiters. Maybe he'd sneak out someday, the way he did with his women, but he was glad now that he didn't have to offend Cassie further.

Cassie plunged into preparations for the show and at the same time kept on the trail of her dead sponsor's heiress with propositions of partnership and appeals to sentiment. When her lawyer reported no reaction to her pleas, she meditated on the possibilities of polite blackmail. The late gentleman had been so experienced in clandestine affairs that he had left no trace of evidence of his past attentions, and her claim would have to be on a personal basis. The problems multiplied, Cassie made giddier and giddier plans, until both her gallery's future and Hugow's show were given hope by an unexpected visitor.

# 11

ALVINE HARSHAWE was in a foul mood the day he set out
to find this Jonathan kid old Earl had told him about. For
weeks he had been lingering around New York, enjoying
himself in his own little sport of driving his agent and wife
crazy. He quibbled and postponed closing the movie deal,
allowed Peg to bombard him with telegrams and phone calls
begging him to return to the Cape.

"My wife doesn't like the terms," he told his agent.

"My agent won't let me leave town till this is set," he
told Peg.

Guests, important English directors, Italian film stars,
"fun people," were due on Chipsie's yacht, Peg moaned,
and he must realize his poor Peg couldn't entertain them
alone. They didn't want to see her, they wanted their lion,
as she knew perfectly well. Alvine knew it better than she
did, and thought it did Peg good to be reminded of it once
in a while. He'd pop up, he thought, just as they were all
bored stiff and ready to go, then watch how they decided
to stay, with the king back on the throne.

But suddenly Peg's telegrams stopped. After a few days
came her cable triumphantly announcing that dear old
Chipsie (Lord Eyvanchip, of course) had felt so sorry for
her loneliness that he had simply kidnaped her to join
the party sailing down to the Caribbean, dropping off at

spots as whim suggested. She might leave the party in a month or even go on to the Mediterranean and then to Paris.

What am I supposed to do with four loose weeks on my hands? Alvine felt like bellowing indignantly across the ocean. He'd be damned if he'd fly over to join her in Paris, if that was what she was counting on. But she had not even suggested it, he thought with some surprise. What could be more baffling to a husband who yearns for his freedom than to have it handed to him gift-wrapped? Alvine pondered over Peg's unprecedented silence, studied her last cable for some clue, and became increasingly outraged.

And then the truth hit him.

It could not be—oh, *couldn't* it?—that for the first time a wife was shaking *him!* Alvine had never believed in fighting to get or hold any woman. Shake them loose little by little was his system, and let them drop off by themselves. Always the good people, the richest and most famous, stayed on his side through all of his divorces, dropped the old wife when he did, accepted whatever new wife he presented. Chipsie, being rich and titled, would never have stopped off had he known Alvine was not there. Chipsie couldn't stand boring wives, having just gotten rid of his own. Why, that made Chipsie a free man now, and this thought brought Alvine up short.

Peg wouldn't go in for any hanky-panky, he was sure of that, at least not for kicks or for spite and certainly not for mere love, but she was a snob. No use kidding himself that she wouldn't rather be Lady Chipsie than a mere author's wife if she had the chance, and the minute he had the thought Alvine knew what the game was. Peg was getting back at him with a ladyship. Alas! His agent had heard talk confirming the suspicion! What made Alvine burn was to think what a smug ass he'd been, so sure he was the one who pulled all the strings. He would never have dawdled around New York, half the time in his house and other times lounging around his agent's cabin cruiser up at City Island, drinking with a couple of actor guests at night, waking up at Port Jefferson or some Connecticut port, then starting all over next day—oh, never would he have enjoyed this except for the pleasure of infuriating old Peg.

But there was Peg hitting it off with old Chipsie and his world of envious enemies chuckling to think the arrogant Harshawe had been kicked out!

Raging about for some way of restoring his vanity, he remembered Earl Turner's talk of the kid who might be his son and he knew that was the answer. Let tricky old Peg have it right between the eyes. Winning a ladyship wouldn't be such a triumph if people knew it was a consolation prize after having her husband bring home a full-grown bastard son. Alvine set out at once to get Earl and find the boy Jonathan. He'd make the first move.

He took a cab from the City Island yacht basin, intending to stop off at the Sixty-fourth Street house and clean up, but it was a hot afternoon and he needed a drink after several days of salt air and bourbon. He dropped off at a dingy First Avenue bar where no necktie was demanded, then made another start downtown, with a few stopovers at some Third Avenue bars.

"Anybody ever tell you you're the spit and image of Alvine Harshawe?" the bartender in the first bar asked, after his second scotch.

"No," said Alvine.

"Of course he's a good bit taller and ten, twelve years younger, ha ha"—what was so funny about that? Alvine wondered testily—"but there's a resemblance, if you were dressed right. Many's the time I've fixed him up after a big night. The screwdriver's his drink."

"Must try it next time," Alvine said and paid his check.

At the next bar, where he ordered a screwdriver, a fish-faced blond man bared shark's teeth and extended a fin, saying, "You don't know me from Adam, but, by George, my mother's one of your greatest fans. I don't read Westerns myself, Mr. Steinbeck, but let me buy you a drink anyway."

"Buy your mother a drink," Alvine snarled and marched out.

He caught a glimpse in a shop-window mirror of an unshaven big bum in a stained white jacket and faded slacks. He smiled grimly, thinking of how Peg would carry on if she saw him going about New York like that. Never mind, he was a free man now, the hell with Peg. A wave of affection for his old pal Earl came over him, and he thought it would be only fair to appeal to Earl, show him that even foxy Harshawe could get in a jam. The trouble was he never took note of Earl's address, being sure he'd never want to look him up. He remembered something about the Hotel One Three and got a cab to cruise around the East Side looking for it, but it was no use. He and the cabby stopped off at Luchow's and had some drinks until a waiter came up with a necktie, suggesting that Alvine put it on. Alvine had a counter-suggestion and stalked out, too outraged to call the inside headwaiter, who knew him well.

Never mind, Earl was bound to be at one of the old haunts. Alvine had a dim recollection of a café Earl had mentioned on Bleecker Street, where the boy Jonathan worked, the place that used to be their favorite bakery lunch, but where was that? The poor good old days in the Village with a mailbox full of rejection slips were blessedly dim in Alvine's memory, and all that he remembered, as they passed the lane of lights on Fourteenth Street, was the feeling of excitement, promise, and youth, a wonderful feeling that he had never expected to recapture. He paid off the cabby, forgetting about Peg and revenge in the sudden joy of the moment.

"Sure you'll be okay, bud?" the cabby called after him for some reason, but Alvine waved him on, amused at the unnecessary concern.

The clock in the Con Edison building beamed down familiarly, and Alvine, surprised that night had come so swiftly, thought then of the old days in George Terrence's apartment on Irving Place when the same clock had beamed in their window and bonged them awake each morning. Old George had been top man then, with his money and family, decent in his way, and it was probably a shame the way they used to exploit him, use his charge accounts, sign his name at restaurants, use his clothes and liquor and girls. Once in a while Alvine had encountered him in later years, and it gave him an inner laugh to see how their positions had changed, George now eager to be host instead of sulking at being "used," as in the old days. Old Earl Turner had had the edge then, for a brief period, having a salaried editorial job instead of being a chancy freelance writer. Where was old Earl right now anyway?

Alvine wandered down toward the square, stopped in a corner bar for a double Johnny Walker to sustain the pleasant glow of memories. When he came out, the neighborhood seemed to him to have changed beyond recognition, old landmarks swallowed up by great new apartment houses and supermarkets. The Planet Drug Store was still there, where they used to drop in for contraceptives, leaving the girl standing, all innocence, on the corner. On such a night

as this, mused Alvine, in such a place he had made his
preparations for a pass at Connie Birch, while she waited
outside, clutching his manuscript. The boy Earl talked of
was surely his, Alvine thought, crossing a side street now,
pleased to recognize the old auction gallery, with the hamburger stand next door now a pizzeria, and the old candy
store now a bar. He looked in, half expecting Earl to be
there with a welcome, but nobody spoke to him, the drink
was terrible, and the seedy-looking customers scowled at
the stranger.

Alvine found himself passing the Planet Drug Store
again and realized that he had forgotten his way around
this neighborhood. He began to be annoyed with Earl, and
the good feeling blurred into a suspicion that Earl had
ganged up with Peg, but that was fantastic, of course, for
Peg was a snob. "Fantastic, fantastic," he muttered, going
down the street. Coming upon his reflection in a window
unexpectedly explained why women on the street gave
him a wide berth. He laughed aloud, thinking again how
embarrassed Peg would be if she could see him looking
like a panhandler. It made him feel good to be a natural
part of this neighborhood instead of visiting it as a well-
dressed slummer. Earl would like to see him like this, that
much was certain.

"Do you know Earl Turner?" he asked in the next bar,
a dark place, clammy and stenchy with stale air-conditioning.

"He hasn't been in lately," the bartender said.

What was the boy's name?

"How about Jonathan?" Alvine asked.

"He'll be around later, maybe, after midnight," said
the man.

Alvine stood at the end of the bar and ordered. He

laughed aloud again, thinking how fantastic it would seem to Earl to come in and find him there. Fantastic, he repeated, absolutely fantastic. There were several empty seats at the bar and at the tables but Alvine did not want to commit himself to such a permanent step, for the customers were not ordinary bar types or even bohemian types but seemed a collection of Rorschach blobs in the watery pink light. Another curious feature of this bar was that no one looked at Alvine or nudged someone to point at him. He was so accustomed to ignoring such attention, staring straight at his drink or at his *vis à vis,* that the absence of it made him look around more carefully, squinting at the blobs to make them form reasonable contours. Good God, I'm drunk, he suddenly decided as the blobs began twinning and tripling before his gaze. This particular kind of old-fashioned plain drunkenness had not happened to him since the old Village days, and now that he recognized it, he was amused and delighted with the game.

"It's the old rotgut," he reflected aloud.

With the fine labels to which he was accustomed at home, he could sip highballs for hours, knowing his Plimsoll line was reached when he retreated into icy silence, subtly insulting Peg's gayer guests by an occasional sardonic grunt that would make them turn anxiously, knowing the king was bored. He would saunter out of the room, bearing his glass, indicating that even drinking with such company was intolerable and that he preferred bed or a really intelligent talk with the cook or the dogs. No crazy, fascinating multiple visions such as his bar tour tonight was affording him. No three-headed long-eared blobs drinking triple drinks. Just boredom, blah blah boredom.

"Rotgut, yes," said the blob next to him. "But I find it has a tang to it that the good stuff doesn't have. They've got a brandy here that is terrific, sort of like sword-swallowing. We'll have some and you'll see what I mean."

The blob turned out to be absolutely right. The brandy was black and brackish, thick and smoky.

"The swords are rusty," said Alvine, gulping. "Instant tonsillectomy. Fantastic."

He found this curious sensation even more charming than the other effects. Instead of going down the little red lane, this raging drink shot up to the top of his head, where it separated the cerebrum from the cerebellum in one clean cut and then bubbled mischievously behind his eyeballs, so that the blobs all around changed their shapes with dizzying speed.

"Are you a darrow, by any chance?" he asked his friend, for the blob was now elongating into a pointed head which might conceivably have made him a Martian or Venusian except that he was too short.

"How did you know?" asked the sword-swallower. "My name is Wright, Percy Wright, but my grandmother was a darrow from Plainfield."

"Did she work nights in a bakery in Perth Amboy?" Alvine asked, intensely interested.

The fellow did not think she had, but he conceded that there were a lot of things about the darrows that he had never known. He did not know how often the darrows came up out of the earth, for instance, but he recalled an uncle who had to have a cement slab over his grave in Maryland because he kept floating out at high tide and indeed had once been waterborne in a tornado right into the village bar that had been his ruin. The wind had blown in the saloon door, and there was the uncle, perpendicular, pushed right up to the bar, ready for a nightcap.

"Fantastic, those darrows," said Alvine, delighted.

Out of the corner of his eye he could see the darrow's head lengthening and then squashing down like an accordion, an accordion with a tiny mustache. Under ordinary circumstances Alvine meticulously avoided that borderline in drinking when he was not master of the situation. He disliked slovenly drinking because he respected alcohol too much, he claimed, to see it degraded, used as a mask, weapon, or means to an end. Tonight was different.

He looked around to see if there were any other darrows present, but the bar was too dark to see well. His companion clung to him whenever Alvine started to leave, for he complained that nobody appreciated him in this bar, his girl friends were always insisting that he wait for them there and then they always came late and latched on to some other guy. It did strike Alvine that whenever his friend hailed a newcomer the person shied away to the farthest end of the bar or else left, probably afraid of darrows.

"Darcy, come have a drink with us!" the friend cried to a girl who walked by, a beautiful little blob of a girl with penetrating oyster eyes, or no, little clam eyes, tiny little Seine clam eyes that cut right through you.

"Not unless you get rid of that bum," said the girl. "You been down to the waterfront?"

"Now, wait a minute, Darcy. Now, Darcy."

The darrow began to cry, and the girl melted away into the Seine mud.

"Bitch," said Alvine, pulling up his friend, who kept sliding from his stool. "They're all bitches, popping off with the first title that comes along."

Rage at Peg came over him again but he couldn't remember what Peg looked like, except for the clam eyes. A fresh drink of the delicious house brandy made him

happy again, and he thought of how Peg would screech
if she saw him bring home all these blobs. His companion
clutched his arm and maneuvered them to a vacant booth
near the bar, where he laid his head down on the table and
sobbed, little hiccupy sobs. Alvine watched his head stretch
and contract like Silly Putty until the rhythm of it made
him sleepy. He tried to keep his eyes open by staring at a
menu card.

"Golden Spur." He made out the words finally. "I used
to know the place once. Let's go there."

The darrow was sleeping now, snores punctuated with
tiny hiccups. A disgusting lot, these darrows, Alvine
thought. He tried to get up, but the other's legs sprawled
out, locking him in.

"Okay," Alvine said, giving up and sliding back. "Might
as well have another brandy."

"The boss says we can't serve you any more," said the
waiter.

"Make it Johnny Walker, then," said Alvine agreeably,
but the waiter had gone.

"Better get out of here before Percy comes to," far-off
voices said, and then other far-off voices sounded familiar,
addressing him by name.

"You get his other arm, Jonathan," the voice said. "Come
on, Alvine, we'll get you to a cab. Here we go."

"Nasty lot, those darrows," Alvine said in the cab
drowsily. "Where the hell were you, Earl, old boy? Looked
for you all day. Let's go to Golden Spur. Old times' sake.
Got to meet my son."

He was peacefully asleep.

"There's your end of the rainbow for you!" Earl exclaimed sarcastically. "You were so hot to find the guy, and
see what you've got now. I don't know what on earth got

into him, but here's your hero for the taking. This is the way it happens."

"He was looking for me!" Jonathan said unhappily. "Don't ever tell him we found him, Earl."

"You think it would bother him?" Earl laughed. "It's material, isn't it? Nothing bothers a genius but lack of material! Come on, we'll get him to bed."

"A good guy is always on the spot," Earl Turner said. "Everybody wants to take a crack at him. He doesn't have a chance. You've got to be a real bastard to get out of a jam, excuse the expression."

Jonathan looked at his notebooks stacked with his laundry package on the unpainted table of his room at the Hotel One Three.

"I should have left word where I was moving," he said. Earl snorted.

"You can't tell a woman you're leaving until you're gone," he said. "Darcy wouldn't have let you get away, and Lize would have tied you up."

Jonathan knew it was true. What worried him was how he could resist capture once they started after him.

"I don't suppose I dare go in the Spur." He meditated. "All those messages on the bulletin board for me to get in touch. I can't go to the café on account of Dr. Kellsey. He's waiting for me to move into his apartment with him. He says he owes it to me."

There had been an unsigned note to "J.J." also, that would have been from Iris, saying, "The past is the past, but what about the future?" Earl had relayed other mysterious messages to him and had brought a letter from George Terrence.

"I can't tell you how disappointed I was when you did not appear for your appointment," it said. "Thinking it over, however, I could understand your hesitancy. We are both, I think, aware of our true relationship, though we have not discussed it candidly. I can see that the secrecy of the relationship would be a burden to you, since you want definite cause to cut yourself from the Jaimison name. I myself should like to sign papers admitting my paternity, which papers could be shown under special circumstances, but for appearances' sake I should like to "adopt" you. This would avoid unpleasant effects on my wife and family, for I would propose this step to Hazel as a sentimental gesture toward her old friend.

"I think this will put you in a much happier position. I shall proceed with these arrangements, confident that you will get in immediate touch with the office. I cannot tell you how much it will mean to me to be united with my unknown son."

Jonathan gloomily handed the letter to Earl. Weighed down with his own problems as he was, he was still able to note with surprise the new sporty jacket Earl was wearing, the natty shoes and pink shirt. Success had gone straight to his back, evidently.

"What about Alvine?" Earl asked, after scanning the note. "He'll be out in another couple of weeks. Every day he asks about you. It's damned awkward, after I laid it on for you."

"He doesn't know how we found him?" Jonathan asked.

"He doesn't remember what happened after he took the elevator in the Big Hat bar and landed in the bowels of the earth with a tribe of darrows," Earl said dryly. "They told him we were expected, so he waited for us. And that's the story he told that made his agent and the doctor hustle him off to the hospital. Oh, he's still mixed up, all right, but it's just shock."

"I haven't got over the shock myself," said Jonathan.

"With Alvine it's the shock of having something go wrong for once in his damn life," Earl said. "A wife leaves him instead of him leaving her. Shock number one. Then the shock of hunting for me instead of me hunting for him. A guy like Alvine can't adjust to upsets like that. He's either kingpin or crybaby."

Earl looked at his watch. Now that he had a wristwatch, Jonathan noticed that he was forever looking at it, as if important people were waiting for him elsewhere. Apparently it was gratifying to use this gesture instead of having it used against him.

"Well, do you want to come along and see him or not? I can see why you don't feel like claiming him right now as your rightful parent, but so far as I'm concerned I like him better as a drunken slob than I ever did as the king of cats." Earl frowned at Jonathan. "Okay, you were looking for a big hero daddy and you back away when you come on him getting thrown out of a bar."

It was the truth, and Jonathan couldn't understand himself.

"I guess I was disappointed on account of my mother," he said. "I couldn't picture her with him. I didn't want to."

"If he hadn't been flipping he wouldn't have even bothered to look for you, just think of that," Earl said. "You would still be hoping to find him, hoping he was your man."

"I know."

"So you've got your wish, and whenever that happens it's always too late and all crossed up. He's got it in his old bull head that a lost bastard turning up in his life will put him one up on his wife. He wants to throw you in her face. I guess that isn't the way you pictured it."

"No."

"I told him I'd bring you up if I found you," Earl said. "Can't say I blame you for chickening out, but I'd like to help Alvine right now. I used to get sore at Alvine always being on top of the world, everything working out for him, but damn it, I don't like a big man down. Funny, eh? I'm used to Alvine always running the show. I'm used to being jealous. That's my security. Alvine's my old North Star, I mean he's got to be up there in the sky."

That was how he felt too, Jonathan thought. He was ashamed to admit that his dream of a father was of a man infinitely superior to John Jaimison, a man it would be a victory to claim, not a responsibility. It was no triumph to be captured himself, to round out some frustrated man's picture of himself as a father. He hadn't asked Fate to send him a great man who appeared to have gone off his rocker and stood in need of a son's tender devotion. Damn it, he'd done his time as dutiful son, yessirring and nosirring. He didn't want to begin that all over with a new candidate. He wondered why it had never occurred to him that his father would expect him to make up to him for the lost years—as if he owed it to him.

"I hoped I'd never see this damn dump again!" Earl exclaimed in sudden petulance. He yanked down the mottled yellow shade on the narrow court window, and the fabric tore off the roll. He swore. "Same view of garbage cans, dead cats, and broken baby carriages. I'm through with all that. Why do I have to rub my nose in it again just for some kid that thought he wanted to find a father and then wants to hide out?"

Jonathan was embarrassed.

"It was getting too much for me," he said patiently." The girls and Mr. Terrence and Dr. Kellsey all expecting to take me over before I'd found out what I wanted. I was so sure Alvine Harshawe was the answer, then coming on him that night blubbering and wild, I couldn't believe it—"

"I couldn't believe it myself," Earl interrupted. "I couldn't believe I wasn't laughing, either, because he'd been so snotty about not wanting to go to the Spur for fear his public would mob him. I could have laughed, but the funny part was that I hated it. Hated seeing him stuck with a punk like Percy, a guy he'd never speak to in his right mind. I'd like to take you up to him, damn it. I'd like to see him get the edge on Peg the way he always had."

"I don't want it that way," Jonathan said.

Earl kicked the fallen shade angrily under the bed.

"If he really thought I was his own son he wouldn't use me to get even, that's all," Jonathan said. "Later on he'd probably admit it was all a joke on her, but the joke would be on me."

This made Earl meditate for a moment. Then he brought out more missives from his pocket and tossed them to Jonathan.

"Dan said these telegrams were forwarded around town to the Spur," he said. "You may have something there about Alvine. Maybe you'll think differently in a week or two when he comes around. Maybe he'll change his tune too. I'm staying at the De Long now if you need me. Don't expect me to come back to this fleabag again."

"It's only temporary," Jonathan said.

"I've stayed here temporarily all my life, boy," Earl said. "Don't get started."

"I hate the word 'permanent,' " said Jonathan. "I've got to pull out of the café job before it's too late. But what can I do? How will I get by?"

"You've got nothing to worry about," Earl said. "You're young, you've got looks, you've got a blue suit and a pair of black shoes, hell, the world is your oyster. All you need is a list of bar mitzvahs, walk right in, eat all you want, help yourself to a fat drink, shake hands, say Irving never looked better. You won't starve."

No use expecting sympathy from a battle-scarred trooper like Earl.

After the door closed, Jonathan looked at the telegrams. All were from John Jaimison, Senior, summoning Jonathan to visit him at the Hotel Sultana on Central Park West as soon as possible.

# 12

FOUR MONTHS AGO Jonathan would have been outraged that his own special city should be defiled by the presence of a real Jaimison. He would have been indignant that the city had broken its promise of asylum and let in the enemy. He would have been shocked that his kind Aunt Tessie had given away his hiding place.

It surprised him that his chief feeling was mild astonishment that these people still existed when they had been erased from his own mind. The letter from Aunt Tessie explained a little.

"I wouldn't have given him the address but I got the idea it has something to do with money. I heard he was going to New York to see a specialist and it struck me he might be wanting to make up to you for everything before he dies. Now Jonny-boy, you take whatever you can get out of him, and don't open your mouth about his not being your own father. Goodness knows he gave you as bad a time as your own father could have, so let him pay for it. You go see him and be smart. Let's see if he'll let go a few dollars at last, ha ha."

Jonathan decided Aunt Tessie's theory must be right. He needn't worry that the old man would have made a trip to New York to retrieve a lost child, when he had not noticed his absence all this time. Nothing to be afraid of, really, in facing him again. If he wanted to atone, let him atone plenty.

Walking toward the park from the Seventy-second Street subway, however, Jonathan had time to worry about what kind of scene he would have to face, supposing the old man had reached a state of sniveling penitence. He might be propped up on his deathbed, surrounded by nurses and weeping Florence, and expecting Jonathan to join in tears of mutual forgiveness. But it was too late to back out now. In no time he heard himself being announced from the hotel desk, and there was his stepmother at the door of 9 B, one hand extended and the other at her lips.

"He's resting," she whispered. "He just got back from the specialist's examination."

At least she showed no signs of weeping.

"Pretty sick, eh?" Jonathan whispered back, tiptoeing into the vestibule.

Florence threw up her hands.

"You know your father," she said.

Jonathan looked startled.

"He will overdo," she said. "So when he had to make this trip I made him promise to see this expert. A hundred dollars a visit, so he must be good. And this hotel—twenty dollars a day, mind you, without counting the garage rent. Well, well, Jonathan!"

As she talked her little brown eyes shopped over his person busily, price-tagging his corduroy slacks and checked shirt, recognizing his old sport jacket and mentally throwing it out. Her frown centered on his hair as if the barbering bore Darcy's own signature. He followed her gingerly through the vestibule. Evidently there would be no deathbed scene, judging from her high spirits.

"My goodness, Jonathan, you certainly haven't got the

New York look yet!" she exclaimed. "I should have thought you'd have a whole new suit by this time. Those trousers—"

"Cost eighteen dollars," Jonathan said obligingly.

If Florence was reducing him to his net merchandise value, Jonathan was just as curious about the obvious rise in the fortunes of the Jaimisons. Packages with the Saks Fifth Avenue label were piled on the hall chair, a new fur stole hung over its back, and the living room revealed not only an expensive view of Central Park but a corner bar cabinet with a full bottle of scotch visible. A closer look at his stepmother showed that she had gotten herself up to hold her own in the great city. The effect was not a New York look but the small-town look multifold. The rouge was redder, the jaw firmer, the coiffure browner and kinkier, the bracelets bigger and noisier, the Alice-blue silk dress bluer and tighter, the patent-leather sandals higher-heeled.

The smell of prosperity was here, Jonathan thought, mystified. A familiar cough announced the emergence of Mr. Jaimison himself from the bedroom. He stood for a moment framed in the doorway, squinting his eyes, mustache and famous Jaimison nose quivering as if testing the psychic temperature of the room. Jonathan squinted back, surprised that his onetime father was shorter and stockier than he remembered, but then he had usually seen him in lordly command of a desk or steering wheel. Without his props of authority the old man seemed at a loss for a moment; then he squared his shoulders and plunged masterfully across the room, arms swinging as if ready to put up a stiff defense. He cleared his throat.

"Well, son," he said, giving Jonathan's hand a firm disciplinary squeeze.

Jonathan cleared his own throat.

"Well, sir," he said and returned the other's bleak smile.

"I guess you never expected to see me in New York City," said Mr. Jaimison, plumping himself down in the regal wing chair his wife pushed toward him. "Never expected to find you here either, for that matter, but that's life, eh? I had this business matter to attend to—we'll talk about that later—and I promised Florence that while we were here I'd let a specialist go over me just to satisfy her, but let me tell you, I'm not as close to the cemetery as you think."

"I didn't—" But there was really no use, as Jonathan knew, in trying to make conversation, for Jaimison, Senior, always pitched right into a strident monologue, which was a deaf man's privilege.

"Yes sir, do you know what this doctor told me? Said I had a little liveliness in the kidneys, perfectly natural in a man of sixty, they say, a touch of firming up in the arteries, usual too, and they tell me I've got the liver of a man of forty. Doctor couldn't believe it. 'You've got the liver of a man of forty—maybe thirty-five,' he says. How about that? Ha ha ha!"

"Ha ha ha!" said Florence, nodding toward Jonathan in an invitation to join the fun.

"Ha," ventured Jonathan, and wondered if he was expected to ask for a peek at this splendid organ.

"Tell Jonathan what he said about your heart," she urged and leaned toward Jonathan confidentially. "I thought it was a heart attack but it was only gas. Ha ha ha."

"Ha," agreed Jonathan and nodded politely while Mr. Jaimison delivered a full medical report, straight A's from sinuses to urine, minuses where it would have been promiscuous to be plus, prophecies of future gains and natural losses declaimed in the cheery manner of a smooth treasurer reassuring doubtful stockholders. When he paused to cough for emphasis, Jonathan coughed in sympathy; when he bared his dentures in a stiff smile, Jonathan arranged one on his own face. For there was no doubt about it, the old man was doing his best to be civil, flailing his olive branch around like a horsewhip, determined to bring up a bucket of bubbling geniality from the long-dry well. But why? Jonathan wondered.

Having finished off the medical report, Jaimison, Senior, launched into an equally gratifying and equally confidential description of his new Chevy, enumerating on his fingers (with Jonathan checking the tabulation involuntarily on his own fingers) the reasons he had chosen this car against other candidates, the real reason being that he never changed his mind about anything, so why would he change his car? During this talk Florence's eyes kept seeking out Jonathan's anxiously for approval, and if he smiled her hard enameled face cracked open wide enough to show a king's ransom in porcelain caps. When she saw his eyes straying in the direction of the bar, she whispered, "The lawyer sent the bottle to us as a gift. Would you like a highball? Okay?"

Extraordinary, Jonathan thought, nodding dumbly. The spectacle of a drink in Jonathan's hands stopped Mr. Jaimison's oration sharply. Forgetting his new warmth, he gave a disapproving snort. He himself never drank except for business, just as he never laughed except for business. It infuriated him that a man could drink half your bottle before your eyes and not even make a fool of himself. If he would only fall on his face, have a fit, or do something to give a non-drinker legitimate excuse to feel superior!

However, an admonitory glance from his wife made him content to mutter only, "More accidents from drunken driving."

"I've never had a car," Jonathan said.

"Throw away your money on taxis, eh." Mr. Jaimison grunted.

"Now, Father," chided Florence, evidently bent on maintaining a truce. She startled Jonathan by giving him a conspiratorial wink, saying, "You know how your father always travels by car, business or pleasure, ever since we bought the Chevy for our honeymoon. He isn't really himself till he's behind the wheel."

No need to remind him of that, Jonathan thought, remembering the blue Chevy tooling up Aunt Tessie's driveway in response to a dozen or more pleas from her for Jonathan's schooling, clothes, or even for simple advice. He recalled how determinedly the gentleman had shunted off appeals by launching into endless travelogues on trips he had just taken with his new wife through the Great Smokies, the New England lakes, the Berkshires, the Adirondacks, Route this and Thruway that, detour here and ferry there, just jump in the car and away, away through those great open spaces between Esso and Gulf. Dizzy from these vicarious tours, discouraged by the inability to interrupt, Jonathan would give up and dreamily observe the caller's evasion tactics. He had a vague image of Jaimison *père,* in the plaid cap and goggles of the early motorist, perpetually gypsying through cloverleafs and underpasses, skyways and byways, oblivious to everything but Stop and Go, knowing it was South by Dr. Pepper signs and Hot Shoppes, North by tonic ads and Howard Johnsons (allowing for the recent exchange of these clues), but happy in the one sure thing that he was safe at the wheel. What a fortress! Nobody and nothing could ever get at a man behind the wheel of his own God-given car. Nor was there any talent in the world as valuable as Mr. Jaimison's superior gift for parking.

"Your father thinks you should have a car," Florence said radiantly, just as Jonathan was musing that he hated the automobile.

"Every good citizen ought to have a car," stated Mr. Jaimison. "Something to show for himself, as I see it."

"Maybe Jonathan thinks owning his own home is most important for a young man." Florence again smiled at him with the coy wink. "Okay?"

Jonathan mumbled something about cars and houses being furthest from his mind, but Mr. Jaimison did not hear him, nor did he hear Florence's murmured explanation that Father should really get a hearing aid, and didn't Jonathan think the high cost would be justified? Jonathan wanted to reply that next to his gift for parking, Father enjoyed his deafness, for all he ever wanted to hear from anybody was "Yes, sir." He didn't want to hear persiflage, or requests for loans, or tales of woe, and the resulting lack of wear and tear on his emotions kept his brow unfurrowed, his eye clear, and his pockets full. What were the pair of them getting at, anyway, with their talk of cars and houses? There must be money in it somewhere, just as Aunt Tessie had prophesied, and Jonathan began dreaming of hundred-dollar bills, or why not five-hundred-dollar bills? Whose face was on a five-hundred-dollar bill? he wondered. For all he knew it might be that of Jaimison, Senior. He'd take whatever the old buzzard offered, he decided, and run.

But Mr. Jaimison had gotten on an even more curious subject as he twirled his cigar. He hoped, he said, that Jonathan had not been permanently discouraged by failing to make good in Silver City. He would admit frankly that Florence had blamed him for not taking a firm hand with him when Jonathan was falling down on his jobs, but the way things were turning out now he would guarantee that Jonathan could go right back home and open his own offices as big as you please and have the town behind him in no time.

"I don't say you could do it alone, mind you," said Mr. Jaimison, "but I've built up a solid business reputation back there, and with me behind you you've got nothing to worry about. I'd retire in another few years from the mills, anyway, and with our own business started I could step in full time. I looked at offices for you in the Gas Building—"

"Offices? For me?" Jonathan thought the drink must be affecting his own hearing, gu'ped it down hastily, and then decided another one would clear his head. He jumped up and poured it, not even seeing Mr. Jaimison's instinctive gesture of disapproval. Florence gave a little gasp and leaped up to snatch Jonathan's glass and plant a coaster firmly beneath it before restoring it to him. Mr. Jaimison watched this operation and Jonathan's greedy gulping of the second drink with tight lips.

"I did not realize that alcohol was so necessary to you, Jonathan," he said.

"Everybody has his own fuel," Jonathan said. "You have to have gas, and I have to have alcohol."

Mr. Jaimison saw no reason to reply to this flippancy. He drummed his fingers on the arm of his chair.

"Now about your office," he began firmly. "I can see that you can be set up by the first of the year. Give you time to straighten out here in New York and get back home and look over the situation. Being on the spot myself will save you a lot, of course, while the lawyers are speeding up the settlement—"

"What's he talking about?" Jonathan asked Florence.

"The inheritance," Florence said. "Your father had to handle the whole thing when nobody knew where you were, and then the chance to buy this real-estate business came along at the same time, so he thought he'd settle that too, advancing you the money himself. Too good a chance for you to invest in a permanent job, so to say."

Jonathan looked from one to the other glassily. Either he was dreaming or they were both crazy.

"I guess you'll be glad to get back home, eh, son," said Jaimison, Senior, with a benign chuckle. "We Jaimisons never like city life. I suppose I've traveled through every sizable city in the country and you can have them all—Detroit, Columbus, New York. Another thing. That money will be a nice little fortune back home, but it wouldn't last you five years in New York. I guess you realize that."

"What money?" Jonathan asked patiently.

"This money we're telling you about," said Mr. Jaimison with a hint of his old irascibility. "The money this party left your mother when he died. Naturally they had to come to me trying to locate her, and I handled it as far as I could till Tessie told us how to locate you, get your signature on things and all that. The way I see it, you'll be set up in a foolproof business for life and can hold your head up with the rest of them. The lawyer—he sent me that scotch you're drinking, by the way—says I've done everything his client would have asked by way of protecting your interests. You'll be seeing him."

Jonathan made an involuntary move toward the bottle, but Florence forestalled him, hastily pouring out a few drops into his glass.

"Jonathan's more surprised than we were." Florence giggled. "Wasn't it foxy of your mother never to mention any of those investments she was making in New York when she worked here?"

"Had me paying through the nose for years, mind you, and all the time this fortune tucked away in New York!" Mr. Jaimison interrupted. "By George, I was mad when I found out, but, come to think it over, it works out all the better all around. Seems her employer invested her money so well that it's mounted to real sizable proportions. A couple hundred thousand dollars is a neat little nest egg, Jonathan, even in these times."

"Whose nest egg? What employer?" Jonathan shouted.

Florence put a finger to her lips, smiling.

"I don't blame you for being excited. Your father didn't write because he didn't know where to find you at first and he kept holding off the lawyer while he sort of got things ready and straightened out the details. The Major, it seems, never knew of your mother's death, so that had to be straightened out."

"Major?"

"Her employer, Major Wedburn," Mr. Jaimison said. "I don't suppose you ever heard of him, either. I never listened to your mother gabbing away about New York, so I daresay it's my own fault for not knowing she was making a whacking lot of money, but—"

Major Wedburn. The man whose funeral was being mourned by the De Long that first day in New York. Claire Van Orphen had said Connie Birch had typed for him. So the Major had left her a fortune in the guise of "investments." Jonathan sat clutching the arms of his chair, trying to keep his thoughts from plunging toward the inevitable conclusion, while Jaimison, Senior, talked on and on, waving envelopes and papers at him, thrusting memos into his hand, and sugaring his voice resolutely.

"Why don't you want your offices to be in the Gas Building, my boy?"

"Because I don't like gas," Jonathan said feebly. "Anyway, I don't need any offices."

Mr. Jaimison was controlling his impatience admirably.

"But I leased them for five years out of my own pocket!" he said. "Naturally I knew you'd settle with me later. There's your real-estate business all set up for you, son."

"Not real estate!" Jonathan cried, seeing Darcy's greedy little face.

"Okay, your father could get you into the bank," Florence said with a firm nod to her husband. "You've got to have everything safely settled. These people trying to get your mother to back them because they had claims on the Major are likely to come after you, and you'd have no protection."

"Once you're dug in they can't get at you," said Mr. Jaimison. "Let 'em sue. Claiming the Major wanted his money used to support a dirty little art gallery. Claiming there's some mistake somewhere."

"Show him the letters," Florence urged. "You'll see that your father was very clever, planning your protection from those sharks."

Jonathan read the letters Jaimison, Senior, thrust into his hand as a final argument. Cassie Bender wished Mrs. Jaimison to be her partner in the Bender Art Gallery, inasmuch as they seemed to have been partners in the late Major's affections. In a later letter Mrs. Bender reminded Mrs. Jaimison of how much they both owed him, and how beholden they both should be to his well-known tastes, creating a monument of sorts to his beloved memory, carry-

ing on his torch, so to speak. A third letter begged the
fortunate heiress to regard herself as heir to the Major's
responsibilities as well as to his rewards, and Mrs. Bender
was confident the Bender Art Gallery was the Major's
prime concern before his untimely end.

"She doesn't know my mother died." Jonathan cut into
the buzz of Jaimison's voice going on about stocks, per-
centages, taxes.

"We ignored her letters, of course," Mr. Jaimison said,
a note of weariness creeping into his tone, for it was only
his wife's admonitory glances and headshakes that kept
his temper down. "As I say, we've saved you all we could."

"But she's right," Jonathan said. "I must talk this over
with her."

"Jonathan!"

This time Mr. Jaimison's honest rage over his son's blind
stupidity was too much for him and he shook his fists in
the air.

"Twenty-five years old, and the boy still can't think
straight! Twenty-five years old!" he exploded.

"Twenty-six," interrupted Jonathan, his courage restored by the exhibition of the old Jaimison temper. "Born
November twenty-eighth, nineteen twenty-nine, just six
months and a half after your wedding day."

There now, see what that brings up, old boy, he exulted.

"Premature, yes, yes," Mr. Jaimison snapped back savagely. "The only time in your whole career that you weren't
backward!"

"Father, now Father!" pleaded Florence with an imploring glance at Jonathan. "All of us having such a nice
reunion here, and the future so rosy, and here we are
quarreling. It does seem, Jonathan, that you ought to be
grateful to your father for protecting your interests after

the way you ran away without so much as good-by, and the lawyer hunting for you too."

"I'll see him myself," Jonathan said, stuffing papers into his pocket.

"But what are your plans? You've got to plan your future, son, all that money going to waste instead of into a nice business," Mr. Jaimison wailed. "What will you do?"

"I'm going into the art business," Jonathan said. "Just like Mrs. Bender said. Sort of a monument to my—I mean to Major Wedburn. Good-by, sir, and look out for that liver."

In the hall he heard his name called and saw Jaimison, Senior, standing in the doorway, mopping his forehead helplessly. He mopped his own brow as the elevator went down, then put his handkerchief away.

"Maybe it was one of the Major's habits too," he re-assured himself.

He came out into the early autumn twilight of the park and sat down on the first bench he saw. He felt giddy. He saw the Sultana lights go on and wondered if it was all a dream. But there were the papers in his pocket. He glanced at the address on Cassie Bender's letter. Her gallery was just across the park.

Jonathan headed eastward.

# 13

CLAIRE VAN ORPHEN looked smaller and older when Jonathan finally paid her a visit. Just a few months made a difference after sixty, he thought, or was it the trimly modern black wool suit, paler make-up, and tidier coiffure that her sister's influence had brought about? To tell the truth he could not conjure up a picture of her old self, blurred as it was by his intense concern with his own problems, and having seen only himself in her eyes.

"Don't you think it's too grand for me?" she asked, with an apologetic wave toward the McKinley plush decor of the De Long Presidential suite. "I've been budgeting and scrimping for so many years I can't enjoy splurging unless I balance it by doing without something else. My sister Beatrice is just the opposite. That's one reason our plan to live together didn't work out."

Jonathan looked admiringly at the sooty but imposing chandeliers, the huge marble fireplace with its electric logs, the balding bear rug sprawled over the faded rose carpet. Arched doors at either end of the room were closed on one side and open on the other to reveal bedroom walls gay with frolicking cupids, bluebirds, and butterflies from a giddier period. There was a combined air of Victorian closed parlors and musty potpourri that seemed deliciously romantic to Jonathan, more luxurious by far than Cassie Bender's bleak modernity.

"It's exactly the way my mother described it when she worked for you," he said. "So this was the place."

"Indeed no, my rooms were much simpler," Claire corrected him. "This was always Major Wedburn's suite, right up to the day he died. He kept it just this way no matter where he was traveling. I took over his lease, thinking of Beatrice, of course, but instead it turns out to be useful for Earl Turner, my collaborator. He has the Major's library there." She nodded toward the closed doors. "You know Earl Turner. Oh dear, I forget. You introduced us."

"I haven't seen him for some time," Jonathan said. "I'm afraid he went to some trouble to contact Alvine Harshawe for me and it—well, it didn't work out as he thought."

"We've been so busy on our scripts, as I told you," Claire said tactfully, remembering that Earl was annoyed with the young man. "He feels we must ride our luck while we've got it. Goodness knows how long we can last. Do you mind ready-made Manhattans?"

"I missed our little parties," Jonathan said, sinking into a titanic overstuffed chair beside her coffee table. "So many things have been happening."

He did look different, Claire thought. Was it the handsome vest or was it something about the eyes? She wished she had not been affected by Earl's and George Terrence's disappointment in him, but it had been naughty of him to get poor George Terrence in such a state, especially since she had been the one responsible for their meeting. And Hazel phoning around like a mad creature, saying George kept confessing to a mysterious past and getting himself analyzed and that she was coming into the city to help with her daughter's career, and why had Claire set him off with that sinister young man anyway? Hazel was a fool, true enough, but still—

"I hope everything is going well," she said, feeling guilty for the many times she had had to refuse his visits in the last few months because of her own new preoccupations. How selfish of her, no matter how mischievous he had been with others, when he had brought so much light and luck into her lonely old age! It was the old ones who were the heartless ones, drawing all the blood they could out of the young and then shrugging them off. Even as she was repenting she found herself peeping at her watch to see how much time she had before the conference with the CBS director.

Jonathan had been eager to share his news with his mother's old friend, but he saw now that her life was filled without him, and there seemed no way to begin again.

"I've had a little luck," he said, but it was no good wasting his dramatic confidence on the polite, strained atmosphere. Besides, people accustomed to advising and helping you were often ruffled when you became independent, as if they liked your need of them more than they liked you.

"I came to ask you about Major Wedburn," Jonathan said. "I should like to have known that man."

Claire could not keep back a laugh.

"You and the Major! I can't think of a funnier combination!"

"I'm sure we would have gotten on," Jonathan protested. "That's why I want to know more about him."

"I'm afraid you would have found him pompous, but he was a great gentleman for all his quirks," Claire said. "Our families were very close. I was touched when he left me the Cecilia Beaux portrait of his grandfather, which hangs in the bedroom."

"My mother spoke of a Cecilia Beaux picture," Jonathan said. "Funny she never mentioned the Major."

"Very strange," Claire said. She and Earl had come to the private conclusion that Jonathan's mother had been a very strange young woman in many ways. She was glad to be asked about the Major instead of Connie Birch, for she knew her disapproval would show.

"He must have been a gay old dog," said Jonathan.

"I don't think anyone could ever have called the Major a gay dog," Claire said. "A man of the world, I grant you, but a most discreet one. I daresay there were women in his life, but he took care that no one knew it."

"Then he could have had a secret affair," Jonathan persisted.

Now what made him pry into that?

"He was a secretive man, very fussy about hiding his lady friends from the world, and from each other," she said, controlling her impatience with the young man's curiosity. "At one time he was courting my sister Bea and myself at the very same time, and we didn't check till years later. He'd been playing us against each other. I suppose he fancied himself a strategist."

Jonathan smiled.

"Sometimes a man has to be," he said, thinking of Lize and Darcy.

"Bea was put out when she found he had left me the portrait," Claire said and sighed. "But then Bea has been very touchy these last few weeks. Quite by chance I bought a new suit at Bonwit's, and it turned out Bea had bought the identical suit that very morning at Bergdorf's. Our minds used to work like that in the old days. But Bea was so horrified at being a twin again that she raged at me. Sent her suit right back. Do you know that I cried myself to sleep for the first time in twenty years? No one can hurt you like your own twin!"

Tears came to her eyes again and she only nodded sadly when Jonathan asked permission to look at the picture.

In the bedroom Jonathan studied the portrait of the Major's grandfather seated at a great desk, quill pen in hand, open record book before him, a pair of black Dachshunds at his feet. He was a stout dark man, and though Jonathan could trace no resemblance to himself, in an odd way he looked familiar. The strong Roman nose, the beetling eyebrows, the bullish shoulders—why, he might have been Jaimison, Senior! He was grasping the pen as if it were a steering wheel, the notebook was a ledger in which he was adding up his toll fees, the keen gaze was searching beyond for the next Howard Johnson. Quite shaken, Jonathan came back to Miss Van Orphen's side.

"The Major looked just like him." Claire answered Jonathan's unspoken question.

"There must have been something else about him," Jonathan mused, "something my mother found and loved."

Good heavens, not the Major too!

"Oh, no!" Claire said, wincing. "You can't do this to my old friend, Jonathan! I don't care how dead your mother is, she ought to be ashamed of herself, stirring up the poor Major's ashes, a fine man she barely knew—no, no!"

"But you yourself told me he admired her so much!" Jonathan protested, confused by her genuine indignation. "You told me he advised her to go back home and marry and have children. You told me—"

"I was making it up!" Claire cried. "I couldn't remember

anything except that he had sent her to me for typing, but I didn't want to disappoint you, so I made up little lies!"

"They weren't lies," Jonathan said. "It was truer than you know. That's why he left his money to her, and now it's going to be mine. I tried to tell you before, but you were always busy on your work. Major Wedburn was my father."

Claire drew a long breath, poured another drink from her shaker, and filled Jonathan's glass as an afterthought. Everything was so upsetting—Bea's recent tantrums, the Terrences in her life again, and now the shock about the Major.

"Why do you young people have to stir up everything?" she burst out passionately and was immediately contrite. "Oh dear, it's not your fault. Forgive me. I should be thinking of how upsetting it must be for you, finding that your mother had so many lovers."

"But that explains so much to me," Jonathan said, surprised that she did not see this. "She wanted to be whatever anybody expected her to be, because she never knew what she was herself. That's the way I am, you see. And now that I know the Major had several different lives too, I understand myself better."

Claire was silent, trying to piece together these missing pieces from the Major's past. It was hard to work up sex jealousy thirty years later, but she could, at least, feel a sense of outraged decency that her first and only affair, a romantic secret between her and the Major, should have its memory fouled by that appalling young woman. How blind she had been not to see it all under her nose, but as usual she always missed the obvious, thinking of the little typist with her wide, eager eyes as charmingly naïve, and herself, ten years older, so worldly-wise! Thinking herself sophisticated with her one love affair in thirty-odd years, when the little country mouse, barely twenty, was having an affair with every man she met as if it were no more than a curtsy! And the Major leaving a fortune to the girl, tacitly admitting his paternity! But then old men always fancied themselves as dangerously fertile, and a girl could persuade the canniest Casanova that his merest handclasp had born fruit. George Terrence, of course— "of course" indeed, when she had never even guessed it at the time—was intent on producing living proof of a guilty past to cover up that brief experiment in homosexuality. Bea had told her about it. Bea always knew those things. Her little circle uptown doted on such tidbits about priggish old gentlemen like George.

"It did seem to me that Alvine Harshawe was the logical man in your mother's life," Claire said. "I understand he admitted it freely to his wife when her divorce suit claimed he was sterile. Of course he can't convince anyone he's sane when he insists on staying on in Harkness Pavilion, soaking up background for a psychiatric play, so Earl says. But what your mother wrote fitted him far more than it did George or the Major."

"I found that what she said fitted everyone," Jonathan explained. "She thought every man she met in New York was Prince Charming and whatever they asked must be the proper thing. She was afraid to seem ignorant or small-town. It's the way I am. That's why we were misfits in our small town. People there—especially the Jaimisons— are *proud* of their ignorance because it's been in the family such a long time."

Claire felt herself melting again under his radiant smile. He shouldn't be blamed for shaking up all these little tempests, and she would say as much to Earl. Considering their own change of luck, they had no right to mistrust the boy's windfall, no matter how preposterous the circumstances.

"I'm investing the Major's money in the way I believe he would approve," Jonathan confided. He handed one of his new cards to her.

"Jonathan Jaimison, Associate Director, Bender Gallery," she read aloud in bewilderment.

"Mrs. Bender thinks I have inherited the Major's natural flair," Jonathan said. "The lawyers consider it a good deal."

Now why should he have to apologize for coming up in the world? Jonathan asked himself.

"But what about your own talent?" Claire said.

"I never could find out what it was," he said. "All I know is that I do appreciate other men's talents, and this way I have a career of other people's talents. I hoped you'd understand."

Claire knew she was squinting suspiciously at the card, trying not to speak out her doubts and warnings, when she should be rejoicing at his news. But that Mrs. Bender! The Major would surely be shocked at such a collaboration. She read in the boy's face that she was failing him, not responding at all as he expected. But he was old enough to know she could not help being loyal to her own generation.

"I'm afraid the Major's tastes in art were totally opposed to the Bender Gallery's," she said bravely. "Winslow Homer was his idol, you know, and he loved Albert Ryder. When the gallery next door had a few Hugow paintings on show I remember the Major getting absolutely indignant."

Jonathan's face clouded.

"I thought of him as more cosmopolitan," he said. "I thought he was someone I'd want to be like."

"The Major was terribly proud of his family," Claire said. "He always tried to go to the family reunions at Christmas in Hartford. And he loved touring around the country in his Lincoln, until the last few years. He was a very conservative man."

Maybe family reunions were different in Hartford, Jonathan thought gloomily, and maybe touring the country in a Lincoln was not as dreary as in a Jaimison vehicle.

"You don't think we'd have gotten on, then," he said.

"I can't picture your having a thing in common," Claire said, shaking her head. "Indeed this all seems incredible, Jonathan."

She was relieved to see Earl Turner come in at that moment.

"Just left the Spur," he told Jonathan. "They tell me you don't come in any more since you made it uptown. Can't say I blame you now the West Coast bums have moved in. The old crowd seems drifting down to The Big Hat."

For a man who had come to success after decades of failure, Earl looked very morose, Jonathan thought. The frozen boyishness now seemed old and dried, petulant more than cynical. The familiar beret was gone, that was it, and the revealed bony bald head added years.

"So Cassie Bender's got you under her wing," he said, tossing back the card Claire passed to him. "It's part of the course. And the grapevine has it that your family came to the city and handed you a fat check."

"Something on that order," Jonathan said.

"Maybe you could advance me twenty until the first," Earl said.

Claire looked at him in amazement.

"Why, Earl, you just got a check for five thousand dollars!"

Earl threw up his hands.

"I can't help it!" he said. "You spend your life thinking in two-bit terms, and that's the only money that's real. Now, when I realize it's my own dough I'm spending it doesn't seem right. With nobody trailing me with duns, nobody hounding me to pay up, honest to God, I get withdrawal symptoms! My whole system is geared for the old way."

"Never mind," Claire comforted him. "It probably won't last."

"It's not just money," Earl said. "At the Spur I started to tell Dan about the new series we're doing for CBS and I saw he didn't believe me, but I didn't believe myself either. Damn it, it was true! I was bragging. It's all right to lie, but a man can't brag when it's true."

He rose impatiently and started toward the library doors.

"I'll straighten out that ending before our man gets here. We have twenty minutes," he said.

"Shall I reserve a table downstairs for dinner?" Claire asked him. "It's roast beef night."

"I can't eat the slops here," Earl said. "We can order tuna-fish sandwiches sent over from the Planet."

"I wish you'd visit the gallery sometime," Jonathan said, unwilling to accept their indifference.

"I can't see how that old warhorse Cassie Bender hooked a smart kid like you for a patsy," Earl observed. "It just doesn't figure."

"She hasn't hooked me. I think of it as the opportunity of a lifetime!" Jonathan exclaimed. "I'll be traveling all over, meeting wonderful people—look at my credit cards!

Cassie arranged everything for me. I know what people say—"

It was no use, he saw by their shocked faces. He picked up his own card and the credit cards he had childishly flaunted and stuck them back in his wallet. It was tiresome having to defend bighearted, overbearing Cassie wherever he went. It was no use expecting these old friends to receive him back into their arms, eager for his confidences. Old people thought only of themselves. Each one alone might be his champion, but together—and he had combined them himself!—they closed ranks, leaving the young intruder outside once again.

"I just wanted to say hello," he said. "I'll run along now."

The boy's feelings must have been hurt, Claire thought remorsefully, but after all one had one's own work and one's own life to live. The young never seemed to understand that. But you had so little time left, and it seemed as if you dared not stop running for a minute. You didn't run to win the prize as you did in youth. Indeed your dimming eyes could not tell if you'd passed the goal or not. You went on running because in the end that was the only prize there was—to be alive, to be in the race.

# 14

Dr. Kellsey was amazed to find himself installed in the larger apartment next to his old one within a month after he'd suggested it to the landlord of Knowlton Arms. He had been talking of this change for twenty years and it might have taken that long again to put his decision into effect. But here he was, books, screen, and pictures moved over in a trice, the studio couch for Jonathan in the living-room alcove, snug as you please, his own couch in the bedroom, empty closet and dressing room for Jonathan, separate door to bedroom so they could have their privacy. Everything settled but Jonathan, and he had left that to the last.

Now the die was cast, the professor reflected, a little frightened at the *definiteness* of things. Jonathan had been evasive when the hint to share his quarters had first been made, but he was a shy lad and would need to see that the place was all ready for him, no trouble was involved, and any responsibility was on the doctor's side. As they were both sensitive fellows they probably would be embarrassed to admit their secret relationship in so many words, but Jonathan must have recognized the facts just as the doctor had.

What worried the doctor was the problem of his lady friend, Anita. She had been urging this move on him for years, as part of her program for his divorcing Deborah and marrying her. A larger apartment would only mean to her that he had surrendered at last, and he would be in for a bad time explaining first the move and then Jonathan. The excuse of "private reasons" was a red flag to women anyway, sure to make them flip.

Pondering these matters sent Dr. Kellsey into a flip of his own for the period between the close of his summer term and the opening of the fall term. He spent this vacation, as he often had done in the past, in civilized drinking, a relaxation conducted in his two-and-a-half room apartment exactly as it had been in his one-and-a-half. It meant days on days unshaven, pajamaed, phone unhooked, incinerator clanking with empty bottles and broken glasses, a copper bowl of quarters by the hall door to hand out to liquor deliverers, delicatessen messengers, then a rehabilitation period presaged by a doctor's visit, drugstore deliveries, valet and laundrymen bringing and taking, a visiting barber, the public stenographer, newspapers, signs indicating reform was under way. Finally, the phone back on the hook, the hand and voice a little shaky but curable by the usual restoratives, the professor was ready to resume a gentleman's life, academic duties organized, the new autumn taken in stride.

He had not heard from his messages to Jonathan but was not concerned—young men were always dilatory—and it gave him time to butter up Anita meanwhile. He had agreed to meet her uptown at five and then escort her to Cassie Bender's preview party.

Pausing for a pair of quick ones at the club made him late at the start, and he had built up an even greater sense of guilt by the time he glimpsed Anita standing in the green glass shadows of the Lever Building. It struck him that she looked uncommonly calm for a girl who'd been kept waiting on a street corner for a good half hour. He had feared to find her pacing up and down, angry little eyes rolling from north to south to wristwatch, lighting a cigarette to place in holder, puff-puff and throw away, then lighting another in that fierce way she had, as if she was cooking his goose, but good, and snorting out smoke like Fafner himself.

"Hi!" she cried, waving her purse at him as merrily as any film star welcoming photographers. "Here I am."

No reproaches for breaking dates. No words about being late. Suspiciously Dr. Kellsey gave her his arm and they turned up Park.

"Good to see you," he said experimentally. Instead of saying, "Well, it's about time," Anita turned on him a radiant smile. Now that he was about to break up with her, he realized that years of familiarity had blinded him to Anita's good points. The sharp gypsy-dark face had good features, nostrils flaring a bit like a nervy racehorse's, upper lip too long and sulky, true, and the thin mouth shirred into a sort of bee-bite in the middle, fixed for a perpetual umlaut. Or an *œuf* or *œil*. More likely *eek*, he reflected. But good chin lines, he admitted generously, good planes, photogenically speaking, decent figure; she always boasted of walking right out of the store in standard size 12, triple-A shoe size 8, 32 bra—oh, there was nothing the matter with Anita's looks except that a mean fairy had taken them over at birth, squinching up everything somehow.

"I didn't mind waiting," she said. "I love watching the characters in this neighborhood. They fit the new archi-

tecture, all spare and bleak and hollow-looking. I'm sure
their X-rays look like the blueprints for a modern sky-
scraper."

"The women with all their organs out and the men with
all their ulcers in," Walter retorted, feeling thrown off by
her beamish mood, unable to utilize his prepared defense.

"No, really, there is a kind of stark purity—a sort of
Mondrian quality that gets me," Anita said dreamily.

"What about a Hugow quality, since this is his day?"
Walter said, falling at once into the clumsy-witted state
that Anita's arch fantasy moods always threw him.

"Now, Walter, please!" Anita twittered. "Hugow has
depth, mystery, all the things you lack, darling, so of course
you wouldn't understand. Oh, poor Cassie Bender will
make a fortune out of this show."

Walter glanced uneasily at the sunny uptilted counte-
nance usually clouded with discontent, and sure to be
when he got around to giving her his news. Yes, she had
the smug well-fed look of someone who had just done in
her best friend for his own good. And here she was with a
good word for Hugow ("terribly overrated" was her usual
opinion of him) and a tender word for Cassie Bender ("a
vulgar nymphomaniac" was her habitual epithet). The
simple exhibition of good humor alarmed Walter much
more than her needling could. In fact Anita's caustic view
of their acquaintances was a major charm for him, blotting
out his own aching jealousy of all forms of success and
permitting him the nice role of bighearted forgiver. ("Now,
now, Anita, let's be fair. No one can be that bad, dear girl,
they must have *something*.") And if she wasn't going to
attack him for his neglect, he would have to make the first
move himself.

"I'm sorry to have missed your calls and our usual Friday

dinners," he began, "but I was busy moving, you see—"

"So they told me at the club," Anita interrupted. "Don't give it a thought, Walter. I understood perfectly."

"But you see a strange thing happened," he went on doggedly. "It turns out there is a young chap in town who is the son of an old friend of mine, that is to say, she was a pupil of mine years ago."

"You do too much for your students, Walter," Anita said. "I've often told Dr. Jasper that that is our only trouble."

Suddenly the reason for her serenity dawned on the professor. Why, of course! She had just left her analyst's couch and had had her ego stroked for an hour by Dr. Jasper! He'd forgotten she had started that again. For a few hours after each consultation she enjoyed a state of glorious euphoria that merely having the money to buy analysis gives some people. Walter began steaming all over at the thought of the intimate revelations in Anita's folder on her "relationship" with himself. No use getting into that old psychoanalysis hassle, though, when there were bigger arguments ahead.

"He's given me so much help in adjusting to our relationship," Anita said somberly.

Help. Adjust. Relationship. How he hated the words, Walter thought irritably. Anita's problem was not a sense of inadequacy in herself but in her feeling overadequate to handle other people's inadequacies. She certainly didn't need a doctor to reassure her of her superiority. What she really wanted was for everybody else to be analyzed into admitting their wretched inferiority.

"He says the reason you don't have the normal philoprogenitive instincts is because you are compensated by being the father image to your students," Anita confided.

Father image!

"Does he think I was born a father image?" Dr. Kellsey exclaimed. "What about the students I had of my own age years ago? Doesn't this shrinker know there are a lot of other images in his old sample case? Doesn't he—"

He stopped, for Anita was giggling girlishly.

"I do think you're jealous of Dr. Jasper," she said. "That always happens and you're afraid I'm transferring."

Transfer! But he mustn't let her throw him. Instead he pointed toward the latest glass building under construction.

"Goldfish, that's what these damn architects would have us turn into!" he declaimed. "But the trouble is that some of us are toads and ought to be decently hidden."

Anita gave a silvery laugh.

"Oh, Walter, don't waste your marvelous epigrams on poor little me," she cried. "There'll be all sorts of clever people at Cassie's who can appreciate your wit properly."

"Look, we don't have to go to this show," Dr. Kellsey burst out. "I'm sick of this Hugow worship wherever I go. I can't stand that faded blond art madam, either. Let's skip it and have a quiet steak down at Costello's where we can talk."

Anita drew a white-gloved hand from his arm and batted her beadies at him reproachfully.

"I didn't realize you felt so hostile toward Cassie Bender," she said.

"Hostile!" echoed Dr. Kellsey savagely.

"And you can't downgrade Hugow's painting. Everyone says he's the best this year," she said.

Now the professor was really angry.

"I'm sick of this new cultural Gay Payoo," he shouted. "I can't stand Picasso or baseball or Louis Armstrong or boxers or folksongs or people's children or new faces, but

if I open my mouth to say so a crowd closes in on me ready
to get me deported. What about a little freedom of thought?
You're as bad as the others, Anita, afraid to have an opinion of your own."

"Just because I don't agree with you, Wally, isn't that
it?" Anita laughed, infuriatingly, above his heckling.
"Come along, you silly boy, there'll be champagne and
you'll love it. La la la."

She was humming "Three Coins in the Fountain" again
and fondly resumed his arm. The shrinker had certainly
filled her up with self-confidence this time, Walter thought,
and he wondered how long before it would start chipping
off like the lipstick and eyeshadow. Whatever was making
her so satisfied made him jealous, but then he was jealous
of everybody nowadays, jealous of the President of the
United States for all that free rent and gravy, jealous of
cops for their freedom to sock anybody who annoyed them,
jealous of students who could skip his classes, jealous of
Hugow or anybody stupid enough to believe in his own
genius, jealous of happy believers and bold infidels, and
jealous of young men with a whole lifetime ahead to louse
themselves up as they wished. Ridiculous to be jealous of
poor old Anita, especially when she had his bad news
coming to her.

"All right, then, let's go," he snapped, taking long strides
to throw off Anita's prim little high-heeled steps, her
thighs never parting as if afraid of wandering rapists. "I
haven't much time because I must see this young chap I
mentioned, the son of my old student—"

"What's his name?" Anita asked. "Who was his mother?"

He had almost forgotten.

"He is Jonathan Jaimison," he said. "Mother was Connie
Birch."

"I can't understand this sentimentality over an old student," Anita said. "You always claim your classes are just one big moronic sea, so what did this one do to stamp her?"

The familiar indications of a fight soothed and warmed Dr. Kellsey. There was chance of a little sport after all.

"It was long before your time, my dear," he said. "I had just come East and barely begun my classes. This girl had a slender talent—"

"You've always hated slender talents." Anita was now smoldering nicely. "Why do you have to waste time on her son?"

They had reached the entrance to the brownstone where Cassie Bender's modern window stood out, bravely anachronistic.

"For very special reasons that I can't go into right here," he said, amused to watch the chipping-off process begin in earnest as Anita, scowling thunderously, drew back and stoned him with a look. "The father image, as you call it, owes something to the father seeker, wouldn't your good Dr. Jasper say? Here is a too permissive young man with no sense of security in a sea of hostilities and unrewarding relationships. It is my plan to help him to adjust or project, rather, by taking him into my home as if he were, let us say, a son image."

"You wouldn't!" Anita choked. "You mean you took that apartment for him instead of for us! You really meant it to be good-by."

Now he did feel guilty and remorseful, for the poor girl looked white and wild under her careful make-up. As soon as she had put his plan into words he realized that he couldn't say good-by to Anita, any more than he could say good-by to his conscience or, for that matter, to his wife.

"It's to help the boy out till he can look out for himself,"
he said cautiously. "Think of him as a lost boy, Anita, without friends or money in this big city, no place to turn but to
that father image you mention. You shouldn't criticize me,
Anita, for feelings you used to scold me for lacking!"

Ha. He was turning the tables on her, and Anita was too
smart not to know it. She was sniffling a little but softening.
They went into the gallery, through the hall to the glass-
roofed patio, where the party was assembling under a
chandelier mobile.

"At least you can be decent to Cassie," Anita muttered
in his ear as the gallery queen swooped toward them, white
bosom bursting from purple velvet beamed toward them
like truck headlights. "I'm so glad you came early," cried
Cassie, clasping a hand of each guest. "The most marvelous
news for you! I want you to meet my new partner, this
heavenly, heavenly creature, Jonathan Jaimison. Darling,
come meet Dr. Kellsey and Anita Barlowe, such distinguished scholars."

"Jonathan Jaimison?" Anita said, looking at Dr. Kellsey.

The young man was far too handsome, Anita thought,
but then that sort of looks always went fast, thank God.
Cassie was crowing over him in that revolting possessive
hungry, sexy way she had, pawing him as she introduced
him. But Dr. Kellsey's face was more interesting at the moment than Cassie's new partner, who was vigorously shaking the doctor's hand.

"I don't think I heard right," said Dr. Kellsey. "Did Mrs.
Bender say she had a new partner? But that can't be you,
Jonathan."

"Yes, it is a surprise, isn't it?" Jonathan said happily. "I
couldn't think of a better use for my money than to buy
into a business like this."

"I'm teaching him everything I know!" said Cassie with a splendid gesture.

"That's so generous of you," said Anita sweetly. "And so like you."

She could tell that her lover was thoroughly unprepared for this encounter, and, whatever the situation was, it comforted her to have him be the one to squirm for a change.

"So you've left the café," Dr. Kellsey said, "and the East Tenth Street apartment."

"I've caged him in the downstairs studio next door," Cassie said merrily. "Wasn't that clever of me?"

"It's best to be near Teacher, isn't it, Mr. Jaimison?" Anita asked Jonathan. "One never knows when one will need a lesson."

She was annoying Dr. Kellsey, she knew, but she felt she had the right. Poor lost boy with no money and no home indeed! A millionaire, from the way he was dressed, and the talk about buying the business!

"I knew his mother, you see," Dr. Kellsey mumbled, trying to collect his wits in the face of Anita's curled lip. "It was a long time ago. I found some old snapshots, Jonathan, that perhaps might help you in your research."

"Good," said Jonathan. "But I've dropped that research. I've been meaning to tell you."

"I see," said Dr. Kellsey, smiling but stricken. "That happens, of course, to all researchers, as Miss Barlowe here can tell you. The researcher comes upon findings that don't fit in with his preconception, so he loses interest in the game."

Anita was pleased and touched to be mentioned and moved closer. She could tell by the professor's trembling voice and nervous mustache twigging that he was immensely disturbed. Jonathan too was aware of a new sarcastic note in his old friend's voice.

"It was a game, as you say," he conceded warily. "As soon as I talked to Mrs. Bender I saw that here was my future."

"It's absolutely miraculous!" Cassie Bender linked arms with Jonathan, enveloping new visitors in her perfumed aura, clutching one, smiling at another, and speaking into a third one's ear. "You've no idea what a flair this boy has! Don't you agree, Dr. Kellsey, that *appreciation* is a talent in itself? Absolutely apart from criticism or promotion or diagnostic approach? Jonathan *appreciates*."

"It must be heaven," Anita murmured.

"Why, I'd never even heard of Percy Wright until Jonathan brought him to my attention. Wright has taken a good deal from Hugow, true, but Hugow's at his peak and Wright is new, one of the new romantics."

"Hard Edge," explained Jonathan.

"But Soft Middle," said Cassie.

"Ah," said the doctor.

"Champagne?" Jonathan motioned toward the bar. "There's scotch if you'd rather."

"I prefer Hugow," the doctor said absently. "Where is he?"

"He still stands up, doesn't he?" Cassie agreed. "But he makes me so mad when he won't come in! He says he can't stand openings and being talked about as if he was dead. He says the kind of people who like him make him want to give up art and drive a hack. Just between us, I'm glad to find a *gentleman* painter like Percy, after my struggles with Hugow."

"We've tripled his prices," Jonathan reminded her. "Sold out, too."

Cassie was loaded, he thought, and more Southern belle by the minute.

"Then you're no longer the little lost boy without friends

or home," Anita said to him with a charming smile, edging away from her escort's savage nudge. "You've found yourself."

"Of course Dr. Kellsey was a great help to me," Jonathan said, knowing he had failed the doctor miserably and wondering how he could atone for getting lucky. "You understood me, sir, and it meant a lot to me."

It meant too much for the professor.

"Ah, but I was mistaken all the while," he said. "It wasn't the father image you sought, after all, but the mother image. And now you've found your true mother."

Too bad Cassie missed that one, Anita thought. Men were so bitchy.

"How much he looks like Dr. Jasper!" she whispered to Walter. "It's amazing!"

"Really, Anita!" reproved the doctor. In his annoyance, the professor rejected the highball offered by Jonathan, suggesting pointedly to Anita that they must leave. It was Jonathan who was the offender now, greeting new visitors as Cassie drew him away.

"You were so right about Mother Cassie," Anita murmured, following Dr. Kellsey to the exit. "She's absolutely clucking today. I suppose she's sleeping with your little hero. Let's go before she makes us look at the pictures. I can't understand what anybody finds in Hugow."

There was his old Anita, the professor rejoiced, the shrinker's salve all worn away and the dear acidulous, embittered girl back again.

"Now, now," he rebuked her gently. "Cassie isn't all that bad, and you can't miss the basic strength in Hugow, crude though it is. Sure you don't want to stay for the crowd? It would be interesting to see how Jonathan handles them in his new role."

"I hate that Spur crowd and Cassie's rich oafs and the disgusting noises the critics make," Anita said. "Let's go to Costello's for a little honest air—unless, of course, you're afraid your wife will be there."

"Nonsense, Deborah would never be in a place like that," he said, which started Anita all over on a very old tack.

"Like that? Like what? You mean it's too good for me and not good enough for your wife? Or maybe she'll be at that new apartment of yours, meant for everybody but me."

It was like old times, before Jonathan had stirred up his life. The professor tucked Anita's hand under his arm when they got into the taxi and gently reminded her that a man's wife did have first rights to his apartment, new or old. By the time they got out at Costello's for steak and quiet talk they weren't speaking to each other.

It was good to be back in the ring.


The Hugow opening was a sensational success by Golden Spur standards. One minute before eight, the hour the party was slated to close, an entire new saloonful of art-lovers roared in from the Muse's farthest reaches. A sea of arms reached in the air for drinks as if for basketballs and passed them over heads of immobilized figures. Museum directors, critics, dilettantes were pushed into the paintings they admired; oldtimers accustomed to snubbing each other found themselves glued together, buttocks to buttocks, lipstick to hairy ear, beard to bra. The barstool artflies took over, and Jonathan's nightmare began.

"Jonathan, you stinker, get out the hooch, you know where the bitch keeps it! . . . Can you imagine that jerk locking up the bar when his old pals walk in? . . . Hugow would kill the guy if he knew they were holding out on his old friends. . . . Get it out, you dirty scab."

The more distinguished guests were being knocked down as they fought for their minks under the mountains of duffel coats, and leather jackets, and there were cries of "Thief! . . . Get the police. . . . Get Hugow! Get a doctor."

Jonathan's efforts to sneak more bottles into the party only reminded his old buddies that he was in a position now to do even more for them, and they despised him for it.

"I got to have forty-five bucks for my loft, Jonny-boy. If I get Hugow to put down a few lines on a card, how much will you pay for it?"

Whatever he said or did was wrong and brought forth jeers, none louder than when Cassie obliged him to announce the doors were being locked. He knew they regarded him as an informer now, but he hated himself too, wishing he could be put out with them instead of putting them out. He had looked forward to this great day as a kind of debut for himself, the more so because Cassie had kept postponing it for greater thunder. He would show his old friends that he was going to be a friend indeed. He had hoped to show Hugow too, but the artist had disappeared on some private binge, and Jonathan found himself agreeing with Cassie that an artist should be more *responsible,* more *mature,* more *considerate.*

"Is that what I'm going to be?" he asked himself, shocked. "Am I going to think Percy Wright is a finer painter because he takes off his hat in elevators?"

Long before the mob had poured in, Cassie, following her usual practice, had siphoned off the plummier guests to her own private quarters for caviar and champagne and inside chatter.

"Do get rid of everybody and come back here," she begged Jonathan. "Tell them I have a headache or passed out or anything."

"Jonny is Cassie Bender's bouncer!" jeered someone as Jonathan tried to guide a sneaker-footed stumbler to the door, and Jonathan was annoyed at Cassie for humiliating him, at the victim, at himself, and at the taunter for speaking the truth. His anger gave him strength to push the intruders outward, though they rushed out as suddenly as they had advanced when word spread that the Jackson Gallery party further down the avenue was still on. There was a hint that Hugow himself had gone to that party instead of his own, which made everyone gleeful.

In the gallery Jonathan stood panting from his exertions, brushing his sleeves, straightening his tie and hair; a regular bouncer, he thought, and his name in gold letters on a door meant just that. He picked his way over the floor littered with broken glasses, sandwiches, and forgotten rubbers to the patio which led to Cassie's exclusive quarters, where the cream of the party was assembled, the big shots he would now be able to swing behind deserving talent, providing the talent didn't double-cross him first. He wished he were going with the mob to the other party, cardless, thirsty, mannerless, tieless, absolutely free.

Immature, irresponsible, he told himself.

Cassie was arranged on her favorite sofa, one plump but shapely leg thrown across the other high enough to reveal chiffon ruffles and a charming suspicion—no, it couldn't be! —of pubic curls, coquettishly hidden as soon as the peek was offered. One gray millionaire sat at her feet for the view of lower joys, while another leaned over the back of the sofa, gazing down hungrily into the generous picnic of her decolletage. Cassie waved her cigarette holder around both admirers and spoke in her Lady Agatha accent of the mystique of art collecting. Jonathan pretended not to see her gracious gesture making room at her feet for him to crouch, look, listen, and learn. He sipped his whisky doggedly, feeling like a child left with the dreary grown-ups while the other boys were having fun in forbidden playgrounds. These important personages of the art world had no value in themselves, only when presented to men like Hugow for their needs. None of them would ever be friends or people in their own right, he thought. Just as he was speculating on how soon he could break loose from his new duties, he saw George Terrence coming toward him, smiling.

"My dear boy, you look as if you'd seen a ghost! Don't apologize, I understand now why you didn't answer my letters, and believe me, I think it's splendid. I've taken up painting for my nerves, on the advice of my doctor, and I will say that there's nothing like it. I don't blame you a bit for preferring it to the law. Even my wife is taking it up. In fact, she just purchased a Hugow from Mrs. Bender, that's why we came."

A lean, lantern-jawed, crew-cut man of distinction, barber-tanned and vested in lamé brocade suddenly detached himself from a manly cluster around the fireplace and reached a beautiful hand toward George.

"Roger Mills, as I live and breathe," he said. "How long has it been—let's see, ten, twenty—no, don't tell me—why, I believe it's nearly twenty-five years, isn't it?" He smiled brilliantly at Jonathan and favored him with the next handclasp. "So you're one of Roger's protégés, too. I've heard about you from Mrs. Kingston Ball, Miss Van Orphen's sister."

"I think you're mistaken about my name," George Terrence said, taking a firm grip on Jonathan's arm as Jonathan was trying to get away. "Terrence is the name. Would you like to meet Mrs. Terrence, Jonathan? She's been anxious to meet you, now that we're so interested in artists."

The trimly dieted little matron summoned from her corner was the same one who had avoided him as Connie Birch's son but was eager to make amends to the promising dealer and was equally pleased to meet the glitter-vested Mr. Gordon.

"Did I hear you mention Claire Van Orphen?" she asked him. "Claire and Beatrice used to call on us years ago. And Mr. Jaimison here is the son of a dear old friend as well as a friend of Claire's. What a lot we have to talk over!"

"Indeed, indeed," said the stranger. "I knew your husband before he was your husband, Mrs. Terrence, when he was quite the gay bachelor, in fact, eh, Roger?"

Mrs. Terrence burst into arch giggles.

"You don't need to remind me, sir," she cried. "George was a very naughty boy when I first knew him and I did my best to reform him. But do you know I do love hearing him tell about his escapades, because sex standards are so much freer now, don't you think, Mr. Gordon, and what shocked us then just seems amusing these days? I really blush at my own ignorance more than at George's naughty affairs. Imagine George using an alias, like royalty!"

Mr. Gordon toyed with the jeweled buttons of his vest and looked from Mrs. Terrence's bisque-matted façade to George Terrence's steely smile.

"Indeed," he said. "So you knew about Roger Mills."

Mrs. Terrence giggled again.

"That was so clever of George. His family owned the Roger Cotton Mills, so sometimes he called himself Roger Cotton and sometimes Roger Mather when he was out on a lark. I nearly died laughing, but it would have shocked me if I'd known it once."

"It still shocks me, Mrs. Terrence," said the stranger.

Jonathan wanted to leave the happily reunited old friends to their reminiscences, but this time it was Mrs. Terrence who detained him.

"My daughter has told me about you," she said. "Really my taking up art, modern art, that is, has made Amy and me much closer, just as it has made George and me understand each other. You must let us come and browse around the newer galleries, Jonathan, because you're the expert and we're amateurs."

"What made you take it up?" asked the stranger, brooding. "Nerves—like Roger's here?"

"Oh no," said the lady. "I knew it was all right because Mrs. Crysler was collecting modern art."

"Don't go, Jonathan," exclaimed George. "Please stay," cried Hazel and Mr. Gordon. "Come sit with me, Jonathan," commanded Cassie.

It was a trap, he thought gloomily. He thought wistfully of the pack of gallery-flies prowling through the night, battering on doors to be let in, brawling and bruising down to The Golden Spur, and he thought those were the real backers of art, those were the providers, the blood-donors, and Cassie's salon of critics, guides, and millionaires, were the free-loaders, free-loading on other people's genius, other people's broken hearts, and, when it came to that, other people's money.

Well, he'd learned something more about himself, and if

all he'd lost was some of Major Wedburn's money, that was okay. He didn't have to save his life by collaboration with the enemy, did he? He found Percy Wright trying to be sick in Cassie's bathroom.

"It's not the liquor, it's my awful problems!" Percy gasped. "I mean, naturally I'm terribly flattered that you and Cassie have taken me up and let me meet these great people, but I still admire Hugow—my master, really—and I want to tell him he mustn't blame me for my prices boosting and those reviewers saying he's through, because he isn't. Would I still be trying to paint like him if he was through, I mean? And if he gets through, where does that leave my work when it's like his?"

Yes, it was a problem, Jonathan agreed.

"I'll make a fortune when my show comes on," Percy said, "but nobody likes my money anyway. You'd think it was leprosy, the way Darcy nags me about it. But how can I stop my stuff from selling?"

"You can buy me out," said Jonathan, inspired. "Be a dealer. That's where you belong. Everybody you like will like you."

"You wouldn't sell," Percy said, cheered at once.

Jonathan handed him a towel filled with ice and a fresh glass of scotch, and the deal was started.

Jonathan hurried down Madison and looked for lights from the side-street galleries along the way where other opening parties had been held. By this time the old crowd must be heading toward The Golden Spur for post mortems and wakes, and he stood waving for a cab. A green taxi was parked in front of a Hamburger Heaven and as he waited the driver came out of the restaurant with a paper bag. He opened the cab door.

"Just the man we're hunting. Get in," he said. "How do you like this job? The best thing I ever painted."

Hugow took off his cap and grinned.

"I knew it," said Jonathan. "You're still in your green period."

"My fare's buying Pernod, a love potion rich debutantes give to taxi-drivers—green, of course."

Iris was hurrying out of the liquor store with her package.

"Darling, we've been looking all over for you," she cried, climbing in. "We've got everything ready for the trip."

"You never guessed I'd be at the gallery," Jonathan said.

"I figured you'd be too smart to stick that one out," Hugow said.

"I was only watching your doodlings pull in a fortune," Jonathan said. "It gets boring."

"Hugow's got it all spent already," Iris said.

It was lovely to be in each other's arms in the back seat of a taxi once again. It didn't matter that she'd been with Hugow, and the truth had no part in love anyway, except for the truth of finding each other at the right moment.

"Not spent, invested," said Hugow, heading the car north. "There won't be any money in art in the year two thousand, so I'm in a new business, the coming one."

Jonathan didn't care what business it was so long as they were all together once more.

"Demolition, that's my business now," said Hugow. "Cab for a hobby, demolition for real. My firm's hoping for this contract."

"The Metropolitan?"

They were passing the Museum, heading for the park entrance.

"We call that a ball job in my business," said Hugow. "The iron ball, that's our god. I'm picking up the lingo too. No art corn, just the simple, brutal words."

"Already it's arty," said Jonathan. " 'Demolition' for 'wrecking.' I've got some money to invest in it myself."

"I'll take it," Hugow said.

Jonathan wondered where Hugow was taking them, but if nobody else wanted The Golden Spur, he'd be the last to suggest it. He wanted to ask Iris where she had been all these weeks, but she was here now. Wasn't that all that mattered?

"Your parents were at the show," he told Iris.

"Parents are getting into everything now, spoiling all the fun," Iris complained. "Now mother wants to go back into the theater, she says, now that she knows about me. I told them all about me so I could leave for good, but instead they wanted to come too. Father painting, mind you! That's what that analyst Dr. Jasper did!"

They were tooling over to the West Side Highway. Maybe Hugow was taking them up to his shack up in Rockland County, where they would freeze to death. Maybe he'd turn around before they hit the bridge and go down to the Spur after all. Iris had her head cozily on his shoulder and was babbling away between sandwiches and drinks about the frightful hazards of getting on good terms with your family after all these years.

"That's why I love you so much," she said. "You simply have no family pride, Jonathan."

"On the contrary, I am very proud of my family," Jonathan said. "The Jaimisons happen to be one of the oldest families in Ohio."

He was very glad that Hugow had turned back downtown, perhaps to the Spur, where they could begin all over.

# ABOUT THE AUTHOR

Dawn Powell was born on November 28, 1897, in Mount Gilead, Ohio. When she was six her mother died, and Powell later wrote that she was "dispatched from one relative to another, from a year of farm life with this or that aunt to rougher life in the middle of little factory towns." She made her way to New York in 1918, and over the next forty years she wrote more than fifteen novels, two dozen short stories, three plays, and articles for such magazines as *Life*, *Harper's Bazaar*, *Mademoiselle* (where she was a book critic for a year), and *The New Yorker*. She married in 1920 and lived in Greenwich Village in New York City, where her literary group included Malcolm Cowley, Edmund Wilson, and occasionally Ernest Hemingway. She was the toast of bohemia's smart set and continued writing until her death in 1965. "True wit," Powell once wrote, "should break a wise man's heart. It should strike at the exact point of weakness and it should scar. It should rest on a pillar of truth and not on a gelatine base, and the truth is not so shameful it cannot be recorded."

*The Wicked Pavilion* and *Angels on Toast* are also available from Vintage Books.

*Also by*

# Dawn Powell

---

## Angels on Toast

Introduction by Gore Vidal

A wicked satire in which two dubious businessmen hustle
each other and assorted wives, mistresses, and hangers-on.

## The Wicked Pavilion

Introduction by Gore Vidal

The site of *The Wicked Pavilion* is a musty but oddly
fashionable café, where everybody who is anybody has always gone —
to get over failed love affairs and pursue new ones, to cadge money,
hatch plots, and puncture one another's reputations. The result is a
mercilessly funny, view of New York high — and low—life.